THE LONG LOOK

THE LONG LOOK

RICHARD PARKS

FIVE STAR
A part of Gale, Cengage Learning

GALE
CENGAGE Learning™

Detroit • New York • San Francisco • New Haven, Conn • Waterville, Maine • London

GALE
CENGAGE Learning·

Five Star Publishing, a part of Gale, Cengage Learning.

Set in 11 pt. Plantin.
Printed on permanent paper.

LIBRARY OF CONGRESS CATALOGING-IN-PUBLICATION DATA

Parks, Richard.
    The long look / Richard Parks. — 1st ed.
      p. cm.
    ISBN-13: 978-1-59414-704-3 (alk. paper)
    ISBN-10: 1-59414-704-3 (alk. paper)
    1. Magicians—Fiction. I. Title.
PS3616.A7567L66 2008
813'.6—dc22   2008019936

First Edition. First Printing: September 2008.
Published in 2008 in conjunction with Tekno Books and Ed Gorman.

Printed in the United States of America
1 2 3 4 5 6 7 12 11 10 09 08

For Carol, who inspires it all

CHAPTER 1
"FAIRY TALES"

Tymon the Black, demon of a thousand nightmares and master of none, came to a sudden understanding. "It's raining," he said. "And I'm cold."

He sounded surprised.

The dwarf Seb was not surprised. The chilling rain had started the moment they reached the foothills of the White Mountains and continued all afternoon. Seb's long fair hair hung limp about his face, and he peered out at the magician through a tangled mat like a runt wolf eyeing a lamb through a hedge. "At last he deigns to notice. . . . I've been cold for hours! At the very least you could have been miserable with me."

"Sorry," Tymon said. "You know I have trouble with some things."

Seb nodded. " 'Here' and 'now' being two of them." While day-to-day practical matters were Seb's responsibility, there was some comfort in complaining. In his years with Tymon, Seb had learned to take comfort where he could.

Nothing else was said for a time, there being nothing to say. Seb, as usual, was the first to notice the failing light. "It's getting late. We'd better find somewhere dry to camp, if there be such in this wretched place."

It was beginning to look like a very wet night until Seb spotted a large overhang on a nearby ridge. It wasn't a true cave, more a remnant of some long-ago earthquake, but it reached more than forty yards into the hillside and had a high ceiling and dry, level floor. It wasn't the worst place they'd ever slept.

"I'll build a fire," the dwarf said, "if you will promise me not to look at it."

Tymon didn't promise, but Seb built the fire anyway after seeing to their mounts and the pack train. He found some almost-dry wood near the entrance and managed to collect enough rainwater for the horses and for a pot of tea. He unpacked the last of their dried beef and biscuit, studied the pitiful leavings and shook his head in disgust. Gold wasn't a problem, but they hadn't dared stop for supplies till well away from the scene of Tymon's last escapade, and now what little food they'd had time to pack was almost gone.

Seb scrounged another pot and went to catch some more rain. When he had enough, he added the remnants of beef and started the pot simmering on the fire. The mixture might make a passable broth. If not, at least they could use it to soften the biscuit.

Tymon inched closer to the fire, glancing at Seb as he did so. The dwarf pretended not to notice. Tymon was soaked and neither of them had any dry clothing. Tymon catching cold or worse was the last thing Seb needed. As for the risk, well, when the inevitable happened it would happen, as it had so many times before.

"I never look for trouble, you know that," Tymon said. It sounded like an apology.

"I know." Seb handed him a bowl of the broth and a piece of hard biscuit, and that small gesture was as close to an acceptance of the apology as the occasion demanded. They ate in comfortable silence for a while, but as the silence went on and on and the meal didn't, Seb began to feel definitely uncomfortable. He finally surrendered tact and leaned close.

"Bloody hell!"

It was the Long Look. Tymon's eyes were glazed, almost like

a blind man's. They focused at once on the flames and on nothing. Tymon was seeing something far beyond the firelight, something hidden as much in time as distance. And there wasn't a damn thing Seb could do about it. He thought of taking his horse and leaving his friend behind, saving himself. He swore silently that one day he would do just that. He had sworn before, and he meant it no less now. But not this time. Always, not this time.

Seb dozed after a while, walking the edge of a dream of warmth and ease and just about to enter, when the sound of his name brought him back to the cold stone and firelight.

"Seb?"

Tymon was back, too, from whatever far place he'd gone, and he was shivering again. Seb poured the last of the tea into Tymon's mug. "Well?"

"I've seen something," Tymon said. He found a crust of biscuit in his lap and dipped it in his tea. He chewed thoughtfully.

"Tymon, is it your habit to inform me that the sun has risen? The obvious I can handle; I need help with the hidden things."

"So do I," Tymon said. "Or at least telling which is which. What do you think is hidden?"

"What you saw. What the Long Look has done to us this time."

Tymon rubbed his eyes like the first hour of morning. "Oh, that. Tragedy, Seb. That's what I saw in the fire. I didn't mean to. I tried not to look."

Seb threw the dregs of his own cup into the fire and it hissed in protest. "I rather doubt it matters. If it wasn't the fire, it would be the pattern of sweat on your horse's back, or the shine of a dewdrop." The dwarf's scowl suddenly cleared away, and he looked like a scholar who'd just solved a particularly vexing sum. "The Long Look is a curse, isn't it? I should have realized that long ago. What did you do? Cut firewood in a sacred grove? Make water on the wrong patch of flowers? What?" Seb waited but Tymon didn't answer. He didn't seem to be listening. Seb shook his head sadly. "I'll wager it was a goddess. Those capable of greatest kindness must also have the power for greatest cruelty. That's balance."

"That's nonsense," said Tymon, who was listening after all. "And a Hidden Thing, I see. So let me reveal it to you—there is one difference between the workings of a god and a goddess in our affairs. One only."

"And that is?"

"Us. Being men, we take the disfavor of a female deity more personally." Tymon yawned and reached for his saddle and blanket.

Seb seized the reference. "Disfavor. You admit it."

Tymon shrugged. "If it gives you pleasure. The Powers know you've had precious little of that lately." He moved his blanket away from a sharp rise in the stone and repositioned his saddle. "Where are we going?"

Seb tended the fire, looking sullen. "Morushe."

"Good. I'm not known there—by sight, anyway."

Seb nodded. "I was counting on that."

"It will make things easier."

Seb knew that Tymon was now speaking to himself, but he refused to be left out. "I know why we were heading toward Morushe—it was far away from Calyt. What business do we have there now?"

"We're going to murder a prince."

Seb closed his eyes. "Pity the fool who asked."

"I never look for trouble. You know that."

The vagueness in his friend's eyes was gone. Seb knew this new expression, and in some ways it scared him more than the Long Look ever could. There was a task at hand and Tymon was devoting all of his considerable gifts to measuring, judging, and planning how best to complete that task, whatever the cost. Seb deliberately kept his tone light. "Yet trouble always seems to find you. Funny about that, isn't it? So. What's the first step for this crime?"

Tymon looked off into the distance at something Seb could not see. "We will need a base of operations. I believe there is an abandoned watchtower on Morushe's border with Wylandia that will do nicely. It'll need some patching."

"I'm not a stone mason, Tymon."

"No need. I'll supply the workers."

Seb didn't ask how or who. He had a feeling he knew. "And then? I assume you have this worked out already."

"We kidnap a princess, Seb. That's how it all begins."

Seb sighed like someone bearing all the weight of the world, which was pretty much how he felt just then. "I'll say this for you, Tymon—you don't do anything by halves."

"I won't marry him and that's final!"

Princess Ashesa of Morushe spurred the big roan viciously, her long red hair streaming behind her like the wake of a Fury. She was dressed for the hunt and carried a short bow slung across her back, but the only notice she took of the forest was mirrored in a glare clearly meant to wither any tree impertinent enough to block her path.

Lady Margate—less sensibly attired—was having trouble keeping up, though she rode gamely enough. A large buck, frightened by the commotion, broke cover and leaped across their path.

"A buck!" shouted Margy, hopefully.

Ashesa didn't even pause. "I won't marry him either," she snapped, "though I daresay if he ruled a large enough kingdom

Father would consider it." She grinned. "At least he's a gentler beast."

"That's no way to talk about your future husband!" Margy said. "Prince Daras is of ancient and noble lineage."

"So's my boar-hound," replied Ashesa, sweetly. "We have his pedigree." There had been almost no warning. Ashesa had barely time to hide her precious—and expressly forbidden—books away before her father had burst in to tell her the good news. The marriage alliance between Morushe and the coastal realm of Borasur was agreed and signed. By breakfast King Macol had the date and was halfway through the guest list. Ashesa couldn't decide between smashing dishes or going on her morning hunt. In the end she'd done both. But now half the crockery in her father's palace was wrecked, and her horse was not much better. Ashesa finally took pity on the poor beast and reigned in at a small clearing. Margy straggled up, looking reproachful and nearly as spent as Ashesa's mount.

"Father could have at least let me know what he was planning, and talked to me about it. Was that asking for such a great deal?"

Lady Margate sighed deeply. "In Balanar town yesterday I saw a girl about your age. She would be even prettier than you are, except she's already missing three teeth and part of an ear. She hawks ale and Heaven knows what else at a tavern near the barracks. Now, if I were to tell her that the Princess Ashesa was going to be married to a wealthy, handsome prince without her permission, do you think that girl would weep for you?"

Ashesa looked sullen. "No need to go 'round the mulberry bush, Margy. I understand you."

"Then understand this—Morushe is a rich kingdom, but not a strong one. Wylandia, among others, is all too aware of that. Without powerful friends, your people aren't safe. This marriage will ensure that we have those friends."

"For someone who claims statecraft is no field for a woman, you certainly have a firm grasp of it," Ashesa said dryly.

"Common sense, Highness. Don't confuse the two." Margy looked around them. "We should not be this far from the palace. Two high-born ladies, unescorted, in the middle of a wild forest. . . ."

Ashesa laughed, and felt a little better. "Margy, Father's game park is about as untamed as your sewing room. Even the wolves get their worming dose every spring."

Lady Margate drew herself up in matronly dignity. "Never-the—" She paused, her round mouth frozen in mid-syllable. She looked puzzled.

"Yes?" Ashesa encouraged, but Lady Margate just sat there, swaying ever so gently in her saddle. Ashesa slid from her mount and ran over to her nurse. "Margy, what is it? What's wrong?"

Ashesa saw the feathered dart sticking out of the woman's neck and whirled, drawing her hunting sword.

Too late.

Another dart hummed out from a nearby oak and stung her in the shoulder. Ashesa felt a pinprick of pain and then nothing. Her motion continued and she fell, stiff as a toppled statue, into the wildflowers, her eyes fixed upwards at the guilty tree. Two short legs appeared below the leaves of a low branch, then the rest of a man not quite four feet high followed.

He wore fashionable hunting garb of brown and green immaculately tailored to his small frame, and in his hand was a blowpipe. He carried a small quiver with more darts at his belt.

Elf-shot . . . ? Ashesa's thoughts were all misty and distant; it was hard to think.

The small man reached the ground and nodded pleasantly in her direction, touched his cap, and whistled. Two normal-sized men in concealing robes and gauntlets appeared at the edge of the clearing and went to work with professional detachment.

First they removed Lady Margate from her horse and propped her against the dwarf's oak, closing her eyes and tipping her hat forward to keep the sun off her face. Ashesa, half-mad with rage and worry, struggled against the drug until her face turned red and the veins stood out on her neck, but she could not move. The little man kneeled beside her, looking strangely concerned.

"Please stop that. You'll only injure yourself, Highness. Don't worry about your friend—she'll recover, but not till we're well away." With that he gently plucked the dart from her shoulder and tossed it into the bushes.

"Who are you? Why are you doing this?!"

The shout echoed in her head but nowhere else; she could not speak. The two silent henchmen brought Ashesa's horse as the dwarf pulled a small vial from his belt, popped the cork, and held it to her nose. An acrid odor stung her nostrils and she closed her eyes with no help at all.

Kings Macol and Riegar sat in morose silence in Macol's chambers. At first glance they weren't much alike: Macol was stout and ruddy, Riegar tall and gaunt with thinning gray hair. All this was only surface, for what they shared was obvious even without their crowns. Each man wore his responsibilities like a hair shirt.

Riegar finally spoke. "It was soon after you broke the news to your daughter, I gather?"

Macol nodded, looking disgusted. "I fooled myself into thinking she knew her duty. Blast, after her outburst this morning I'd almost think she cooked this up herself just to spite me!"

Riegar dismissed that. "We have the note, and the seal is unmistakable—"

The clatter on the stairs startled them both, and then they heard the sentry's challenge. They heard the answer even better—it was both colorful and loud.

"That will be Daras." Riegar sighed.

The Crown Prince of Borasur strode through the door, his handsome face flushed, his blue eyes shining with excitement. "The messenger said there was a note. Where is it?"

Riegar scowled. "Damn you, lad, you've barged into a room containing no fewer than two kings, one of whom is your father. Where are your manners?"

Daras conceded a curt nod, mumbled an apology and snatched the parchment from the table. For all his hurry the message didn't register very quickly. Daras read slowly, mouthing each word as if getting the taste of it. When he was done there was a grimness in his eyes that worried them. "Wylandia is behind this, Majesties. That's certain!"

Macol and Riegar exchanged glances, then Macol spoke. "Prince, aren't you reading a great deal into a message that says only 'I have Ashesa—Tymon the Black'?"

Daras looked surprised. "Who else has a reason to kidnap My Beloved Ashesa? The King of Wylandia would do anything to prevent our alliance." Daras said Ashesa's name with all the passion of a student reciting declensions, but he'd seen his intended only twice in his life and had as little say in the matter as she did.

Macol shook his head. "I know Aldair—he'll fight you with everything he has at the slightest provocation, but he won't stab you in the back. And Morushe and Borasur have so many trading ties that it amounts to alliance already. Aldair knows this; his negotiating position for Wylandia's use of our mountain passes is quite reasonable. We are close to agreement."

"If Aldair is not involved, then the kidnapping is not for reasons of State. And if not, then why was there no ransom demand? Why taunt us this way?"

Macol looked almost pleased. "A sensible question, Prince. Your father and I wonder about that ourselves. But no doubt this villain will make his demands clear in time, and I'll meet them if I can. In the meantime—"

"Of course!" Daras fairly glowed. "How long will it take to raise your army? May I lead the assault?"

"There will be no assault." Riegar's tone was pure finality.

"No assault!? Then what are we going to do?"

Macol sighed. "Prince, what can we do? Our best information—mere rumor—puts Tymon in an old watchtower just inside the border of Wylandia. Even assuming this is true, do you honestly think His Majesty Aldair will negotiate tariffs during an invasion?"

"Has it ever been tried?" Daras asked mildly.

Riegar looked to heaven. "Sometimes I pray for a miracle to take a year from your age and add it to Galan's. I might keep what's left of my wits."

"My brother is a clark," snapped Daras, reddening. "Divine Providence gave the inheritance to me, and when I'm king I'll show Wylandia and all else how a king deals with his enemies!" Daras nodded once and stalked out of the room.

Macol watched him go. "A bit headstrong, if I may say."

"You may." Riegar sighed. "Though it's too kind." He winced suddenly.

"Are you ill?"

"It's nothing. Comes and goes." Riegar relaxed a bit as the pain eased, then said, "I've been thinking. We both know that Aldair won't tolerate an army on his border, but if the situation was explained to him, he might be willing to send a few men of his own."

"I dare say," Macol considered. "If a man like Tymon the Black really is operating in Wylandian territory without permission, Aldair's pride would demand he do something about it. Yes, I'll have a delegation out tonight! After that, all a father can do is pray."

"As will I. But there is one other thing you can do," Riegar said. "Would you be good enough to post a guard on Prince Daras's quarters tonight?"

Macol frowned. "Certainly. But may I ask why?"

King Riegar of Borasur, remembering the look in his son's eyes, answered, "Oh, just a whim."

Prince Galan of Borasur strolled down a corridor in Macol's Castle, a thick volume under one arm. He didn't need much in the way of direction, though this was his first visit to Morushe. The fortress was of a common type for the period it was built; he'd made a study in his father's library before the trip. Finding his brother's quarters was easy enough, too. It was the one with the unhappy-looking soldier standing beside the door.

"Is Prince Daras allowed visitors?" he asked, smiling. The guard waved him on wearily, and Galan knocked.

"Enter if you must!"

The muffled bellow sounded close enough to an invitation. Galan went inside and found his brother pacing the stone floor. With both in the same room it was hard to imagine two men more different. Daras was the tall one, strong in the shoulders and arms from years on the tourney fields he loved so well. Galan by contrast had accepted the bare minimum of military training necessary for a gentleman and no more. He was smaller, darker, with green eyes and a sense of calm. When the brothers were together, it was like a cool forest pool having conversation with a forest fire.

"It's intolerable!" Daras announced.

Galan didn't have to ask what was intolerable. He knew his brother's mind, even if he didn't really understand it. "Macol and Father don't want a war. Can you really fault them for that?"

Daras stopped pacing. He looked a little hurt. "You think I

want a war?"

Galan shrugged. "Sometimes."

Daras shook his head. "Remember the heroic tales you used to read to me?" He apparently caught the reproach in Galan's eye and so amended, "I mean the ones you still read from time to time? Even among all the nobility and sacrifice, the excitement of combat and rescue, I can see the destruction in my mind's eye. What sane man wants that? No. I blame Father and Macol for nothing except their shortsightedness. By the by, I called you a clark today in front of Father."

"It wouldn't be the first time. And not wholly wrong."

"Even so—I was angry and I'm sorry. I envy you in a lot of ways; you know so many things, whereas I know only one thing in this world for certain—wanted or no, a war with Wylandia is inevitable. I'd rather it be on our terms than Aldair's."

Galan changed the subject. He held up his prize. "Look what I found in Macol's library."

"A book. How odd."

Galan smiled. Sarcasm was another thing his brother knew for certain. "Not just a book. Borelane's *Tales of the Red King*. I told you I could find it."

"How did you know it was in Macol's library? I was present when you asked him about it and even he didn't know."

Galan thought about that question for a minute, but finally shrugged. "I can always find a book if it exists, you know that. I always manage, though I don't know how. It's strange."

"More like one of the rather feebler forms of wizardry." Despite his comment, Daras had begun to show a little more interest once he had heard the title. "Perhaps . . . ," he said, then finished, "perhaps you can read to me later."

"It'll have to be later. I'm for Wylandia tonight. Macol and Father are sending a delegation to Aldair. Father thought his message might carry more weight if a Prince of the Blood went along."

"Not me, of course," Daras said bitterly.

"Be reasonable, Brother. You've no patience for diplomacy; action suits you better."

"It suits all men better."

Galan swallowed the casual insult by long habit. He'd long ago given up seeking approval from his older brother. He'd never quite given up wanting it. "We wouldn't want to do anything to endanger Ashesa." Her name brought back a little of the envy he'd always felt for Daras. The first time Galan had ever seen Ashesa was barely a year before, when Morushe's royal family paid a state visit to Borasur. He'd spent a month afterwards writing bad poetry and staring at the moon.

"No," Daras agreed, though his thoughts were plainly elsewhere.

CHAPTER 2
"A TIME FOR HEROES"

Ashesa awoke in a room fit for a princess—a near perfect copy of her own. The big four-poster bed and the tapestry of the "Quest for the Sunbeast" were both in place; she was beginning to think she might have dreamed the whole abduction until she saw what was wrong. There were books, and they were not hidden.

She got up, still a little wobbly, and examined the first of them. They weren't hers, of course. She checked a few pages of each, just enough to know they were real books. She closed the last one and checked the door. It was barred, of course.

Someone's gone to a great deal of trouble to make me feel comfortable, was the first coherent thought Ashesa could put together. Her head still ached and it was easier not to think at all. There was an arched window in the east wall and she looked out.

The room was in a high tower somewhere in the mountains—somewhere, some mountains—and even in the dying light the view was breathtaking. The earth looked folded almost like linen in a press, and one peak snuggled up to the next with a bare knife-edge of a valley between them. The window was barred too, but the glassed shutters worked. She opened them and took a breath of cool, head-clearing air.

Someone knocked on her door.

Odd manners for a kidnapper. And there was another coherent thought. She was almost pleased. "I'm afraid you'll have to let yourself in," she said.

Nothing happened. Ashesa put her ear to the door and heard a faint creaking like an old oak in a breeze. The knock repeated.

"Come in, damn you!"

She heard a scrape as the bar lifted, then the clink of silverware. The door swung outward and there stood a figure in a black robe and hood, carrying a tray of food and wine. His face and hands were both covered—his face by the hood, his hands by leather gauntlets. He looked like one of the pair who had helped kidnap her. Ashesa stepped back, and the figure came in and set the tray on a little table by the bed. Ashesa considered trying to slip past him, but two more figures just like him stood in the corridor, steel spears glinting. She turned to the tray bearer, looking regal despite her rumpled condition.

"I demand to know who you are and why you've brought me here." Her jailor only shook his head slowly and turned toward the door. Ashesa stamped her foot and snatched at the hood. "Look at me when I speak to—"

There was no face under the hood. A stump of wood jutted through the neck of the robe, around which a lump of clay had been shaped into a crude likeness of a head. A piece of it fell to the floor and shattered with a puff of yellow dust. Ashesa screamed.

"Normally they don't wear anything, but I didn't want to upset you. I see I've failed."

In that moment Ashesa was more startled by the strange voice than by what she had just seen. She turned to look. A slightly chagrined man stood in the doorway. He was just past the full blood of youth, with features as fine and delicate as a girl's. His dark eyes were reddened and weak, as if he spent too many hours reading in poor light. None of these details registered as strongly in Ashesa's mind as her first impression—the man had an air of quiet certainty that she found infuriating.

"Very . . . considerate," Ashesa said, recovering her poise with great effort. "Would you please tell me *what* that is and *who* you are?"

He patted the simulacrum fondly. "That, Highness, is a stick golem. I learned the technique from a colleague in Nyas; you should see what he can do with stone. . . ." He stopped, clearly aware that Ashesa had heard as much as she cared to on the subject. "My apologies, Highness. I am called Tymon the Black."

Ashesa almost screamed again. She scrambled to the other side of the bed and snatched up a heavy gilt candlestick from the table. She waved it with all the menace she could scrape together. "Stay away from me!"

"My reputation precedes me," the magician sighed. "What is my most recent atrocity?"

Ashesa glared at him. "Do you deny that you sacrificed a virgin girl to raise an army of demons against the Red Company?"

Tymon smiled a little ruefully. "To start, they weren't demons and she wasn't a virgin. Nor did I 'sacrifice' her . . . exactly. The Red Company took a geld from half the kingdoms on the mainland, so I don't recall hearing any objections at the time. No matter; it's water down the river. You must be hungry, Highness. Have some supper."

In truth, the aroma from the tray was making Ashesa a little giddy, but she eyed it with suspicion. Tymon apparently noticed the look.

"Be reasonable, Highness. Would I go to all this bother just to poison you? And if I *were* in need of a virgin there are certainly others easier to hand than a Princess of the Blood, common knowledge and barracks gossip not withstanding."

"You are a beast," she said.

"Red eyed and howling every full moon. So I've heard."

Ashesa shrugged and sampled a beef pie. It was delicious. She poured herself some wine as Tymon dismissed his stick-figure servant. He found a chair and sat watching her, while she in turn glared at him between mouthfuls.

"Well?" she asked, finally. "Aren't you going to tell me why I'm here?"

"You didn't ask, so I assumed you weren't interested. Pesky things, assumptions," he said. "Let's see what others might be floating about, besides that silly misunderstanding about virginity. . . . Ransom? There's a common theme. Will I force your doting father to surrender half his kingdom to save you?"

Ashesa took a sip of wine so he wouldn't see her smile. "No," she said from behind her goblet.

Tymon looked genuinely surprised. "Why not?"

"Because we both know you wouldn't get it, break Father's heart though it would. And then there's all this. . . ." She waved a capon leg at the room and furnishings. "That tapestry alone is of finer quality than my copy, and I know how much that one cost—poor Father nearly had a stroke. You obviously have great resources at your beck, Magician. That rules out any conventional ransom short of greed and that's *one* sin I've never heard spoken of you. So. What do you want?"

There was open admiration in Tymon's eyes. "You have an exceptional mind, Highness. It's really unfortunate that Prince Daras will never allow you to use it. From what I've gathered of his philosophy your duties will be to produce heirs and be ornamental at court."

"You seem to know a great deal about matters that don't concern you, Magician, but you still haven't answered my question. I wish you would because, frankly, I'm baffled. I hope for your sake it's more than a whim. They'll search for me, you know."

"And find you, too, since I was good enough to leave a note. I've also bought supplies openly; my location is common knowledge to half the hill crofters on the border. Diplomacy and protocol will delay your father, but unless I've misjudged the man, Prince Daras will be along soon."

Ashesa was stunned. "Are you mad? As well to draw a map and have done!"

"No, Highness. I'm not mad, though it often seems so—even to me. But to avoid wearying you I'll speak plainly—I kidnapped you so that Prince Daras will try to rescue you. And he will try. His nature doesn't allow for any other option."

"But why—" Ashesa stopped. She knew. It was there for her to see in Tymon's eyes.

"Quite right, Highness. I'm going to kill him."

The man Macol selected to watch Daras was a veteran: solid, trustworthy. A competent guard. Not a competent diplomat. The scope of the orders he had received in King Macol's throne room were quite beyond him.

"I want you to guard my son's quarters tonight," said King Riegar solemnly. "He is not to leave his room."

"But," added King Macol, "Prince Daras is an honored guest, not a prisoner. Treat him with respect."

Riegar nodded. "Certainly. But he may have it in his head to do something foolish. Use whatever force you must, within reason."

"But," again added Macol, "Prince Daras is heir to the throne of Borasur. He must on no account be harmed or you'll answer for it."

"Just keep him there," said Riegar.

"Without hurting or offending him," said Macol. "Now. Is all that clear?"

"Yes, Sire," the man lied. Later, as he stood at his post in the corridor, he placidly awaited the inevitable.

"Guard," Prince Daras called out, "lend some assistance in here, there's a good fellow."

The guard smiled and walked right in. The bump on his head was no less than he expected, and he was grateful for it. It seemed the simplest solution to a very complicated problem.

Princess Ashesa climbed the long spiral staircase to the top of Tymon's fortress. Her hooded escort thumped along behind her like a child on stilts. Ashesa wasn't fooled. She'd stumbled once and the thing had snapped forward, supporting her, faster than she would have believed possible.

They passed several doors along the way. All unlocked, most empty, but Ashesa couldn't resist looking for something that might help her escape. One room was full of echoing voices in a language she didn't understand; another held a dark gray mist that she could have sworn was looking at her. None of them contained anything useful.

Ashesa ran out of doors and stairs at about the same time. She and her golem escort stood on the parapet that wrapped around the outside off the highest level of the tower. The thin mountain wind whipped the golem's robes tight against its stick frame until it looked like a scarecrow flapping in a field. Ashesa looked over the railing and got a little dizzy.

"Too far to jump," said the wind.

Ashesa jumped anyway, but only a little. She didn't clear the railing.

The dwarf sat before a small canvas on the other side of the platform. He had changed his woodland green for an artist's smock stained with the remnants of an exploded rainbow. Upon closer inspection Ashesa could tell that the rainbow was merely streaks of paint. The dwarf concentrated on the canvas and painted with long smooth strokes, unperturbed by the gusty wind.

"That depends on your reason for jumping," returned Ashesa grimly. She put her hands on the railing.

The dwarf smiled, though he still wouldn't look at her. "A noble gesture, but it wouldn't keep Daras out of Tymon's web even if the prince knew about your plummet from the tower. Revenge has a longer pedigree than rescue."

"He's very certain of himself, your master."

"About some things," the dwarf said, and he looked a little melancholy. "Tymon can't help it."

Ashesa considered a new tack. "How much is he paying you? Whatever your price, my father will meet it. Just help me escape and warn My Beloved Daras."

The dwarf cleaned one brush and selected another. "Would your father be willing to offer me the lucrative and entirely appropriate position of Court Foole?"

"Certainly!"

"Yes," the dwarf sighed. "I thought he might."

Ashesa frowned, and, even as she spoke the words, she wondered how many times they had passed her lips and her thoughts since the kidnapping. "I don't understand."

"Then I will explain. My story is simple, Highness—my mother died at my birth and my father sold me to a troupe of acrobats and thieves when I was seven. By twelve I was the best among them at both skills, but I still wore a cap and bells at every performance. Can you guess why?" He studied the canvas. "And when I couldn't abide that anymore, I took to the streets on my own, and that's where Tymon found me. We understood one another. Now he pays me with a little gold and a lot of hardship and aggravation, but part of the price is respect and an appreciation of my talents that totally ignores my height except when it's actually important. That's coin beyond your means, I'm afraid. Consider—we've been conversing for the better part of two minutes and you haven't even asked my name." He swirled the brush-tip in a puddle of gold.

Ashesa stood in the presence of the man who'd kidnapped

her, and yet for a moment she almost felt as if he were the injured party. It made her angry. "Very well, then: what is your name?"

He touched his cap and left a speck of gold there. "Seb, at your service," he said, making a quick dab at the canvas. "Up to a point."

"I'd like to know where that point is. Tymon won't tell me why he plans to kill My Beloved Daras. Will you?"

"My Beloved . . . that's not what you were calling him during your little ride." Ashesa flushed but said nothing. Seb shrugged. "I know—it's the proper title for the betrothed and you do know your duty, even if you don't like it. So. Why not 'to prevent the marriage'? You suggested it yourself, Tymon says."

The princess shook her head. "If he merely wanted that, killing me would have worked as well and been a lot less bother. I don't flatter myself by thinking he'd have hesitated."

"He wouldn't," confirmed Seb. "Though it would grieve him bitterly. As it will when Daras is killed."

"But why? Why does Daras deserve to die?"

Seb smiled ruefully. "That's the saddest part—he doesn't. At least not in the sense of anything he's *done*. He's not a bad sort, really. A bit headstrong and hot-tempered, but that's not a crime. Rather it's who he is, and what he is, and what that combination will make him do when the time comes. It's all here, Highness, if you care to look."

Seb moved to one side so she could see the canvas. Ashesa's mouth fell open in surprise when she recognized the portrait. It was Daras, mounted and armored in an archaic pattern. He held his helmet under one arm, his lance pointed to the sky.

"It's lovely," she said honestly, "but why the old armor?"

"That's the armor of the time of the Lyrsan wars. When the folk of the western deserts pushed east against the Twelve Kingdoms. That's when Daras should have lived. That was a time for heroes."

"Daras isn't a hero," Ashesa snapped. "That takes more than winning tournaments."

"More even than rescuing one princess," the dwarf agreed. "It's rather a full-time pursuit. It might even take, say, a long, bloody war with Wylandia."

Ashesa put her hands on her hips. "Do you really expect me to believe that Daras would start a war just so he can be a hero?!"

"Tymon and I have discussed this and agree that he wouldn't be starting it, to his way of thinking. But the seeds are already there: real intrigues, imagined insults . . . mistrust. All waiting to take root in his mind until he firmly believes that Wylandia struck first. You see, Daras is already a hero in many ways. He's seen the soul of it in his brother's stories, and in that soul he sees himself. And why not? He's brave, strong, skilled in warlike pursuits and little else. All he lacks to make his destiny complete is the one vital ingredient—need. If the need is not there, he will create it. He has no choice. And neither do we."

Most of the blood had deserted Ashesa's face, and she trembled. "You can't be sure! And even if you were, what right—"

"Tymon is sure," interrupted Seb calmly. "It's his greatest power, and greatest curse. He knows, and he can't escape the responsibility of knowing. That gives him the right."

"I . . . don't . . . believe . . . you!" Ashesa spat out each word like something foul.

Seb smiled. "Oh, yes, you do. Though you don't want to. It's far better to see this tale as history no doubt will—a foul crime done by foul folk. Forgive me, Highness, but I'm not as kind as Tymon and see no reason why this should be any easier on you than the rest of us."

Ashesa's hands turned into fists and she took a step toward

the dwarf. In an instant the golem was between her and Seb, and the dwarf hadn't even blinked. Ashesa took several deep, calming breaths, and after a moment the golem moved aside. She groped for some thread of sweet reason to pull her thoughts out of the pit. "But . . . but Daras can't start a war on his own! Only the king can do that! Even if what you say is true, there's still time. . . ."

While she spoke Seb made several deft strokes on the canvas, and when she saw what the dwarf had painted there her words sank into nothing.

"Time has run out, Highness. King Riegar—rest him—died in his sleep last night."

In the portrait, Daras wore the plain gold crown of Borasur.

Prince Daras had never been on a quest before and wasn't quite sure what to expect, but at least the scenery felt right—it was wild and strange. The forest that bordered the mountain foothills was very different from the tilting fields and well-groomed game parks he was accustomed to: the grass grew high and razor-edged, brambles clawed at his armored legs, and trees took root and reached for the sunlight wherever the notion took them. Daras stepped his charger through a tortured, twisty path, and when an arrow hummed out of the trees and twanged off his armor, that, too, seemed as it should be.

"Hah! Villains! At you!"

Daras spurred forward along the arrow's course as if his mount was as armored as he was. The second arrow showed that notion in error; Daras barely cleared the stirrups before the poor beast went down kicking. Another instant and Daras was among his attackers.

They were men, of course. Forest bandits with no other skills and without enough forethought to lay a proper trap or the sense to avoid a well-armed man in plate armor, even if he was alone. None of that mattered to Daras once the attack began. They were bodies attached to rusty swords, meat in ragged clothes for the blooding, characters in a play of which Daras was the lead, existing only for their cue to dance a few steps and then rush through their death scenes. It wasn't how he thought it would be; it wasn't horrible. Daras never really saw their faces, never noticed their pain as he turned clumsy blows and struck sure ones, killing with the mad joy of a new-found sport. When it was over it was as if they had never lived at all.

Rather like a tournament, only they don't get up.

After the last bandit fell, Daras, cat-like, lost interest. He cleaned his sword on a dead man's tunic, verified that his mount had expired, then had a sip or two of weak wine before he resumed his quest on foot, whistling.

Ashesa didn't know what was different at first that morning. She only knew that something was not right. After a few moments she was awake enough to notice what was missing. Her clothes. The mantle and overdress she had laid out on the table the night before weren't there. In their place were two rather ethereal strips of cloth embroidered with crescents and stars and glyphs of a rather suggestive nature.

Tymon sat in her chair, looking unhappy.

"Magician, where are my clothes?" she asked, as calmly as she could manage.

He waved his hand at the table. "There, I'm afraid. It's the traditional sacrificial garb of an obscure fertility cult. You wouldn't have heard of it."

"And you're one of them?" she asked, though her calm wasn't holding up very well.

He shuddered delicately. "Certainly not. But, as much as the prospect would delight *me*, I don't think Prince Daras expects to burst in and find us discussing history over a cup of tea. I

Don't.

Ashesa lay down reluctantly and let the twig-fingered guards shackle her to the cold stone. As the last manacle clicked into place she heard a yelp like a hunting horn cut off in mid-note. Tymon wasn't smiling now. There was something like worry on his face, perhaps even a touch of fear. Ashesa couldn't have imagined that a moment before.

"Prince Daras is early. . . . I'd better hurry and get into my costume, Highness. Won't be a moment."

The magician hurried off into the temple, leaving Ashesa alone with the golems. There was a commotion at the gate and Ashesa turned her head to look just as the gate burst open and something very much like a brown rag sailed through, cartwheeling end over end to smash against the stones. Prince Daras of Borasur strode through.

His entrance made Ashesa skip a breath; she'd forgotten how handsome he was, but that wasn't all of it—a glory seemed to shine around him, like a saint etched in stained glass. He saw her then and rushed forward, all smooth motion and mad joy.

And this is what Tymon wants to destroy.

She heard Tymon but could not see him. "Stop him, my Pets!"

The golems set their halberds and charged. Ashesa finally recovered her wits. "Flee, My Beloved! It's a trap!"

Daras, of course, did nothing of the sort. He veered to the right and a golem's headlong rush carried it past. Daras struck a trailing blow without breaking stride and the golem's clay head exploded.

Ashesa watched, horrified but unable to look away. There was a battle-light on Daras's face, and his eyes were bright and wild. Ashesa's breath skipped a second time.

He's enjoying this!

The truth of it was like a cold slap in the face. It wasn't the rescue. It wasn't even herself as anything but an excuse. The prince was consumed with a mad ecstasy born of the clash of weapons and pleasure in his skill. He destroyed golems. He would destroy men with as little thought and the same wild joy. Ashesa tried not to think anymore, but it was a torrent held too long in check and the dams were breaking.

This is what Tymon wants to destroy. . . .

The second golem thrust past Daras's parry by brute force and the prince twisted his body like an acrobat. The halberd merely sliced a thin red line across the front of Daras's tunic and the prince's return stroke left the golem broken and still.

A voice issued from the temple. It was Tymon and it wasn't Tymon—it boomed like thunder across the valley. "Now you must die!"

Ashesa strained to turn her head and saw Tymon step out of the shadows of the temple. He wore a robe decorated with glyphs like the ones on Ashesa's costume, and in his gloved hands he carried a long curved knife. It glowed with a blue balefire that still could not penetrate the blackness under Tymon's hood.

Prince Daras studied the magician's knife, then looked at his own sword. Grinning, he dropped the sword and pulled his own long dagger. Ashesa wanted to scream but nothing came out—it was as if an invisible hand clapped itself over her mouth.

The fool, she thought wildly, *the bloody, senseless fool!*

What happened next was filled with terrible beauty. Daras charged the magician, and this time it was Tymon who danced aside to let him hurtle past like a maddened bull. Tymon's blade flicked out and then there was another line of red on the prince's chest. Daras snarled like a berserk, but kept some caution as he stopped himself and slowly circled, looking for an opening. Tymon kept just out of reach, reacting with a speed Ashesa wouldn't have expected of him. The glow on Daras's face built to new heights of rapture, as if the magician's surprising skill fanned it like the bellows of a forge.

It was like the sword dance Ashesa had seen performed at her father's court—the flash of steel always averted, always eluded as if it was nothing more than a dance for her amusement instead of a fight to the death. Tymon's knife traced its path through the air like a lightning flash, and Daras's dagger slashed and hummed in a silvered blur.

Then everything changed.

Tymon broke from the fight and sprinted toward the altar. "The sacrifice must be made!"

What?!

The wizard hurtled toward her, his knife burning away the distance to her heart. Ashesa closed her eyes.

Someone screamed and Ashesa opened her eyes again, surprised. She had meant to scream but never really managed. Who?

Tymon. He lay sprawled at the foot of the altar, Daras's weapon buried almost to the hilt in his back. Bright, impossibly red blood oozed from around the steel. Ashesa felt a little sick, a lot relieved and a bit . . . well, guilty. Guilty for wondering why Tymon's trap had failed, and for wondering—just for an instant!—if it should have failed. And why the mad dash to the altar? Unless Tymon had lied to her. . . .

Prince Daras grinned down at her, his chest heaving like a bellows. "Did—did you see that throw?" he chortled. "Thirty paces, easily. . . ." Daras seemed to forget about the throw all at once, as he got his first good look at Ashesa. The grin turned into something else.

Ashesa shivered. "For the love of heaven, stop staring and get me loose! There may be more of them."

"You're in no danger now, My Beloved Ashesa," Daras said, placing a hand on her bare shoulder. "And first things first."

"Get me loose." Ashesa repeated, all sweet reason. "We have

to get away from here."

Daras nodded. "In time. His lackey today, Aldair himself tomorrow. That's the order of business. Right now there are other matters to attend to."

Ashesa spoke very clearly, very urgently. "You're wrong, Beloved. Wylandia had nothing to do with this. I must tell you—" She stopped. Daras's hand had departed her shoulder for a more southerly location. "What are you doing?!"

He looked a little surprised at her attitude. "That 'other matter' I mentioned. Surely you know that tradition demands a price for your rescue?"

"We're not married yet, Beloved," Ashesa pointed out.

Daras shrugged. "A rescue is a separate matter altogether, with its own traditions and duties. Binding, too. I'm afraid we don't have any choice."

That word.

Later, perhaps, she wondered how so very easy it would have been for the matter to have turned out differently. It wasn't the act that Daras demanded, or even her feelings about Daras himself that mattered in what came next. It was the one word Daras had used. That made all the difference.

Sometimes, in those dark hours between waking and sleeping, when night closes in and the sound of their own heartbeats is much too clear, people have been known to wonder how close to the edge of the abyss they dwelled, and what it would take to push them over. In that moment, strapped to an altar under a warming sun, Ashesa became one of the lucky ones. That question would never trouble her again.

She looked at a soft patch of grass nearby, perfect for paying her debt. Very close to where Tymon's dagger had fallen to lie mostly hidden. Yes, it was perfect.

"Free me," she said, "and you'll have your reward."

For a while, Ashesa did not remember what happened next.

She refused to remember. When the weight of it brought her back to her senses against her will, Ashesa found herself leaning on the altar, trying to clear away a red haze from her mind. She tried not to look at Daras's body, tried not to see in her mind's eye the stunned surprise on his face before all expression ceased. Ashesa pulled herself around the stone until she came to Tymon's limp form, then her mouth set in a grim smile and she yanked the robes aside.

The blood came from a punctured animal bladder, and the stick skeleton was dappled with thick, blackening drops.

"Damn you!"

Tymon stepped out of the temple again, but this time it was really him. Ashesa glared at him and all the world behind him. "No one will believe you," she said, pale as snow and twice as cold.

Tymon obviously considered the suggestion in questionable taste. "Did I suggest such a thing? No, Highness. But they will believe *you* as you relate—tearfully, I advise—how Daras fell in the rescue, slaying the fiend and freeing you with the strength of his dying breath. Will I spurt green ichor? I should think I would."

"I saw the fight—the real fight—while it lasted. Daras was good but your golem could have killed him easily!" she accused. "But you knew I. . . ." She couldn't finish.

"What a mind," repeated Tymon with deeper admiration. "But you need to understand that what you say is only partly true, Highness. Once Daras took my bait he was finished, one way or the other. For your sake I would consider and take comfort in this—you can't kill a dead man. But I was curious about you, I admit it. Not everyone has the talent for knowing *what* must be done *when* it must be done. No, Highness. I didn't know. Add another sin to my head because I wanted to find out."

Ashesa saw the dwarf Seb coming down the mountain path. He led two geldings carrying travel packs and two more saddled to ride, and he played out a grayish cord behind him from a large spool mounted on a stick.

"A few matters to attend, Highness," Tymon said. "The first involves something new in the art of destruction. I think you'll be seeing it again." He nodded and Seb struck a flint to the cord. It sizzled with life and burned its way back to the tower. In a moment there was a dull roar and the earth trembled. The tower swayed on its foundation and then collapsed. Flames licked the exposed beams and flooring and soon the whole thing was burning merrily.

Ashesa stared. *Heavens.*

Tymon pulled a vial from his robe and poured an acrid black liquid on the golem. There was an instantaneous, nauseating stench and the cloth, wood, leather and blood all hissed and bubbled and melted into a smoking mass.

Seb stared at the remnants of the tower wistfully. Tymon laid a hand on his shoulder. "Sorry, but you knew it was only temporary. My magic would have to die with me. Expectations, you know." He turned back to Ashesa. "As cruel as assumptions in their way. They killed Daras as surely as we did."

"What about me?" Ashesa asked dully.

"Don't worry. If you'll wait here I've no doubt that King Aldair and Prince Galan will follow the beacon of flames right to you, combining against the common foe under the push of a father's love. Have you met young Galan, by the way? A kind, intelligent lad by all report, though given to idle dreaming. Who can say? With a firm hand to guide him he might even make a king."

Seb handed Ashesa a cloak and she wrapped herself against a sudden chill. Seb turned to the magician and said, "Master, we'd best be going."

Tymon and Seb mounted and rode out through the gate without a backward glance. Ashesa gathered the cloak tighter about her and settled down to wait. As she waited, she thought about Tymon, and Daras, and herself. Maybe she would talk to her father about Galan. Maybe. They would still want the alliance, but that didn't matter just then. She would meet Galan again, and she would decide. *She* would decide. Her father, whether he realized it or not, would just go along. She didn't really understand what was different now, but something was, and it wasn't because of her crime as such. It just came down to choice. Once you knew it existed there was no end to it. And no escape from it either.

Forgive me, Beloved, but Seb was right—this isn't a time for heroes.

Yet, if not for heroes, then for whom? Ashesa didn't know, but she feared the answer.

CHAPTER 3
"FLAWS"

Some hours after Tymon and Seb took their leave from Princess Ashesa it was raining again. After a while Seb began to wonder if it had ever really stopped. That, perhaps, all the time they had spent arranging the death of Prince Daras and, by extension, the lovely weather they'd enjoyed for the task, were both no more than the remnants of some half-remembered dream. In a way, Seb hoped that was the case. It was one thing to know what needed to be done, and to do it. It was quite another to enjoy the act.

"Do you think she will be all right?" he asked.

Tymon shrugged, and a raindrop fell off his nose. "I'm not sure I understand the question."

"We laid a great burden on Ashesa's shoulders," Seb said. "It may have been her choice but it was our doing. Haven't you thought about what it might mean for her?"

"Yes. I'm afraid time will tell that tale, since I cannot. I hope so . . . for what little that may mean."

"The Long Look cannot see her future?"

Tymon sighed. "The Long Look shows what it will, always. I believe it shows me what I need to see. It's been reliably uncooperative on matters where I'm merely curious. I do know this much—we will meet her again."

Seb's spirits, not very high to begin with, sank a bit. "This thing isn't finished, is it?"

"No. That, I hasten to add, is just my opinion. But I'm sure I'm right."

Seb started to ask about that, then decided that, right now, he really didn't want to know. They rode in silence for a while and Seb, because it was his responsibility, considered what to do next.

There was no cave for refuge this time, but Seb didn't mind so much. Their exit from their lodgings had been inevitable as always but, for once, planned in advance, and Seb made sure to be better prepared this time. They wore oilcloth cloaks against the wet, and there was a good tent of the same material among their baggage, as well as a good supply of food, enough for at least a fortnight. Seb tried to judge the hour, and considered that there was still some bit of daylight left. It was best to make use of it and be as far away as possible from the watchtower valley before nightfall.

Seb finally called a halt and made camp. Much later, with the campfire nearly burned out and the rain stopped, Seb made a confession.

"After the events of the last few days I've decided to keep a journal."

"Why?" Tymon asked.

"Because I think there should be another version of events other than history's. At least in some small regard. Would you like to hear the beginning?"

"The burden of history does fall heavily on us," Tymon said. "Yes, I would."

Seb began to read in the failing light:

"My name is Seb. For the past ten years, I have been servant and assistant to Tymon the Black, known throughout the Twelve Kingdoms and the Far Isles as the wickedest man on earth.

"I had a mother. All men do, they tell me, but I never knew her. My father sold me to a group of traveling thieves and jon-

41

gleurs when I was six. Something else you should know that my father didn't—I'm a dwarf. Not that it would have made any difference, except perhaps to dicker up the price a little. My new family would have paid more, if they'd known I'd reached my full height. Acrobatic dwarves—for so I became—are fine diversions when cutting a man's purse."

Seb closed the leather-bound journal. "That's how it begins. What do you think?" he asked.

Tymon stretched his long legs in front of the fire. He gnawed a rabbit bone thoughtfully for a moment then tossed it on the dying flames. The sparks flared briefly on the evening breeze and then faded. "It's a little slow," he said. "But well spoken and certainly promises interest for later. Is that all you have?"

Seb nodded. "So far. I've been meaning to do this for a long time."

"Then by all means you should. Don't spare me in the telling, Seb. I wouldn't."

"Nor will I." Seb looked thoughtful for a moment, then he smiled a wistful smile. "Besides, it's not as if anyone will believe a word of it."

Tymon nodded, somber. "So long as you understand that. By the by, I almost forgot to ask: Where are we going?"

Seb felt a chill. "I've come to hate that question."

"There's no need to worry yet. I don't think we need a place now so much as we need time. Quiet time to rest and consider. Any place at all that will supply that will do."

"No," Seb corrected firmly. "Any place at all that is *dry* will do."

The meeting was Macol's idea, but that it took place in King Macol's library was at Galan's request. Galan had spent most of his eighteen years in libraries of one sort or another, and it was in such places he generally felt most at peace and secure.

Not today. Galan put his elbows on the long table and then covered his face with his hands for a moment. "I am at a loss, Your Majesty. I really am."

King Macol sat across from him, looking a bit bewildered himself. "Still, it was good of you to see me now."

"My advisors argued against it," Galan said. "Strongly."

Macol shrugged. "If they had done otherwise you'd have been ill-served. You are vulnerable now, and should not be making hasty decisions or fielding questions that may have lasting significance. Yet I must ask, and yet you came. Why is that?"

"You were my father's friend," Galan said. "I would like for you to be mine."

Macol smiled. "Well and frankly spoken. For the sake of your father's friendship I will do the same with you, at least this one time: Riegar and I were friends, true friends, and I mourn his loss greatly. Yet he himself would have said that the only reason we could remain so all that time was that the interests of my kingdom and his were very often the same. I think that will remain. I hope so. But you have to think of your kingdom—for so it is now—first and last in whatever you do from now on. That is what I have done and will do where Morushe is concerned. Borasur deserves no less."

"I will remember what you've said, Your Majesty. Whatever else may fall. So. Morushe still wants the marriage?"

Macol nodded. "That at least has not changed, Prince. I think it serves both our kingdoms well."

Galan waited, but Macol didn't say anything else. He seemed to be waiting himself.

Now I must be guarded in speech and heavy in consideration. Father always was, and I see the same in Macol. But I never expected the burden to fall to me.

"Speaking as Galan, I think so too. But as the Crown Prince of Borasur, I cannot make any commitments until after my coronation, Your Majesty, as surely you can understand. Also, I must return to Borasur tomorrow."

"Certainly," Macol said. "But I ask you to consider that this is a time of transition. The more you can show that you have the reins of succession firmly in hand, including trading alliances, the less likely it will be that any . . . instabilities may arise."

Galan smiled at Macol's delicacy, but his meaning was clear enough. The same thought had occurred to Galan, and to say that there were few pretenders to the throne of Borasur was not to say that there were none at all. "Will Ashesa agree?" Galan said. "I know it isn't, strictly speaking, necessary. But I would like to know."

"Then you'd best ask her yourself," Macol said. He looked thoughtful. "I once believed this a simple enough matter, Prince. Lately I've had second thoughts, at least about the simplicity. Though, oddly enough, Ashesa has been asking about you since her deliverance. I don't pretend to know what it might mean, Prince. I am only her father."

"May I see her before I leave?"

"Certainly. But whether it's a wise thing for either of us is beyond me."

Galan smiled faintly. *So it begins. Damn you, Brother, and Father both, for leaving me with this mess.* He thought of Ashesa then, and added the coda, *And damn me most of all, for finding this joy to weigh against what should be an unrelieved burden of grief.*

"I should raise an army."

Molic of Riverfold, now calling himself "Prince Molic the Seventh" for no reason that any reputable genealogist could fathom, dreamed aloud as he stirred his supper. The stew was coming along nicely; there was even some meat today, thanks to a clumsy snare and an even clumsier rabbit.

His old servant Takren would have stirred the pot himself, but he was too busy trying to patch the patches on Molic's boots. "What army would that be, M'Lord?"

"The one that places me on my rightful throne at Borasur, of course! How does one raise an army, Takren?"

Takren paused to bite through a length of thread as he considered the matter. He had only four teeth left in his head, but those were surprisingly sharp. "For those who do not owe you fealty? Wages and a share of the loot is customary."

Molic considered this notion and found it wanting. "Our coffers are empty, and I would not want my kingdom looted. What else?"

"You could lead a popular uprising."

The pretender demurred. "The usurpers who hold the throne now are too popular as it is. Think again."

"I am. I am thinking the idea of an army may not be practical under the circumstances. Your kinship to the royal house is certainly real but, sad to say, distant and dilute."

" 'One drop of royal blood is as good as a flood,' " Molic said, quoting an old saying that he had only recently invented. "My claim is as good as theirs."

Takren looked about their modest cottage. "But your coffers, if I may say so, are somewhat lacking by comparison, M'Lord."

It was a familiar scene between them, played out over the years for want of a better one. Takren could play his part in his sleep. Sometimes he thought that Molic actually did. It was true that Molic's family was very distantly related to the royal family, and counted as minor nobility. Yet the reality was that his family had also, through gambling, feuding, and general foolishness, gradually lost their standing in the world to the point that now Molic, the sole living representative of that family, was little more than a glorified farmer, and not a very good one, truth be told. Takren, who remembered when the family's priorities strayed more toward getting in the harvest than tracing pedigree, stayed out of habit and at least the chance of semi-regular meals now that Molic, second son and dotty at that, remained. Time and an outbreak of Black Blood fever having done for the rest. The worsening of their circumstances didn't affect Molic in the least, except to feed his romanticism. Kings often came from hovels in his mind's bright world.

"Have some stew, Takren. Then help me plan my coronation."

"Seb, you don't understand. The problem is not that the Long Look has struck again. The problem is that it *hasn't*."

Seb chewed on the last bit of roasted duck and sighed contentment. "If this is what you consider a problem I am more than happy to see our troubles multiply like rabbits."

"I'm serious, Seb."

"And I am not? This is the first peace we've had since, well, ever, or at least as far as I can remember. Is there something about you that simply rejects happiness out of hand?"

From Seb's point of view, Tymon's concerns made no sense. This was their second week as the guests of a remote and sparsely populated sect of scholar monks with which Tymon had some prior association. Seb didn't know what that association was, and, at the moment, he didn't particularly care. It was enough that their lodgings were simple but comfortable, and the food much better than passable. Messengers arrived almost daily in the course of the monastery's affairs, but none of which seemed to concern Seb or Tymon. Indeed, the news that came with the runners was remarkable in its utter unremarkability.

"If you say the world is too quiet, I'm going to have to throw this bone at your head. Fair warning."

Tymon's pacing continued unabated, though he shrugged as he paced. "Even chaos has its periods of quiet potential. Then, of course, that potential reasserts. It never stays peaceful for long, Seb. Chaos returns. Just as the Long Look will return."

"What if it doesn't?" Seb asked.

Tymon blinked, and for a moment or two, he forgot to pace. "What do you mean?"

"Just what I said: what if it doesn't return? What if you're free? What if whatever Power blessed you so horribly has gotten bored with the game? You must admit that it's possible."

"Gladly. I'll also admit that the Great Wurm of Golondan could roast you a mutton joint with his fiery breath, too, and serve it on silver, but you'll pardon me if I wager against it."

Seb almost smiled. It had been a long time since he had seen Tymon so obviously uncomfortable. He would have enjoyed it more, except for the nagging feeling that Tymon's lack of optimism was entirely justified.

"No doubt you are right, but let me ask this: if you worry, and disaster strikes, how are you better served than if you had not worried at all? Does it change what happens?"

"No."

Seb shrugged. "Well, then. This place has the largest library I've ever seen, and that includes more than one king's palace. Don't tell me you haven't thought of taking advantage of it."

"Well . . . ," Tymon admitted, "I did notice a treatise on the 'Esthetics of Traditional Midwife Curses in the Lyrsan Period.' It's been a long time since I've read for pleasure."

Seb shuddered only a little. He even managed a smile. "Then I'd say you're overdue. Now wouldn't be too soon to begin."

Tymon looked thoughtful for a moment or two, then resumed pacing, only now he paced off in the general direction of the library, and Seb watched him go. Later, for want of something better to do, Seb found himself sketching in the gardens, in the company of a young monk more curious than amiable.

"You don't fit," the monk said. He was an earnest young fellow; his head was shaved but his face didn't need to be. Seb had ignored him when the boy first came to watch him sketching the mountain monastery's east wall; indeed the view held most of Seb's attention, with the garden and its well-tended trees contrasting so vividly with the sheer drop to the valley far below. The rough stone wall was too low for defense and hardly necessary considering the topology, but it added even more visual interest.

"Fit where? Here? I agree," Seb said, without taking his eyes off his work.

The boy shook his head. "You're not a dwarf."

Seb badly smudged a line, swore softly, and turned to the lad in annoyance. "I'm a fully grown man under four feet in height. If that's not a dwarf there must be some new definition of the term I'm not familiar with," he said.

The young monk looked enthusiastic. Seb cringed. He knew that look. He'd seen it in Tymon's eyes often enough. The monk confirmed his fear. "It's my specialty," he said, "or rather, I hope for it to be one day. I'm a student of the normal deviations of the human form. My name's Col, by the way."

"Seb. And I don't fit," Seb said, using some gum resin in an only partially successful bid to correct the line. "Apologies."

The boy reddened a bit. "I meant no offense. It's just the characteristics are so rare. Your proportions are perfect for your height; there's almost no distortion in either arms or legs."

"Seen a great many dwarfs, have you?"

The admission was grudging. "Well . . . no. But the texts lead me to suspect that, even for a dwarf, you are unusual."

"Col, I suspect you're right. But Master Seb is a guest, not a subject or supplicant. As such, he might find your comments more rude than interesting. Just a thought."

The abbot stood under the archway leading into the garden; neither Seb nor the monk had heard him approach. His head was shaved, as was Col's, and he was dressed in the same simple brown robes, but on the abbot they looked somehow more . . . well, "regal" was the only term Seb could think to describe it. And why not? The Alerian Order belonged to no one kingdom by agreement of all; the abbot was the closest thing to a king the monks recognized.

Seb noted the boy's stricken expression and couldn't resist a little smile. "I'm not really offended, Master Abbot. I see the same enthusiasms in my friend Tymon, with as little guile in the telling. I'm rather used to it by now."

The old man nodded. "I dare say. Col, I think you have other duties to attend. Am I right?"

Whether he did or not, Col used the pretext to take his leave as hastily as possible. The abbot found a stone bench near Seb's easel and settled down. "I have something I need to discuss with you, Master Seb."

Seb nodded. "I wondered when you would get around to that. Have we worn out our welcome?"

"Hardly. For Tymon's sake you would always have a place here, should you need it," the abbot said. "Yet it is because of Tymon that you will probably never have leisure enough to enjoy this."

Seb smiled. "Irony. I seem to run across that a lot. So. You have information?"

The abbot smiled now. "It seems the rumors of Tymon's death aren't spreading as widely, nor are as widely believed, as he might have hoped. This is not an eviction, Seb. It is fair warning."

Seb put his charcoals down. "I don't understand you, sir."

"Could you be more specific?"

"You know who we are, yet you shelter us when Tymon has a price on his head payable anywhere from Nols to ancient Lyrsa itself."

The abbot shrugged. "We have gold, when we need it. What we crave most is information, and the contemplation of that information that leads to understanding. In his own fuddled way, Tymon is one of our better sources. He's worth more to us for himself than for his hide, if you'll pardon my bluntness."

"Yet there's more to it, if you'll pardon mine," Seb said. He frowned. "Tymon was a student here, wasn't he?"

"Did he tell you that?"

"I'm assuming again. And I think I'm right."

The abbot shrugged again. "You may continue to think so. It's not for me to say."

"You know what happened to him. How this all started."

"Yes."

"I want to know."

"Yes," the abbot said amiably. "I imagine you do. Tymon will tell you when he's ready. Or rather, when he can."

"I don't suppose you'll explain that last bit?"

The abbot was still smiling. "It's always a risk to assume, Master Seb," he said, "but I must say you have the gift."

CHAPTER 4
"VISIONS IN A CRACKED GLASS"

Seb made preparations for leaving. It was one of the many things he was good at, though it wasn't one of his natural talents. He'd just had an incredible amount of practice. He made lists of travel stores and made certain that the types and amounts would be available at a moment's notice. He saw to their packhorses and mounts, making sure they were well-fed, groomed, and rested. He checked their belongings, making certain that all necessities were either already packed or quickly to hand.

All was ready, and had been for the last three days. Seb certainly was. Once the notion of leaving had gotten into his mind, there was no way he could find peace in his surroundings.

Yet Tymon would not leave.

He wouldn't say why, either. Seb knew Tymon had spoken to the abbot on several occasions after that day in the garden, but there was no sense of urgency about Tymon at all. Seb found himself watching the comings and goings of the ubiquitous messengers with growing unease. Any one of them could have been something other than he or she seemed, sent on some pretext to the monastery with gold in their dreams and assassination on their minds. Tymon listened politely time and again as Seb pointed this out. Then he would say, "Not yet," and that would be that until the next time Seb could not hold his tongue.

Has he finally gone mad?

Seb knew that Tymon surely had enough reason. Tymon was

at heart a kind, gentle man. The realities and actions the Long Look had forced him into had not hardened him; far from it. Seb understood to the core of his being that, one day, the burden would drive his friend insane, and he dreaded the day when that eventuality unfolded. Yet dealing with Tymon's gentleness of spirit was simply one more aspect of his mission that Seb assisted him with, where he could. Now he could not help, indeed had no idea what the specific problem was. And yet there was nothing about Tymon that Seb could definitely mark to a growing madness. Tymon seemed as placid as an ox, and with about as much tendency to move, unprodded.

Seb ran over his lists one last time and, because he could think of nothing else to do, he went looking for Tymon. Seb found him in that same east garden, perched on the wall above the valley. Seb approached cautiously; a startled Tymon could easily fall off and, tempted as Seb might be now and again to push Tymon off a high wall, he certainly didn't mean to do it by accident.

"We're not leaving yet," Tymon said, without turning around.

Seb sat on the bench. "I didn't ask," he said, which was true enough. It was also true that he had been about to ask, as he and Tymon both knew full well.

"Perhaps I could be a shade less irritating if I knew why we aren't leaving when we both know it's dangerous to linger," Seb said.

The question seemed to puzzle Tymon. "Why? Is that what this is about?"

"What else? You're being enigmatic. I hate that."

"Sorry. I don't mean to be. You keep asking me if we're leaving, and I say not yet. You ask when and I say that I don't know. And that, friend Seb, is no more or less than the truth. We probably should go; I don't dispute that. Yet I can't help feeling that I need to wait, that it's very important that we do not leave yet. I don't know why."

Seb got up from the bench and scrambled up the wall to sit beside Tymon. "There's been no Long Look yet, has there?"

"No. Why do you ask?"

"Because I wonder if that's the problem. When the Long Look strikes, you always know what to do. Or rather, what you need to accomplish to prevent what the Long Look is showing you. Plans must be made. Am I right?"

Tymon shrugged. "As far as my understanding goes, yes."

Seb looked smug. "Yet there's been no Long Look. Consider this, Tymon: maybe without the Long Look you simply have no concept of what you should do about anything. Stay or go, read this ancient tome rather than that one. Climb this wall or sit on that bench. Everything's a decision, and all directions are your own. It's complicated, and sometimes frightening. The Long Look has become your compass. Without it, you're adrift as a merchant ship with a broken rudder."

Tymon looked thoughtful. "You might be right, Seb. It certainly sounds plausible."

"So why don't we test it? Why don't we leave? Now?"

Tymon looked back out over the ribbon of a stream in the valley far below. "Because," he said, "It's not time to leave."

Seb again considered pushing Tymon off the wall. It was a very serious notion, and Seb liked to think he gave it due consideration. He made himself consider the consequences. Seb also pictured Tymon dwindling from man to speck and then nothing, out of sight, out of life. Seb pictured that last bit for a good long while. He settled for one single swear word as he hopped down to go check on the horses one more time.

Takren didn't like his master's visitors from the first. The larger one was, in Takren's considered judgment, a well-dressed butcher. He stood by the doorway, thick arms folded, his gaze wandering from Molic to Takren and back again as if the order had already been given and the only thing remaining was to decide which one of them would be most satisfying to slaughter first.

The other stranger, in Takren's even more considered opinion, was worse. He was even better dressed than his servant, in fine hose and a satin jerkin. He wore no heraldic device that Takren could see, but there was no doubt he was of the nobility. There was an air of casual command about him; an unaffected manner that only those born and raised to power could carry off well. His dagger and sword were jeweled and of fine make, but far more than merely decorative. The visitors had politely refused offers of food and drink. Now the stranger kneeled before Molic and spoke in a somber, deferential tone, but Takren wasn't fooled.

Molic, of course, was fooled. He knew no other state of existence.

"This is most exciting," he said. "I look forward to speaking to you again, My Lord."

Another bow, even as the man rose. "Your Majesty," he said. The voice did not change. The noble backed away a discreet distance and then turned to go out the door. His servant nodded, absently, and followed. Molic was grinning like a fox.

"It's going to happen, Takren. The day we have prayed for is at hand!"

Takren listened very carefully until he was sure he heard their guests ride away. "What day is that, My Lord?"

"My army. My subjects have come to my aid!"

Takren swore very softly. "I gather you refer to our mysterious guests, My Lord. Might I inquire their names?"

"They begged leave not to announce themselves until the time is right. I granted it, as that is such a small thing in return for their loyalty."

"Indeed," Takren said. It was all he could do to keep the word from becoming another question. He knew there was no point. "Is the time yet set for this marvelous event?"

Molic looked at him a little strangely. "Takren, if such were not totally ludicrous, I would swear I detected a hint of sarcasm in your manner."

"Your Highness is certainly correct," Takren said, "about it being ludicrous in the extreme. I ask only to better serve."

"Well said. Don't fret, Takren. I promise that, when the time comes, you will be first to know. Or perhaps third. One must leave a certainly flexibility in one's plans in the early stages."

Takren nodded. "One certainly must."

Galan was the first to break silence between himself and Ashesa. "You did not love my brother, did you?"

Lady Margate sat at a distance that was close enough for propriety and far enough for discretion, supposedly sewing. Ashesa and Galan sat together on a bench by the tower window, looking out together at a fine summer morning. Galan wasn't sure why he asked the question. He considered it a profoundly silly one. The match between his departed brother and the Princess Ashesa was arranged, as all such marriages would be. And nearly everyone had heard of the tantrum Ashesa had thrown when the arrangement had been announced; indeed, the incident was growing to nearly legendary proportions.

She must think me a fool.

If Ashesa thought anything of the sort, it wasn't obvious. In fact, the question seemed to startle her. She reddened very slightly, but soon that faded and her composure came back. She appeared to give the question due consideration for several long moments, and Galan was a little surprised to see that the question seemed to pain her. "No, Prince. I did not," she said finally. "I would like to think that Daras and I could have come to some understanding in time. Perhaps . . . perhaps more. I do not know, and fate decreed matters otherwise."

Galan sighed. "I am to be king now. I didn't want it, but fate decreed matters otherwise there, too. Your father still wants the alliance."

Ashesa looked grim. "And what do you want, Prince?"

"As Crown Prince, I want what my father wanted—the alliance. For myself. . . ." Galan hesitated, but only a moment. Galan knew himself well enough to know that, if he did not speak now, he might never speak at all. "For myself, for Galan, I want the marriage. To you."

She didn't say anything for a while, and Galan stumbled on, "I am not my brother. I'm not as handsome, nor as bold and brave. My hand turns better to a pen than a sword, albeit I can use either at need. I will be king, the Powers willing, but most of all I would wish to be what will make you happy. I wish that more than anything."

Ashesa stared out the window. She might have smiled a brief, sad smile. Galan wasn't sure. "I don't know what will make me happy, Prince," she said. "But if you are not your brother, well, that isn't altogether a bad thing. If Daras was brave, he was also reckless. If handsome, he was also vain in his way, and I do not think he cared for me at all. No matter. I'm not looking for happiness now; I'm not sure it exists. But if my wishes mean anything to you, know that I have no objection to the marriage. You may tell my father as much for me, if he asks."

It wasn't exactly a tearful expression of undying devotion, but to Galan it was more than he'd dared to hope.

"I hope I never give you cause to regret this, Highness."

"Nor I you," Ashesa said. She did not look hopeful.

Ashesa continued to stare out the window long after Prince Galan took his leave. Lady Margate concentrated on her sewing, and waited.

"What do you think of Galan?" Ashesa asked finally.

Her nurse warmed to the subject. "He's not so ill-favored as he seems to think, even measured by Daras's lofty standard. Green, yes, but time will cure that if he isn't a total fool. He's well-spoken, polite and respectful. I rather like him but, more to the heart of the matter, I think he's completely besotted with you. That is a good quality in a husband-to-be, to my mind, politics and necessity aside."

Ashesa blushed slightly. "I like him, too. I didn't really expect that."

"Why not? Once you got past your anger you may have even found Daras not so bad. Pity."

"More than you know," Ashesa said softly.

"You're being mysterious, child. Save that for your betrothed. There's something you're not telling me. A secret? Yes, of course. We all have them. Some are best discarded; this may be one."

Ashesa smiled. "If I solve that particular puzzle, Margy, I promise you your share of it. For now, I think I'll keep it right where it is."

Tymon missed sleep, or rather, the parts of sleep having to do with oblivion. He remembered those, perhaps through the haze of nostalgia, as being the best parts and now gone forever. It had to do with his art, he knew. Deep, untroubled sleep was something not so much lost as paid out as part of the price of his quest for mastery.

This night the sacrifice seemed a bit excessive.

Tymon waited in a place that didn't really exist as part of the material world. He knew he was asleep, or rather unconscious. His body lay in his quarters at the monastery, breathing yet inert, because whatever could be said to be Tymon himself—

soul, avatar, spirit—sat on something that looked like a stone bench, beside what looked like a flowing willow, beside what looked like a dark, slow stream, and he waited, because in that infinitely distant place there was nothing else he or anyone else could have done. That was the reason for it being there, wherever "there" was. He knew the signs. He had been summoned. It wasn't the Long Look. It was much worse.

"I am here," he said.

"You think I don't know?"

Amaet appeared beside the willow tree. Tymon had thought her beautiful when he had first seen her many years ago. Now he knew that his perceptions were correct but still not to be trusted where she was concerned. She was beautiful, yes. Her hair was blacker than a cold, starless night and almost as long. Her face and form together were a masterpiece to shame even the best human artists. All this was true, and all unimportant. Amaet looked the way she did because she chose to. She could choose otherwise. Tymon had seen that, once. He wasn't sure he could do the same again and keep what few shreds of sanity he still cherished.

"You teach me my place yet again, Amaet."

Amaet sighed, and somewhere in the real world a lover's heart broke. "Such a self-infatuated thing you are, Tymon. Not all the music plays for you. Not even the song of the lash."

"Yet I still find myself beneath that lash. Metaphorically speaking."

"As is everyone, Magician."

"Even you, Amaet?"

Tymon didn't know he was going to say that before he did. He wondered why he dared. Perhaps it was the frustration of waiting so many weeks when every instinct he possessed told him it was now the time for doing, and might soon be too late to make a difference. The world was in motion now, as it always was, and Tymon knew he could not escape his part in it by hiding in the abbot's garden, however pleasant that might be.

She looked at him. Tymon thought she smiled. He wasn't sure then or later. "Especially me, mortal. You carry a rock; others carry mountains and can no more discard their burdens than you. Everyone serves as strength allows. It wouldn't hurt for you to remember that now and again."

Tymon kept silent and, because he could still do no less, he waited.

"It's time," Amaet said. And she told him what he needed to do.

Tymon listened, and then he nodded. "I understand. But why didn't you send the Long Look instead?"

"Because I don't send the Long Look," she said. "You do. And I did grow weary of waiting." And then she disappeared.

After a moment or two the bench, and the stream, and the willow, and then Tymon himself began to do the same. He sighed, thinking of all the questions that would again go unanswered, only now there was a new one. No matter. Tymon knew that, for now, this was all the explanation he was going to get.

Seb paused by the saddle packs, resting for the moment from the chore of packing for travel, feeling yet again as one trying to push twenty cats into a ten-cat sack. "Will you tell me again why we're leaving now?"

Tymon yawned, though as far as Seb knew he'd done little for the last two days except sleep. He was like a cat himself that way. Tymon blinked. "Oh. Sorry. We're leaving now because that will give us just enough time to reach the bridge over the Ald River by sunset of the third day from today."

"You're too literal at times," Seb said. "I know you don't do it to annoy but, trust me, it often does annoy, and very much indeed. Now then: why is it important that we reach said bridge on said day?"

"I don't know."

"Any thoughts on what we might do there once we arrive? Should I pack something for a picnic lunch or something for a battle?"

"Again, I don't know. Sorry, Seb. I do know this isn't much help to you, and sometimes I consider making things up, just to have something to say to you when these things happen. But I don't. I'd mean well, but it just doesn't feel right to me, and more often than not that's all I have to go on. All I can say is that I have reason to suspect that the proper course will be revealed at the proper time. If not. . . ."

"If not, what?"

"I don't know that, either."

Seb sighed and, at least figuratively, reached for another cat.

Unlike most of his friends who were born on the small farms and fishing villages on Borasur's coast, young Koric had always wanted to see more of the world than the parts of it he knew by heart. When Lord Molic's old servant came to him one evening after chores to say he had a special task for him, the lad was overjoyed. Now, two days later and much farther from home than he had ever been in his life, Koric was no longer quite so certain that his joy had been well-placed.

The road north had been rising steadily all day and, after the previous two days, Koric was discovering that walking around Lord Molic's farm on his daily routine and walking hour after hour down a hot, dusty road was not the same thing at all. Oh, the scenery varied somewhat, but it was hard for a farm lad like Koric, more than passingly acquainted with trees and rocks, to become too enthused about more trees and different rocks. Especially when he was hot and thirsty and had so very far to go, and nothing was quite as, well, different, as he had expected.

"It's as if everything's different, and yet nothing is."

"Rather heavy thought for such a weary traveler."

Koric looked around, startled. A large oak tree spread magnificent shade in a small meadow just beyond the road, and seated in that shade with his back to the oak was another traveler. He was dressed all in black, though the sable was somewhat muted by road dust. His clothes were of fine make, as was his pack and the sword and scabbard leaning against the tree. He wore a wide-brimmed hat pushed forward on his nose so that Koric couldn't quite see his face.

"Your pardon, My Lord, I didn't see you there."

The stranger pushed his hat back. The man's hair and eyes were even darker than his clothes, though the smile he turned on Koric was friendly enough.

"My name is Aktos and I am no one's 'lord.' Some days even I don't obey me," he said.

Koric couldn't stop from smiling. "I often have that problem. I give myself good and considered advice, but seldom take it."

Aktos smiled again, indicating the shade. "Well, if you'll accept the suggestion of a stranger better, he would point out that the road is very hot, this shade is not, and neither condition will change much for the next hour or so. I advise rest. I really do. I have some water. Would you care to share?"

It occurred to Koric that the stranger could be a thief, but Koric also knew he didn't have anything worth stealing. He also knew that his dress and equipment, functional as they both were, didn't count for much to a man of such obvious means. And the water sounded wonderful. He had been looking for a stream to fill his own shrunken waterskin for the past few hours without success.

"That I would, and my thanks. Though I'm afraid I can't repay the favor, having nothing to share."

Aktos shrugged. "The day is young and we both, I suspect, have a long way to go. Perhaps we could share that instead. For now, sit. The road isn't going anywhere."

The water and the company were both very good. Later, when they started walking together, Koric thought the miles seemed to pass faster, and said so.

" 'Time shared is time divided,' a wise man once told me," Koric said.

"A bit of a problem, since there always seems precious little enough time without dividing it with everyone you meet," Aktos said. "Although I think it a compliment, nonetheless."

Koric smiled. "Well, some sorts of time should be divided. Travel time. Work time. Unpleasant time."

Aktos looked thoughtful. "That could be. Yet what is pleasant and what not is often a matter of hindsight, and things that seem pleasant at the time might show a darker nature farther down the road."

Koric couldn't quite see it that way at the moment. As they walked north, the road had shown itself less traveled, and the forests grew thicker and closer. Yet that in itself seemed an improvement. Fewer travelers meant fewer opportunities for highwaymen, who seemed to favor the riskier but more lucrative byways farther south. The wildness of the forest merely meant that now the road was shaded over by oak and aspen and much more cool and pleasant walking. Koric and Aktos kept up a brisk pace, and Koric wasn't nearly as tired as he expected to be.

"I think I've told you all there is to know of me," Koric said at last, "but I still count you a mystery."

"All men are mysteries. Some have explanations, some do not, but in neither case is that mystery really revealed. Consider, I know much about you, yes, but I still don't know why you came to be on this road, at this time."

"Didn't I mention that? I'm running an errand."

"Fetching a pail from a well is an errand. Traveling the north road from the coast all the way to the foothills of the White Mountains is not an errand. It's more in the nature of a great undertaking. Especially for one who, I rather guess, has never been so far from home before."

"Is it that obvious?"

Aktos laughed without breaking stride. "Yes, in a word."

"You're a man of great experience, I can see, though compared to me anyone would be. What could I teach you?"

"Something I don't know, of course. I'll do the same: what do you want to know about me?"

Koric thought about it. "Well, for a start, where were you born?"

"In a pig sty in Nols. Or close enough."

Koric frowned. "I thought—" He stopped.

Aktos smiled. "Nobility? Royalty traveling in disguise?" Koric reddened, and Aktos smiled broader. "See? By telling you one thing I learn another. You're a romantic. I didn't know that before. Suspected, perhaps. But did not know."

"Yet . . . you dress so well."

Aktos shrugged. "I've done well for myself over the years, but all through my own efforts, I assure you. I have no advantage over you by birth, Koric. Maybe rather the opposite."

"I hope one day to do as well," Koric said.

Aktos didn't say anything for a moment. Then he said, "Be careful of your desires, Koric. They're harder masters than any man or woman you can serve in this life."

"I sense another story there," Koric said.

"You may yet hear it, but not now. My turn: where are you going, Koric? I confess you've aroused my curiosity; I've been on this road many times, and I've never seen you on it before today."

Koric considered. Takren had made him swear to reveal the message he carried to no one, but since Koric couldn't read, there was precious little chance of that. Koric didn't see how he could reveal the nature of secrets he did not possess. "I'm on an errand, as I said. My master's servant sent me to deliver a message to a man at the Kuldun monastery. I don't know what it's about; I don't need to know."

Aktos nodded. "Quite right and proper for a messenger," he said, and that was all. Still, there were silences and there were silences, and it seemed to Koric that the one now coming from Aktos was of the sort that might be broken, if caution or simple manners had not argued against it. He wasn't sure which one was responsible, but now his curiosity was aroused.

"It is a very long way," he said, "and what stories I've heard of the monks of Kuldun do give one pause."

Aktos shrugged. "Much is said of them, true enough. How much of the telling is true. . . . well, who can say who has not been there himself?"

It was nearing sunset. They walked through a place where the trees were very thick indeed, and beyond that Koric heard the roaring rush of swift water over stone. The trees parted ever so slightly and Koric came first to the bridge. It was built of wood and rope, but it was wide and solidly made for the traffic of cart and horse it was doubtless built to carry. Koric looked down into a deep rocky gorge through which a river not so much ran as poured, like water from a pitcher, in a series of waterfalls that ended further downstream as the river turned wide and dark.

"What river is this?" Koric asked.

"The Ald, I think."

Koric blinked. "You think? I thought you had been this way many times."

Aktos sighed. "I'm afraid I lied about that. This is the first time I've set eyes on it."

Koric heard the whisper of steel on leather, and he turned to find a very sharp dagger at his throat. "You will please give me the message you're carrying," Aktos said. At that moment, frozen as it was in Koric's memory, the only image that really remained was Aktos's smile. It hadn't changed. His easy, friendly manner had not altered one bit. Yet the dagger was still at Koric's throat.

"What are you doing?!"

"You're too new from home to have developed a proper mistrust of your fellow man, and I'm afraid I used that, Koric. In my trade it's often required to use the tools at hand," Aktos said.

"Y-Your trade?"

"Mercenary, assassin. Call it what you will. I was hired to intercept you and discover whether you carried a message and whether it was written or memorized. This I have done. I was also hired to recover the message, if written. Which I am now doing. Please hand it over."

"Takren said—" Koric hesitated, trying to remember what it was that Takren had said. Something about a matter that was unusual and yet somehow routine. Something about not giving the note to anyone except the man he described.

Aktos shifted the blade a mere fraction, but Koric felt the sting of its tip and his bowels almost loosened then and there.

"Takren is not here, Friend Koric. This blade is. One way or another I will have what I came for. Don't force me to kill you now."

"Why is killing the lad later so much more preferable?"

They both looked to the other end of the bridge, but Aktos did not move the knife. A tall, dark man, darker of hair, clothes, and trappings than even Aktos, sat there on a big dun horse. He wore a sword and dagger but did not seem to be paying much attention to either weapon. Koric heard Aktos draw one slow breath and let it out even slower.

"Tymon the Black," he said, so softly that even Koric almost didn't hear. Aktos looked down at him. "Koric, this matter may be more important than you or I knew."

CHAPTER 5
"MET, BUT NOT WELL"

"Tymon the Black," whoever he was, sat very still on his mount. Aktos shifted his grip on the dagger as if he just could not find the perfect hold. Koric, still stunned from the first turn of events, couldn't decide where to turn his attention, albeit the image of the dagger at his throat was never far from his mind.

Tymon sighed a gusty sigh, audible even at that distance. "You haven't answered my question. Why the delay? Was it really preferable to wait rather than kill him when you had the chance?"

"I still have the chance," Aktos said. If he had been a whit more alert Koric might have noticed the tinge of fear in Aktos's voice, albeit he hid it well.

"You were going to kill me, weren't you?" Koric said. He meant it to be a question but it just didn't turn out that way.

"Yes," Aktos said. "Now do be quiet. I'm negotiating, or hadn't you noticed?"

Koric had not. But now he made it a point to notice everything possible. The gleaming edges of Aktos's knife. The depth of the gorge and the water below, and how much chance he would have of surviving if he could pull away from Aktos long enough to jump. None, he decided. He turned his attention to the rider. For no reason other than desperation, he thought hope might reside there.

Aktos raised his voice just enough to carry the distance. "What business is it of yours, Magician? Why do you interfere?"

"The message he carries is intended for me," Tymon said. "I call that reason enough. Though I'll point out that I have not—in point of fact—interfered. Yet."

"Don't try to frighten me, Magician."

Tymon smiled. "Why would I want to frighten you?"

Koric could now plainly see that Aktos was already frightened, for all his talk. That, as far as Koric could see, only made him more grim and determined. Koric reconsidered the gorge.

Tymon continued. "Consider—you have been accompanying the lad for some time, by my information. Surely you could have found out what you needed to know and done the deed before now."

"I choose my own time and pace," Aktos said.

"Even the Powers are not so unconstrained," Tymon said. "But let that pass. I submit that you were reluctant. You don't really want to kill this boy."

Aktos chuckled. "I never want to kill anyone, but I've not let that stop me. I've found that those in my profession who enjoy taking life never last long. They don't know when to stop. They get careless."

Tymon dismounted. He came to the foot of the bridge but advanced no further. "Do you know when to stop, Aktos?"

Aktos took a step backward, pulling Koric with him. "You know who I am. I find that disturbing."

Tymon smiled again. "Are you suspecting that your employer has betrayed you? Is that possible?"

"Considering their nature? Very possible. Though I don't think it likely; I can't see the point." Aktos took another step backward with Koric following, though it was not as if the lad had a choice. A few more steps and they would be off the bridge. "We're leaving now, Magician. Don't try to stop me."

"Don't try to leave and I won't have to. I'd like to make a bargain."

Aktos laughed. "I'm sure you would."

Tymon sighed. "Aktos, one way or another you will listen to me. Which way will it be?"

"I said we're leaving. We are. I'm taking the boy and the message he carries."

"I can't let you do that."

Tymon whistled. Aktos, startled, looked around, but nothing seemed to happen except that Tymon's mount trotted a few steps forward to stand behind its master.

Revealing a second riderless horse standing just within the forest.

"Damn sneaky—"

That was as far as Aktos got. Just as he released Koric long enough to set himself in a knife-fighter's stance a small black and green blur somersaulted over the railing of the bridge and knocked him sprawling. He bounced off the opposite railing and fell in a tangled heap. Aktos was still trying to untangle himself and draw his sword when the blur resolved itself into a small man about four feet high, a small man who drew a small hunting sword that was only a little longer than Aktos's dropped dagger. The dwarf kicked the dagger over the edge of the bridge and set his own point at Aktos's throat before the struggling young man could get his own blade clear of its sheath.

"Well done, Seb."

The dwarf nodded an acknowledgment, but kept his blade point steady all the time. Tymon strolled across the bridge and stood looking down at Aktos. The assassin's eyes had a trapped look. "Now then, Aktos . . . about that bargain? It can wait. Young man, may I have the message?" He held out his hand to Koric.

Despite his relief, Koric wasn't sure what to expect. He did know that what actually did happen afterwards was not something he would have imagined, left to his own devices. Tymon took the message from him and read it, though he didn't seem either surprised or concerned by its contents. After that a sense of resignation seemed to come over his former friend Aktos. Then about an hour later they all sat around a campfire in perfect amity, having supper.

Seb was an excellent cook.

Aktos ate, but his mind was clearly elsewhere. "I thought you were going to kill me, Magician."

Koric scowled. "You were going to kill me," he said, and Aktos shrugged.

"If I'd simply taken the message, Takren would have known he was suspected. If you simply never returned he'd have assumed you met with some misfortune and sent someone else. It was nothing personal."

"It was to *me*," Koric muttered.

Tymon sighed. "Don't go on about it, lad. You're safe, and Aktos's current predicament may work to our mutual advantage."

"I'm waiting to hear about that part myself," Aktos said. "You spared my life, and I want to know why. I know you don't trust me, and you're wise in that."

Tymon waved his hand in dismissal. "This has nothing to do with trust, Aktos. If you were one of your warped associates you'd have gone off into the gorge with a slit throat, which is what I assume you had in mind for our young friend here. I won't kill you without a good reason. We're alike in that."

Koric felt a little sick, but he kept silent. There was too much going on that he didn't understand, so much indeed that he wasn't even certain what questions—if any—he should have been asking.

Aktos shrugged. "I'm listening."

"I've seen the message you were sent to intercept, so you

have officially failed. I take it your employer will be very cross with you."

Aktos shrugged again. "Could be."

"So I propose that we don't let him find out."

"I haven't said it was a 'he.' Or anything else concerning the person," Aktos pointed out.

Tymon nodded. "Properly discreet, and so noted. But then, I knew who you were, so you might believe me when I tell you that I already know who your employer is. You needn't name him to me. I ask only that you observe the letter of your agreement with this person."

"How can I do that now?"

"By bringing him my message. Which really will be mine, strictly speaking, as I will write it while you watch. It will concern trivial matters that will put your employer's mind at rest. It will duplicate Takren's script so well that I fancy he himself couldn't tell the difference. We'll also keep the boy with us so his reappearance at the farm doesn't raise your employer's suspicions."

By then Koric was more afraid of Tymon and Seb than he was of his would-be murderer, but he couldn't keep silent. "I never agreed to that!"

"You will agree," Tymon said, "or I'll kill you myself and save Aktos the bother." He didn't raise his voice or change the tone of his words in any way, but Koric didn't doubt him for a moment. Neither did Aktos, apparently. He looked almost touched.

Aktos sighed. "I must ask, then: why would you do this for me?"

"It's not for you. This will serve us both. Are we agreed? Your only other option is to attempt to overpower and slay us now. Or pretend agreement and then creep back to attempt the same later. I would advise against either course."

Aktos glanced at Seb, who grinned at him. He looked away

quickly. "I wasn't paid for any extra effort or risk. Very well, I agree."

Tymon nodded. "A wise choice."

Koric just looked around at all of them as if he were the only sane person in a parliament of the mad.

Seb pretended to sleep as Aktos gathered up his blanket and pack and slipped away from their camp early the next morning. Then Seb sat up, yawning. Night was in full retreat from a hint of dawn. Seb got up, rolled his bedding, and started to prepare breakfast. He allowed himself the peace and lack of complication such routine activities often created for him, but it didn't last. It never did. After a few moments he gave up and allowed himself to notice that Tymon was up, sitting on a fallen log, watching him.

"Good morning," Seb said. "If indeed it is."

Tymon yawned. "We have Takren's message. We're alive to scheme another day. I call that good enough for any given morning."

Seb glanced in the direction Aktos had taken—south. "Can we trust him?"

"No, so it's a good thing we don't have to do so. Aktos, despite his profession, is a relatively sane young man who does not take his work personally. He will do what's in his own interest, and so I suspect he'll keep his bargain for that reason."

Seb frowned. "Suspect? You don't know for certain?"

Tymon shook his head. "I do not."

Seb started to say something, thought better of it. "What's so important about that message?"

"There's going to be an attempt to steal the throne of Borasur by Prince Molic."

Seb frowned even deeper, if that were possible. " 'Prince' Molic? You mean that addlepated farmer? If we're thinking of the same person, he couldn't steal a melon."

"This isn't a melon, Seb. This is the sort of thing that only a simple soul like Molic very well could steal. With the right help."

Seb's frown cleared away. "Help. You mean Aktos's current employer."

Tymon nodded. "You grasped that. I thought you might."

"Well, hiring an assassin certainly wasn't Molic's notion. By all account he's a sweet old daffy with the mental acuity of a butterfly."

"And the bloodline of a king, albeit very dilute. Worse, he's in the direct line of the current ruling House. Not even the most powerful nobles of the kingdom can make the same claim. That makes him dangerous."

"Not to us," Seb said pointedly.

Tymon said nothing. Seb didn't expect anything else. He finally sighed. "How are we going to stop him?"

"I haven't a clue."

For a moment Seb just stared at the magician.

"Excuse me. . . ."

They both turned. Koric was sitting up on his blankets, listening. He had apparently been doing so for some time.

"I realize that I'm just a small bit of nothing in all this, but I've just come very close to dying for no good reason that I can see. If there is one, I'd like to know what it is."

Seb grunted. "To tell the truth, so would I."

Tymon wasn't very helpful. "My boy, I'm not really sure how you fit into this, except as a nuisance. That concerns me. I wonder still if it might not have been better to let Aktos work his will on you."

Koric looked a little pale. Seb glared at his friend. "Tymon, you're scaring the lad."

"Good. If he's not afraid of the mess he's in, then he's a damn fool, and that's the last thing we need now." Tymon

73

turned back to the boy. "You were to deliver a message to me from Takren, who happens to be an old acquaintance of mine. That should have been the end of it, Koric, and I don't think Takren would have sent you if he'd thought otherwise. He was wrong, and I apologize on his behalf. So there you are."

Koric was still pale. Now he looked confused, too. Seb smiled at him. "You should feel honored, lad. He's seldom so straight-forward."

Tymon frowned. "I don't know how to put it plainer than that."

Seb nodded. "More's the pity there. Let me try: Koric, on Molic's farm you might not have noticed, but out in the wider world great matters are afoot. They always are. It is your misfortune that this one seems to be occurring on your doorstep. Do you know what is contained in Molic's letter?"

"Only as much as I heard you speak a moment ago. I didn't open it."

"Can you read?" Tymon asked.

Koric hung his head. "I have my letters, but little practice."

"Then I will read for you." Tymon unfolded the parchment. " 'To Tymon of Nols from the Servant of the House of Molic, Greetings.' " Tymon waved his hand slightly, saying, "The rest of that concerns matters of our earlier association; I won't weary you with the details. This is the important part. 'I fear there is a threat to usurp the throne of Borasur. My master is innocent in this but not uninvolved. I do not know if there is anything you would or can do, but I thought you should be aware if you are not already. I do not know the person responsible. I think I should, but I do not, and they carry no badges or devices that I've seen. Please answer if an answer there may be. Takren.' "

Tymon refolded the parchment. "Most of the rest you know as well as we. Have there been visitors to Molic's farm?"

Koric looked from one to the other for several long moments.

Seb noted his hesitation. "I can understand that you've little cause to trust us," he said. "But you know Tymon is your master's friend and looked to him for aid. Trust that, if not us. We are trying to help."

Koric nodded, looking doubtful but resigned. "There have been a few. They were strange men. I-I did not care for them."

"Oh? Why not?" Seb asked. "Did they mistreat you?"

"They barely spoke to me except to ask for water and a bite of fodder for their mounts."

Now Tymon looked interested. " 'Asked'? Not 'demanded'?"

Koric shook his head. "They were very polite, which was a surprise. It was their eyes that worried me." The boy hesitated again, then continued. "I've seen that same look in my older brothers' faces when I was younger. Like when they were about to play a nasty joke, that joke is going to be on me, and they can't wait to see my pain. These men were full of secrets, and they were not pleasant secrets."

"Hmmm." Tymon looked thoughtful. "Takren said there were no heraldic devices or badges. Did you see anything of the sort?"

"They wore nothing in plain sight that would indicate their allegiance, but when I watered their horses I noticed an emblem stitched into one of the saddle blankets—a swan spreading its wings to fly. Takren wouldn't have seen it."

Seb and Tymon exchanged glances.

Tymon looked thoughtful again. "House Dyrlos. Not in the direct line. But the next best thing."

Seb sighed. "Why am I not surprised?"

Tymon came to a decision. "I must speak to Takren."

"What of your bargain with the assassin?"

"I intend to keep it," Tymon said.

Koric went pale again, and even Seb drew back a bit. "Tymon, what do you mean?"

Tymon ignored them both. He reached into his pouch and

pulled out a slim case. He opened it to reveal pen and ink. "There's some blank parchment in my saddle bag, Seb. Would you bring it to me?"

Seb obeyed, but he kept his eyes on Tymon all the while. Koric looked as if he wanted mainly to run, if he could have picked a good direction. Seb brought the parchment and Tymon selected one of the smaller pieces. He wrote quickly, then sealed it with a bit of wax softened in Seb's campfire. "Koric, come here."

Koric came forward, warily, and Tymon placed the parchment in his hand. "My lad, you're going to deliver another message, this time to the abbot of the monastery at Kuldun. And if you must talk to strangers on the road, at least this time pick your company more carefully."

"Were you . . . singing?" Tymon asked.

A few hours later, with Koric well on the road to Kuldun and themselves the same on the southern road, Tymon waited for Seb to say what was on his mind. Seb seemed unusually hesitant; so much so that Tymon felt compelled to start the avalanche himself. Not that Seb's tune was just an excuse at conversation; Tymon couldn't remember the last time he had heard his friend sing.

Seb shrugged. "Sorry. It's an old song. I was afraid I'd forgotten the words."

"I was distracted, I'm afraid. I didn't hear the words. What is the song about?"

The dwarf shrugged again. "Love. Hate. Loyalty. Betrayal. Death. The grand themes."

As explanations went it wasn't much, but it was more than Tymon needed. "You really thought I was going to kill him, didn't you?" he said, bending down to avoid a low branch.

"The thought did cross my mind," Seb said dryly.

"Mine too. There. Are you satisfied?"

"No. I'm not disappointed, mind you. I'm rather relieved, and I did feel sorry for the lad, away from home for the first time and already up past his neck in a hornet's nest. So. Just what have you done to the poor boy?"

Tymon smiled. "I sent him to the abbot, with a request that he help our young friend make productive use of his stay. I think teaching him to read better is a fine place to start."

Seb rolled his eyes toward heaven. "They'll educate the lad, see if they don't. He'll discover the musty secrets of book and scroll and never be content with field and sky again. They'll turn him into Brother Col! Maybe death would have been kinder."

"I think not," Tymon said.

The dwarf sighed. "It was a joke."

"Of sorts," Tymon grudgingly admitted. "If it had been necessary, I would have done it, Seb. If I had been sure. Removing Aktos and Koric would have simplified matters but I don't know if simplicity is what we want or need. I took a chance making that bargain with Aktos. I did the same again by sending Koric off for tutoring, on faith that he won't break and run the first chance he gets, which could be disastrous for everyone. My reasoning said to kill them both."

"Then why didn't you?"

"Because my instincts disagreed, and right now they're all I have to go on."

Seb blinked. "All?"

"Yes," Tymon said. "The Long Look has deserted me. We may have to solve this dilemma with only our own devices."

Seb just stared, and after a moment Tymon nodded. "You once said I was cursed, Seb. I'm beginning to think you are right."

Seb sighed deeply. "Perhaps we'll know more after we talk to

Takren," he said.

"Perhaps," Tymon said. "If only I could be sure that would help."

Duke Laras stood on the parapet looking down at the docks beyond the outer walls. His father, the previous Duke, liked to pretend that the docks weren't there. That the family's livelihood was something that appeared magically as their right and due as Children of the House of Dyrlos. Laras, as tall and fair as his father, was far different in that regard and many others. Laras paid attention to the docks, and the charter of perpetual trade they represented. He noticed when ships were sailing undermanned, or cargos did not match their tallies. Laras prided himself on paying attention, as the strengthening family fortunes could well attest. That was why the scrap of parchment in his hand now was so puzzling.

"I don't understand it, Vor," he said.

Vor leaned against a stone crenelation some few feet away, his thick arms folded across his chest.

"Is the old man's script that abominable?" he asked. "I'm surprised he can write at all."

Laras doubted that his vassal was really surprised. For one thing, it was not so uncommon for men at the level of overseer or dockmaster to have their letters; often that was how they achieved their positions in the first place. And for another, Laras well knew that Vor did not like surprises. They worried and upset him, and Vor was currently in neither state.

"It's not that. It's the subject. Takren talks of harvest and hopes for a visit. Ramblings of his declining years. It's just not that important. Why send one of the few farmhands, and this close to harvest?"

"Old men ramble," Vor said. "It's their nature. Especially when they scent mortality coming closer, I hear. Such maudlin sentiments might have overridden his judgment."

"Still, it is curious."

"Do you think that hired blade of yours might have misled you?"

Laras shook his head. "I don't know. I don't think so. This could be a code of some sort. After all, Takren never names the person to which this was intended. Don't you find that the least bit odd?"

Vor shrugged. "In this one matter you are too subtle, Your Grace. Takren is a foolish old man and no more. You were wise to be cautious, but this is doubtless nothing."

"Doubtless," Laras said, but he did not look so certain of it. "Still, one lashes a cargo to the deck before a storm, not after. We will keep watch. I want you to see to it personally."

Laras tore the parchment into small pieces and watched them flutter off on the breeze like brown butterflies over the water of the bay. Laras watched them go.

"Your moment is close at hand, now, Duke. Your father would be proud."

"My father was a fool," Laras said.

Vor looked away. "I would not say so."

Laras smiled. "Certainly not. But he was my father and I stood in his corpulent shadow long enough. It's my prerogative to tell the truth about him when it suits me. He would have delayed the moment forever, searching for the right time to take the revenge that his father charged him to gain. That's the difference, Vor. I don't care about revenge for a slight two hundred years old, and that more imagined than real. Molic will take Galan's place on the throne of Borasur because I believe this is for the greater good of my House."

"Molic will be removed when necessary."

Laras frowned. "Why should it be necessary? I don't care who wears the crown, so long as House Dyrlos has the power to control its own destiny. That is what this is about, Vor. Nothing more."

"It is enough," Vor said.

Laras watched the last piece of fluttering parchment fade out of sight. "More than enough. Everything."

Tymon and Seb reached Borasur after two days of unhurried travel. Tymon was under the opinion that hurrying would serve no purpose, that events were unfolding at a pace that would allow some time for reflection. Seb was aware that this was only Tymon's opinion, and the fact of this was weighing very heavily on his mind.

One thing to do monstrous acts for a good cause when you know you're right. What if you only believe you're right?

Seb knew that far too many people in the world had absolutely no trouble with that subtle but important difference. Seb wasn't one of them, try as he might to ignore it. There was a line he had never crossed before, and Seb wondered what Tymon would ask him to do now, and whether it would be in him to obey. It was a new worry, and Seb didn't like it one bit.

Their meeting with Takren—conducted in secret on a hillside in the dead of night with no fires lit—failed at both drama and in setting Seb's mind at ease. Takren had not written more in the letter out of fear of discovery; he simply didn't know much more than he had told them. In fact he was chagrined to hear what Tymon had to tell him about House Dyrlos.

"I'm a fool," Takren said. "But it never occurred to me to ask Koric if he had noticed anything. Speaking of which, why isn't he with you?"

"He is safe, Takren," Tymon said, "but I deemed it wise that he not return here for a while. I've seen to his lodging in the meantime."

Takren nodded. "I thank you for that. I should have known

there would be danger. I should have suspected House Dyrlos. I'm too old for intrigue, old friend, though I suspect this is something I would never have been young enough for."

"Why should you suspect House Dyrlos?" Seb asked.

"Because there has always been bad blood between them and the Royal House of Borasur," Tymon said softly.

Takren nodded. "Quite right. Ever since the Succession of Nyldur . . . or usurpation, depending on who you ask."

Seb looked from one to the other. "I'm not well versed in Borasurean history and I gather you both know this story. Would one of you please tell it to me? And quickly, mind—the night won't last forever."

"As dynastic struggles go, this is a short one," Tymon said. "About two centuries ago, the last king of the Molkoran royal line of Borasur died without heir. There were two Great Families with close ties of kinship to the Crown—Dyrlos and Kotara. The origin of each was just obscure enough that it was very difficult to settle the matter of precedence between them. So the lords of both Houses agreed to put the matter to the Priests of Amatok, and each lord swore to abide by the priests' decision, for the good of the kingdom. The priests chose Kotara, whose lord, Nyldur, became the first monarch in the Kotaran line. This is the one to which Molic claims kinship."

Seb shrugged. "I can understand House Dyrlos's disappointment, but—"

"But that wasn't the end of it," Takren said. "There was a rumor, widely believed, that the Priests of Amatok had been bribed and the outcome foreordained."

"Ah. . . . Civil war? Burning and pillage?"

Tymon shook his head. "Oddly enough: no. The rumor alone would have been enough for most, but the Lord of House Dyrlos had given his word and he was, for those times, a very honorable man. He wanted proof of any bad faith and there was none. So he abided by the decision with as much grace as he could muster. Later he challenged the Kotaran royal house on some other pretext and took to the judiciary field himself. He was slain in combat by the king's champion."

Seb nodded. "Now I understand their annoyance. Still, people will talk. You'd think after two centuries the matter would be forgotten."

"Some people cannot release a grudge, Seb, as we well know. They cherish a hurt as others cherish a lover. Especially a wrong as delicious as this."

Seb frowned. "Wrong? You mean . . . ?"

"Oh yes. The rumor was accurate in at least one regard—Galan's ancestor was not closest in kinship to the Royal House of Borasur. The crown should have gone to House Dyrlos."

Chapter 6
"Thwarted Justice"

Tymon sat by the dark stream, on the stone bench. The stone was cool. The dark waters, when Tymon dipped his bare toes into the silent stream experimentally, were cool as well. Tymon wished some of that cool could reach his mind, now fevered as it was every day and night. He came to the Meeting Place, as always, without prior intent, and again, as always, he did not know if Amaet would be there. He didn't really know if he wanted her to be there, since her arrival in his life had always tended to complicate matters.

Tymon finally decided that what he wanted was not coolness, but clarity. His own supply was shockingly low.

"I don't know what to do," he said.

"No. You don't."

Amaet was there. Tymon had not called her—if Tymon making his own presence known and hers desired could be referred to as a summons in any case—but she came. And so far she had not been very helpful.

"Amaet, are you a Power?"

She sat beside him on the bench. Tymon couldn't suppress a shiver, though of excitement or fear he didn't examine too closely. "You never asked me that question before."

"I thought I knew. I thought there was no need to question. Now there is. Will you answer me?"

"Perhaps, if you will answer a question of mine. What is a Power?"

Tymon blinked. "A Power is one of the Seven Immortals. Most people consider them deities and worship them as best they can."

"If you know so little of them, how do you know what is acceptable worship?"

Tymon sighed. "That question keeps the priests and priestesses in happy argument for much of their careers. More than that I do not know."

"You ask if I am a Power. If I am, what does that mean? Do you worship me? What does that change?"

"Are you a Power, Amaet?" he repeated, as if he hadn't heard.

"Perhaps."

"That's not an answer."

Her face could have been marble, for all the expression there. "On the contrary—it is a very fine answer. Is it my fault that you ask the wrong question?"

"It could be my imagination," Seb said, "but you seem especially surly this morning."

Seb had made tea, and thanks to Takren there was fresh bread and butter, but Tymon wasn't especially interested in any of it. He sipped tea and nibbled at the bread, his face set in a deep scowl.

"Umm," he said.

"Tymon, I'd like an explanation. Your last utterance is the most you've said all morning, and if that frown of yours goes any deeper your skin is going to crack."

"I feel small and simple," Tymon said. "It is an extremely annoying feeling, and one that, concentrate as I might, there's no way to banish. I hate it."

Seb sat cross-legged before the fire and poured a mug of the strong greenbush tea for himself. "Now you know how the rest of us feel, making our way from day to day. It's no feast of pleasure, is it?"

Tymon poured the dregs of his cup into the fire. "No. How do you manage?"

Seb sighed. "We don't, a great deal of the time. It's amazing we've done as well as we have. So. What happened last night? And don't say 'nothing.' You're no liar and I'm no fool."

Tymon shrugged and told Seb about the Waiting Place, and Amaet, and a few other things that he had never mentioned before in their time together. Seb listened, though from the expression on his face Tymon could not decide if his friend was surprised, angered, hurt, or astonished, or a bit of all at once. He did keep quiet as Tymon spoke, letting the magician speak until he clearly didn't know what else to say.

"My" was all he said at first. Then he asked, "That's all she said?"

"Almost. Before she departed, Amaet looked at me very intently, and she said, 'Consider a pebble. It is a small thing, unimportant as anything can be. Yet if the wrong pebble shifts under the wrong boulder at the wrong time, an entire mountain might fall. And who knows what the mountain was a prop to?' "

"Another way of saying that everything is important. Or not."

Tymon sighed. "That's not very helpful."

"Your . . . well, what shall we call her? Goddess? Power? Guardian spirit?"

"Call her Amaet," Tymon said. "She may be one or all of those things, but her name is the only one I'm reasonably sure of."

"Amaet, then. Her homilies seem rather simple and useless, and yet. . . ."

Tymon finished it. "And yet I can't escape the feeling that I've just had something very important explained to me as simply as a creature such as Amaet can do so, and my feeble mind simply cannot get the measure of it. I haven't felt this way

85

in a long time, Seb. I repeat—I don't like it."

"I think I'd enjoy your confusion more," Seb said, "if I didn't realize how dangerous it is. So, I ask today as I've asked before: What now?"

Tymon considered. "And I say again: I don't know. Worse, I can't escape the feeling that the time when knowing would make a difference is fast drawing to a close."

The Lord of House Dyrlos bowed to very few people, but one of those very few not only had him bowing, but currently on all fours on the nursery floor.

"G'up, horsey!"

Laras obligingly shuffled forward a few paces. He tore a hole in his woolen hose, but he barely noticed. He was using all his concentration to make sure his small rider kept her seat; a neat enough trick for all her squirming and bouncing.

"G'up!" repeated the tiny voice, imperious.

"The horse rears!" Laras announced, then rose up slightly even as he reached behind him and plucked the young rider from his back and swung her around into his arms while she giggled and squirmed.

"Horses are tricky things, Lytea."

The voice came from the doorway. Laras smiling, cradled his laughing daughter in his arms as he rose. "Listen to your mother, sweetling. And some horses are trickier than other." Laras kissed his daughter's gold ringlets and, since there was no one around to comment on the lack of decorum, he bussed his wife as well. It was an arranged marriage, as all such were. Mero was the child of a prince of Nols and Laras saw no more than her portrait before she had been brought to live at Balanar. Yet from that day forward Laras had counted himself a very lucky man. He cradled his daughter with his left hand and used the other to rub his back.

"She is growing well, Mero; a few more months and she'll be too heavy for her father."

"Get a real pony then," Lytea announced. "I keep it in my bed and feed it summerleaf!"

"That's just because you don't want to eat your summerleaf like a good girl," Mero said. "You need to learn to eat good food and become a big strong girl before you take care of a pony."

"Then fwat pony eat?" Lytea asked with flawless logic.

"Apples and hay," Laras said, swinging her about, "or seaweed and fish, if it's a seahorse. I thought I saw one yesterday, playing beyond the breakers. Do you want to go look?"

"Yes!!" Lytea shouted.

Mero smiled at her husband. "Why don't we all go?"

"Lovely idea. . . ." Laras started to shift Lytea to his shoulder to ride when he saw Vor approaching down the hallway. His eyes were down; he moved quietly. Laras didn't even need to ask. He handed the child to her mother. "Will you take her on ahead? I'll just be a minute."

Mero glanced down the hall, and when she saw Vor her mouth set in a hard line, but she said nothing. She took the child and set out for the staircase without looking back. Laras sighed, and waited.

"Your Grace—" Vor started, but Laras cut him off.

"What happened?"

"I don't know, and there's the problem. Takren left the farmstead last night, and I don't know where he went."

"What do you mean you don't know? He probably just slipped off to the privy."

Vor shook his head. "I mean he eluded me, Your Grace. I failed you."

Laras looked thoughtful. "Walk with me a moment." He followed his wife and child, but at a very sedate pace. Vor fell into step behind him. "This is disturbing," Laras said.

"I'm a fool. I actually thought he *was* going to the privy, and kept more distance than I should. But then he slipped away so quickly. Much more quickly than I thought he could move."

Laras nodded. "Exactly. He either knew he was being followed, or was taking care not to be followed. Either case raises disturbing questions."

"Do you think he's working against you?"

"I don't know. I do know that we can't afford the luxury of time and effort to find out. That doesn't leave us much choice. When it's done, put one of our people in Takren's place so there are no more surprises. See to it, Vor. I know you won't fail me again."

Vor nodded. "I am yours to command as always, Your Grace, but are you certain about this matter?"

Laras came out onto the parapet where his wife and child were waiting for him in the sunlight. Lytea was pointing and laughing in delight at a pod of dolphins beyond the breakers while Mero held her up so she could see. Laras looked at them both, and his smile was pure contentment. "Very certain," he said.

Seb expected nothing new from his meeting with Takren, but then a chance for any news at all seemed worth the effort. Tymon's inaction worried Seb more than any one of a number of monstrous or merely odd acts that the magician had been known to commit.

More than that, it was a lovely morning. Seb moved through concealing hedgerows with his normal caution, but he still managed to step through a patch of sunlight now and then, and feel the warmth of it on his skin. It was still summer but there was a cool edge to the breeze that knew autumn was coming soon. Out in the fields Seb could see the hayers at work with their scythes, getting the winter's fodder in. He was close now; the scent of apples was on the breeze. Takren's morning inspection of the ripening apples in the orchard was a good time to meet; the orchards were Takren's special province and he usually walked them alone. Besides the discretion of it, Seb felt sure he might at least get an early apple out of their meeting.

Seb reached the edge of the closest hedgerow and looked out into the orchard.

Damn!!

For a moment Seb was certain he had shouted aloud, but all was quiet. A man had just pulled a dagger from Takren's back; Seb saw the streak of red that marked it and did not need to see what had just happened to know, know without any doubt at all. The man had taken Takren unawares as he reached up to grasp one of the lowest-hanging apples, fat and golden on its branch. The fruit only now fell from Takren's nerveless fingers as the old man started to slump.

In an instant Seb's own dagger was in his hand; he measured the distance in his mind's eye and prepared to throw at the murderer's broad back. It would be a long throw but nothing Seb hadn't done before, and well.

Die, you murdering bastard!

The man did not die. Seb's dagger remained in his hand; he had not even shifted to grip the point, his preferred throwing style. Seb wanted to kill the man, wanted as much as he could remember wanting anything. Takren was a smug old sod but Seb liked him immensely. He deserved better than this. He deserved revenge. Yet revenge was a luxury Seb had not been able to afford for a very long time. No matter how angry he was now, Seb had to consider the larger picture: he was too late to help Takren. From the position of the blow and depth of the bloody streak Seb had no doubt that the old man was dead before he fell. The murderer was no common thief; he examined the old man to be sure of him but no more. Why? Why kill Takren? Who would want or need to, and in a way that clearly spoke of necessity, not anger?

I kill this man and I've just slain a messenger. Who wrote the warrant is what we need to know.

Seb crouched down behind a mulberry bush as the assassin cleaned his knife on the hem of the old man's robes. The man looked carefully about to make sure he hadn't been seen. Then he quickly slipped into the hedgerow not six yards from where Seb was hidden. Seb glanced at Takren's fallen body, then the retreating back of the assassin. After a silent prayer for Takren's forgiveness, he followed the old man's killer.

Later Seb's report was pithy and short. "Straight to Duke Laras's holdings in Balanar. He didn't so much as stop for an ale."

"Such misplaced dedication," Tymon said softly.

They sat together on a small grassy hillock, while some distance away, on a larger, flatter hill, Takren's body was being buried according to the Rites of Martok. Or rather, Tymon sat. Seb paced back and forth like a caged wolf.

Tymon and Seb were in plain sight, but no one seemed to notice them. Seb knew Tymon had done something to make them escape the notice of the mourners, but he didn't much care. He saw the bundle—small, smaller than he had expected—being lowered into the ground and he did not care if Molic's household saw them or not.

"I should have killed the bastard when I had the chance," Seb said.

Tymon shook his head. "You did the right thing. It was safe to assume that House Dyrlos was behind Takren's murder. If you had killed the assassin there's a good chance everyone else would know, too."

Seb finally sat down, hard, on the grass beside Tymon. "Why

would revealing the criminal be a bad thing?"

"His name is Vor," Tymon said softly.

Seb blinked. "Vor? Who are you talking about?"

"The bastard you were referring to. And he is—literally. A child born on the wrong side of the blanket, rejected by an uncaring father whose wife, understandably, did not care for the reminder of her husband's dalliances. House Dyrlos took him in; the old duke raised him almost like a second son."

Seb looked at him. "That sounds almost like the Tymon I remember: long statements of absolute fact at almost no provocation. Has the Long Look returned?"

"No. But once I knew of House Dyrlos's involvement it made sense to learn as much about its folk as possible. Or did you think I did nothing but contemplate smoke?"

"Frankly, I didn't know what you were doing while I was out and about on your errands. Fine—now I know his name. So?"

"You know more than that. Think of your own past, Seb. Think what might have happened if House Dyrlos had taken you in when you needed it, given you the comfort and belonging you never found. Now tell me, in that case, that it would not have been your dagger in Takren's back if you thought your House was threatened?"

Seb didn't strike Tymon. It took an effort, but he did not. "That may be as you say. If there's a point to this I'd love to hear it."

Tymon sighed. "How do we judge, Seb? How do we find the authority within ourselves to say yes to this, no to that? In our view Vor killed a harmless old man. What right have we for revenge? How shall we answer that, Seb? We've done far worse."

"And prevented even greater tragedies. Whatever we did, we did for good reason. You know that."

Tymon nodded. "I know. Yet without the tyranny of the Long Look I am free to wonder: Is any reason really good enough? If you had slain Vor perhaps you would have also slain any chance we'd find out what Laras's reasons are, assuming he is responsible."

"If we had the tyranny of the Long Look, it's possible you could have foreseen this and prevented it."

Tymon sighed. "The Long Look was never so unambiguous as you seem to think, Seb. There was always the chance of error; we were cautions and, dare I say, fortunate. More, the revelations seldom had much to say about individuals as such. More likely it would have shown me some terrible Twelve Kingdom–wide tragedy that only Takren's death would prevent, and I'd have been compelled to slay the old man myself. As hells go, I think I prefer this one."

Seb didn't have an answer for that. They watched the rest of Takren's funeral together in silence. When the rites were done and the mourners finally departed, Tymon rose. "Come on."

"Where are we going?"

"I need to speak with Takren."

Seb blinked. "Takren is dead, Tymon."

"Seb, I do know that. I'm not quite mad . . . yet. Sometimes I feel myself dancing perilously close to it, but not quite over the edge."

"Necromancy?" It wasn't something Seb really associated with Tymon, but he had long since learned not to put much beyond the pale where Tymon was concerned.

"Something close enough," Tymon said, "that the difference probably isn't worth mentioning."

They walked past Takren's grave. Tymon bent down and picked up a small clot of dark earth, but he did not stop. The mourners had only recently traveled the same path. Seb worried for a bit that someone might see them, but then he detected a faint shimmering at the edge of his sight, and realized that, whatever working of air, haze, and distance that Tymon had applied to them on the hill, the concealment was still working.

"Where are we going?" Seb asked, keeping his voice low.

"To the orchard. What I have in mind will work best there, if it works at all."

Soon they had reached the place. Normally, Seb did not look when Tymon worked magic directly. Not that it happened very often, but Seb did not like it when the world as he knew it was forced to change part of itself. That someone could remake the world even a little bit was unsettling, and hinted of things best left to the Powers. This usually wasn't a problem, because most of the time Seb couldn't even tell when Tymon had either changed something of the world or delved a better understanding. He neither declaimed long passages from moldy books nor sliced the air and smoke with a staff or made gestures mystical or grotesque. Tymon just read for a while from one book or another, very intently, then looked thoughtful for a moment or two. Then the thing—whatever it was—was done.

Not this time.

Tymon stood before the very apple tree that was Takren's final contact with the living world, and he spoke to it. Seb wanted to point out that Tymon was talking to a tree, but he could no more bring himself to say it than he could to walk away.

He says he's not mad. I wonder if he is truly the best judge of that—

"Here, Seb?"

"Huh?" Seb realized dully that Tymon was pointing to a spot on the ground just near the tree-trunk. "Where it happened? Yes . . . right about there."

Tymon nodded and moved to the spot, then raised his hand. There was an apple hanging just a few inches from his fingertips; Tymon reached for it but stopped just short of touching it. He looked puzzled for just a moment, and Seb felt a chill. It was Takren's last pose, as he reached for the apple and was slain, just as Seb remembered it. Tymon stood that way for several long moments, then he sighed, shuddered, and lowered his hand again.

"Done," said Tymon.

Seb blinked. "What's done?"

"Takren's life. I'd suspected as much. I wanted to be sure."

"Takren is dead, Tymon." Seb felt almost foolish repeating this one more time, but there were instances dealing with Tymon when holding onto the facts as Seb understood them was the only defense he had.

Tymon shrugged. "Yes, his life is over. I knew that. But was his life finished? That's a separate matter."

"I've seen bottoms of wells more clearly than that, Tymon. When you're dead your life is finished."

"When you're dead your life is over, true. Yet had you done what you expected to do? Were you happy with yourself as best you could be? Was it time for your soul or spirit or potential of transcendence to move on? Was it *finished*, Seb?"

Seb blinked. "Oh. I do see. And was Takren finished with this life?"

Tymon looked thoughtful again. He could have been working magic or he could have been remembering. In either case, after a moment he smiled. "Takren was a complex mind but a simple man. He died in the place he loved most in the world, doing what he loved to do. The last thing he reached for was an apple, and his life ended so quickly that he never knew that he didn't grasp that apple. That one perfect moment is frozen for him forever, Seb. That much I know, from what you told me and from what I've learned here and now. Yes, Seb. As far as such a thing was possible, Takren was finished. Not everyone dies so well."

"Why did you need to know?"

"Because he was my friend. Right or no, that would have been reason enough to take revenge, if revenge was needed. It isn't needed, so now we're free to leave."

"What has that to do—" Seb began, then stopped. "We're leaving?"

"I have to regain the Long Look, Seb. Curse or not, there's too much potential on the move now. Too much chance that all we've worked for over the years will be destroyed. As much as I owe Takren, I owe more to the ghosts of those who have died to prevent the horrors shown by the Long Look. I think I know where the Long Look can be found, and I have to go there. But first I had to decide between doing what I think I have to do and avenging Takren, because the two goals are not compatible."

"Why?"

Tymon seemed to be choosing his words carefully. "Because my choices were to kill Laras or to use him. So today I came to find what I owed Takren to find out which way the balance turned. Now I know."

This wasn't exactly the Tymon of old, but it was a Tymon prepared to act, for reasons he understood as the right ones. He could be wrong, and disastrously so but, Seb knew, even with the Long Look that had been possible.

Seb made his choice, because he always had one to make. He looked grim. "Tell me what you want me to do."

"Only this: you are going to deliver a letter, which I have already prepared." He held up a sealed square of parchment.

Seb blinked. "That's all?"

Tymon smiled like the Reaper himself. "Ask again," he said, "after I tell you where I want the letter delivered."

Lady Margate wasn't so much angry as disappointed. She stood now in the doorway of the stable from which Princess Ashesa had planned to make her departure.

"Child, this will never do."

Ashesa, caught in the act of loading her saddle pouch with provisions, didn't bother with concealment now. She still wanted to hide her intentions from her nurse, but she didn't see how. Lady Margate may have looked like a silly old woman but Ashesa knew better; Margy was no fool, and treating her like one wasn't going to change that. "I need to see Galan, Margy. In person and private. A letter won't do."

Lady Margate smiled, but her eyes were like black stones. "I knew you were smitten, child, but the boy just left. He'll have to visit most of his outlying districts in a show of force before he can even return to Tonara proper for the coronation. Give him some time to settle his affairs."

"It's not about that, Margy, and I can't," Ashesa said. "I've been thinking of this for days, and if I wait now I may wait forever. This is important. Please don't try to stop me."

"I don't intend to stop you. When I said 'this will never do' I was referring to your lame excuse for a disguise."

Ashesa looked at herself, or as best she could without a mirror. Her red-gold hair was hidden by a dark hood; her jerkin and hose were those of a squire. Such were always about on their masters' business; no one gave them a second glance. That wouldn't be true in Ashesa's case, or at least, not now.

"You last pulled this stunt when you were twelve. It barely worked then. It won't now, Ashesa, though I suppose that's another reason I shouldn't call you 'child' anymore. But it is my considered opinion that even the most near-sighted highwayman in the Twelve Kingdoms will not believe you are a boy."

Ashesa considered. "Well, the roads are fairly safe in that case."

"Not that safe, Highness. I'd talk you out of this if I could, but I know well the futility of trying to prevent anything you've a mind to do. You've more than your share of royal foolishness, for all that I love you deeply. No. You will go escorted or not at all."

Ashesa protested. "Any of Father's men would talk, and I must go in secret!"

"And you will, but you will leave the matter of your escort to me. You will wait—not long, I promise—until I have arranged it. Or by All the Powers I'll tell your father before you get well out of the gates, and there are horses in his stables a lot faster than that one. What do you think would happen?"

"He'd lock me in the north tower until my wedding day, at the very least." Ashesa sighed. "Please, Margy. . . ."

"I'll do it, Highness. Don't test me."

Ashesa considered her alternatives, decided there weren't any. "All right, Margy—have your way. But please hurry."

So far, to Galan's mind, being a king was more trouble than it was worth. "So this is 'procession.' My father used the word once, and it sounded like something foul. I begin to see why."

Galan rode with his chief advisors at the head of a column of thirty landed knights, from baron rank to earl, with twice as many men-at-arms and lesser knights riding on the wings and as rearguard. In the train were servants, cooks, yeomen of the hunt serving as both scouts and foragers, blacksmiths, armorers, farriers, and others besides whom Galan, try as he might, could not quite attach a function to. His father's body had been sent back to Borasur under the escort of the late king's personal guard so that his mortal remains could be expediently placed in the royal crypt. The official funeral would not occur until just before Galan's coronation. At the moment, Galan wasn't at all sure when either would occur.

"Necessity, My Prince," Albon said. He used the word "necessity" a lot. Albon was just past middle age, of the knightly class and a veteran, but he had since turned his considerable talents to administration, where he was, to use the tournament jargon, high lance.

Galan had not been so far removed from the day-to-day functioning of the kingdom that he didn't realize what a shrewd group of men Riegar had brought into his service, and he was not fool enough to squander their advice. Still, three weeks from the day he had left Ashesa at Morushe, Galan didn't think he was one mile closer to home. The road was interminable, the showy raiment he wore was hot and uncomfortable, and the expense of maintaining such an honor guard made Galan's stomach hurt, for all that much of their food and lodging was provided by the noble Houses he "visited" on the procession.

"Necessity?" Galan repeated the word, trying to decide what there was about the sound of it that annoyed him the most. "Isn't this just for show?"

"Yes. Which is far more important than you think, My Prince. You are the heir to the throne by right; I think all the noble Houses agree to this, albeit some might be more enthusiastic than others. Your escort is large as befits your station but, more to the point, it is a show of force, presence, and control. You show your steel but offer your hand for the Oath of Fealty. The nobles swear allegiance and we pick up more escorts as we go. Finally, we ride into Tonara in pomp and with the full—and present—backing of the noble Houses. The coronation proceeds smoothly from there."

"Lord Albon, I dare say you could find a political advantage from a visit to the privy."

Albon thought about it. "Easily, My Prince."

Galan nodded. "My father was wise to listen to you. I'll do the same."

"I am honored by your confidence." Albon signaled to Tals, another of Galan's counselors riding at a discreet distance. The younger man rode up to them bearing a parchment map of the region they were traveling. Albon studied it for a moment then nodded, satisfied. "Patience, Highness. We have stops here and here," he said, pointing to two fairly small but ancient fiefdoms. "Tollors and Pokai are not very powerful these days but they do have influence; we can't afford to overlook them. As their resources are not infinite we'll stay as long as protocol demands but no longer. Even so, in a week's time we'll be able to reach the ducal provinces of Korsos and Maltai. Once those two worthy gentlemen swear fealty and their escorts join us, we'll be more than ready to proceed to Tonara with or without House Dyrlos in attendance."

Galan sighed, and winced as he shifted a bit in the saddle. "I can last that long. Though the royal rear end may have other ideas."

Vor pointed at a squiggle that represented the Kor River. "Here, at the ford. We can attack the vanguard from the cover of this ridge. Whatever we do, it must be here," Vor said.

Laras studied the map Vor had put before him on the table in the great hall. "This is dangerously close to Korsos," he said, "and I know beyond question that the duke is loyal to House Kotara."

Vor nodded. "My point, Your Grace. Once Galan's escort joins forces with the duke's retinue there, the prince will be too strong to attack directly. The procession has given us time to muster, but there is a limit to how many troops we can move without undue notice. Our contact in Pokai will send word when Galan departs, so we can move when the time is right."

"Efficient," Laras said dryly, "but hardly the mark of a popular uprising in favor of Molic."

Vor smiled. "Already considered. Our hired foot will be wearing peasant garb over their mailshirts. It won't fool anyone but, even if we have to commit our own horse, it will cloud the issue enough that, once Molic is safely crowned, our version of events will be the one that survives."

"Impressive, Vor." Laras considered. "With timing and enough surprise, our own horse may not even be needed."

"As long as everyone remembers that the point is to slay Galan, not defeat his entire escort. Once Galan is dead, loyalties will be in flux in any case. I doubt if we'll have to face the entire escort at that point, though keeping our reserves ready is still wise."

"Certainly, but the nobles will want to see to their own holdings before they worry about the succession. That will leave us free to act and present them with their new king before anyone can argue." There was a predictability to the nobility's way of thinking that Laras found very reassuring.

"One thing, Vor. I want you to remain here and look after my lady and children. If anything goes wrong I trust them to your care. I'm going to see to the attack personally."

Vor frowned. "Of course I'll obey, but wouldn't it be wiser to remain here?"

"Perhaps, but if you are discovered everyone would know it was my doing anyway, so my presence changes nothing. And if we are committed to destroying House Kotara I want to be there. I owe my fool of a father that much, if nothing else. Are your men ready?"

"They await only your word, Your Grace."

Laras nodded. "Well, then. It is given."

He said it easily enough. All the reasons had been explored, as well as the risks. There was nothing else to consider. It was the right thing, the only thing, to do. Laras knew that, but it didn't change the sick feeling that lingered in him long after the words were out.

Chapter 7
"Honor, Glory, and the Mess They Made"

Molic stood on top of a sharp ridge of land near the Kor River. "I am so pleased," he said. "It's all so wonderful."

Duke Laras, mounted at the head of his personal guard, listened politely, though he kept a firm hand on the reins and intently scanned the crossing of the Kor River, visible from their vantage point among the oaks on the ridge. "How so, Your Majesty?" he asked.

His Soon-to-Be-Majesty spoke with a sort of pathetic eagerness. "No one ever listened to me before," Molic said. "I mean, they listened, but it's like they didn't hear me. Even the simplest things. My claim to the throne. The correct pronunciation of my titles. That sort of thing. I'm glad that all that's finally over."

"A glorious day, indeed . . . yes?"

A scout ran up to kneel at Laras's stirrup. "One of their outriders discovered us on the north side. I think we killed him quietly enough, but there are more about and they may notice he's gone before long."

Laras frowned. "Galan is being inconveniently prudent, or well advised by people who are. Tell Nassen's men to advance as far as they can, right to the treeline if they can do it without being seen. We may have to move sooner."

"Aye, Your Grace."

The scout bowed and hurried away, and Laras turned his full attention on the Pretender. "When you're on the throne, Majesty, there will be Masters of Protocol whose sole joy in life is the correct rendering of your titles. I will see to it personally."

"You are a loyal subject, Duke . . . ?"

Laras smiled. "I'm sorry to beg your indulgence once more, Sire, but our time is not yet. I promise to reveal all soon." Laras couldn't help but be amused at the fact that Molic didn't even recognize one of the most powerful dukes in the kingdom on sight. Still, it was a convenient failing.

Molic shrugged, the matter clearly already well on its way to forgotten. "So be it."

One of Laras's personal guard was the first to spy the column. "Here they come."

At this point "they" were little more than a black spot in the distance, then a line, then a snake, then a column of mounted men with spears glinting in the sun as they rode out of the trees sheltering near the Kor. Laras judged the distance. "I wish we had more archers, Merak."

The guard nodded. "Or better ones, Your Grace," he said. "As things stand. . . ."

"We can't risk a volley that might miss and would certainly warn. You have a good eye, Merak. No, what archers we have today have another task."

Laras watched the column grow even closer. He waited for the inevitable moment. Not the attack as such, but the moment when Prince Galan's column reached the banks of the Kor and there would be no time to recall Nassen and his mercenaries even if Laras wanted to. Until then, all options were open. After, there was no turning back. He didn't have to wait very long.

Now. We are committed.

Soon the first mounted riders of Galan's vanguard splashed into the Kor. Nassen, as instructed, let the first few riders pass. Prince Galan's personal guard was clearly visible as they reached the river ford. Laras heard the muted shout as Nassen's men broke cover and advanced. Just that quickly the battle was joined.

The vanguard heard the commotion behind and turned about, hesitating only a moment in their confusion, but in that moment Nassen's small company of archers loosed on them, striking several down before they could rejoin the embattled column. The other end of the column was fouled beyond the riverbank, choked off from the battle by the land and the press of bodies in front of them. So far it was going according to plan.

"Is he dead?" Molic asked, excited.

Laras, watching the battle from the ridge, shook his head. "No, Sire. Not yet. His guard is pressed hard but they fight well as we expected. Still, hemmed as they are by our spearmen they cannot use their mounts to best advantage."

What he didn't say was that the dilemma worked both ways; on the attack Nassen's men could not form a proper line of spears without giving Galan's men a flank to strike at; with their skirmish lines as they were the confusion worked against both sides. The ambushers' main advantage was surprise and that, as Laras knew well, would not last.

Hurry up and kill him, Master Nassen!

The thought made Laras feel a little ashamed of himself; he wasn't sure why. He shrugged it off.

The fighting was fiercest around the prince, and Laras expected to see the banner fall at any moment, but it did not happen. Laras was impressed despite himself when he realized that Galan wasn't waiting to be butchered like a veal calf, but had drawn his own blade and, though not the warrior his brother had been, clearly knew how to use a sword. Twice Laras saw the blade extend when one of the mercenaries managed to grab rein or saddle of the prince's horse, and twice the attacker fell back. Once he even fell over.

"Is he dead yet?" Molic repeated, hopefully.

Laras gritted his teeth. "No, Sire. He is not. Patience."

Laras gave a counsel that he did not believe. Patience was losing as, the duke now realized, were Nassen's mercenaries.

Merak pointed. "The outriders are returning, Your Grace!"

Laras saw them too. Groups of scouts coming in twos and threes, doubtless alerted by the commotion, were spurring hard to relieve the column. Worse, a dozen or so knights wearing the blue phoenix of House Tandas had found another way down the bank, avoiding the choke point at the crossing. One fell to an arrow as they crossed but the rest spurred on toward the embattled prince, where a clump of mercenaries had formed, pushed back by a hard defense.

Merak voiced Laras's thought. "If they hit that mob from the rear we're finished."

Duke Laras nodded. "You have the horn?" Merak grinned with excitement and held up a large hunting horn, the agreed signal for the reserves. "Well then, at my command—"

Merak's gaze grew wide as he shouted a warning. "Your Grace!!"

A lone rider burst through trees, then practically threw himself from his saddle to grasp Laras's reins. The guard pressed forward and the duke had his sword halfway from its sheath before he recognized the man.

"Vor! What in the Name of the Powers are you doing here?!"

"Y . . . Your Grace. . . ." Vor's face was flushed red, though whether in shame or exhaustion or both Laras could not tell. "We are betrayed!"

Merak held up the horn. "Your Grace, we dare not delay!"

Vor shook his head. "No! No. Please . . . please read. Hurry!" He forced the parchment into Laras's hands.

Laras unfolded the parchment and, with one last hasty glance at the battlefield, began to read. The message was very short but the duke's reading of it seemed to take forever. At last he looked up, and his face was white as death. "Where was this found?"

Vor took a deep breath before he answered. "In the nursery," he said. "Pinned by a small dagger to Lytea's crib as she lay sleeping. She could almost reach out her hand. . . ." Vor didn't finish.

Duke Laras looked stunned, and more than a little afraid. "Apparently rumors of Tymon the Black's death were in error. Damn it all, how, Vor? *How* was this done? Where were the guards?"

There was nothing but shame in Vor's expression. "In place and awake, Your Grace. As for how, well, as I consider who wrote the message, I can easily guess. I had to bring it myself; I trusted no one else with this."

Laras just stared at the parchment for several long moments, then glanced back at the battle. The mercenaries were hard pressed, but the right attack in enough force could still tip the scale. "You were right to come, Vor." He turned to his men. "The horn, Marek—put it away."

His officer had halfway raised the horn to his lips. Now he just stared at his leader, blinking like an owl. "Your Grace?"

"Now, Marek. And send the word down the ranks—we're leaving."

"Leaving?" Molic stared at his ally, uncomprehending. "The battle is not over."

"For us, it damn well is," Laras said. "I am sorry."

Molic ran forward, grabbing at Laras's reins. "No! You can't! It's not done!"

Laras didn't seem to notice him. He just looked at the battle, wistfully. "I'm afraid it is, Your Majesty. I see that Nassen has fallen. Good. Now I can only hope that he didn't inform his men who had hired them, but that wasn't his way, and so we depend on the discretion of a mercenary captain. In either case it can't be helped now."

"What are you talking about?" Molic asked. "It's not finished. It's not!"

Laras frowned, as if trying to remember something important. "Oh, yes. I'm afraid it is very much finished. Vor, let's be gone."

"A moment, Your Grace," Vor said, his anger and frustration still evident. "No one has said your name, but Molic has seen your face. I'm afraid that just won't do now." Before Laras could protest, Lord Vor drew his sword and cut Molic down. One stroke without fanfare or hesitation, though it seemed almost like an afterthought.

After his initial surprise at Vor's deed, Laras felt strangely sad. Molic was a fool and worse, but Laras had found himself becoming somewhat fond of him. "The risk was minimal. Was that really necessary, Lord Vor?"

"Molic's claim depended on our being able to enforce it directly, and that's impossible now. You know as well as I that one plan may fail, and from the ashes may rise a better one. But not if the loose ends of the first knot are left dangling. I'm afraid His Late Majesty qualified as one such."

Molic was dead. There was nothing more to say, or to do. Duke Laras was somber as he recalled his men and rode away as the tide of battle turned against the hired soldiers dying on the banks of the river.

Tals, Albon's second, rode up and dismounted just as the healers were finishing. "Well fought, Your Highness. Albon would have said so."

Prince Galan winced as one of the healers gave one last pull on the bandage on his upper arm. "Father insisted on weapons practice even though I had little interest or aptitude. The man's wisdom continues to astonish me." Galan looked at one still form only a few yards away and felt a rush of nausea that he barely contained, remembering. "Sir Albon is dead, isn't he? He died defending me. As did several good men."

Tals removed his helm and nodded, then wiped away a trickle of sweat and blood with one gauntleted hand. "I'm sorry, Highness. We were taken unawares and that is inexcusable."

Galan took a sip from a wineskin and felt a little better. He looked around at the carnage. "This wasn't a chance encounter with a Free Company, not within my own borders," Galan said. "And we had no warning because they were waiting, hidden. They knew we were coming."

Tals sighed. "That was my conclusion as well, Highness. Still, it is very strange."

"What is? That someone would seek my life?"

Tals shook his head. "No. Your pardon, Highness, but Albon taught me that a counselor's main duty is to speak truth as best he understands it. There is more than one faction that could find some advantage to a dynastic void; indeed there are such in any kingdom. No, I was speaking of the rather pathetic disguises the ambushers wore, and the very fresh hoofprints we found on that ridge." Tals pointed to a section of high ground just opposite the fording place. "The tracks are muddled, but we estimate about twenty horse, maybe more. Whoever was there had a good view of the battle."

"And could have changed the outcome," Galan said, looking thoughtful. "Why?"

"Why what, Highness?"

"If they were in league with the ambushers—and I find their presence hard to explain otherwise—why didn't they attack when it would have mattered? We were hard pressed there at first and for quite a while after. A charge might have made all the difference, and not in our favor."

"A very good question, Highness, to which I have no answer," Tals said. "I'm sorry."

Galan smiled weakly. "No need, you of all people. Your shield was at my side today more times than I can recall. Did you find anything else?"

"Just a dead farmer, Highness. Probably used as a guide and then slain when his work was done, poor sod."

"Indeed," Galan said. "Someone has a lot to answer for. I intend to see that they do."

Tals hesitated. "There's another matter that I would bring to your attention right now, since the greater ones must wait in any case."

"What is it?"

"Sir Lokara of House Tandas also fell today. His two squires were due to be knighted when we reached Korsos. Under the circumstances they have requested that it be done now and, in the absence of their lord, that you would do the honors."

Galan smiled a little wistfully. "I was always meant for either monastery or university, Tals, as you well know. I never won my spurs nor thought I would miss them, and only a knight may create another knight. Much as I hate to disappoint anyone who fought for me today, I cannot in good conscience grant what I do not possess."

Tals smiled. "Well spoken, Highness. And anticipated." He raised his hand and three knights approached. Galan recognized them all, and knew the nobility of their Houses and their service to his father. Earl Caras carried a bare sword across his arms, Lord Moltai a belt and scabbard, and Earl Nond a pair of golden spurs. Galan looked from one to the others in total confusion.

"What does this mean?" he asked finally.

Tals broke into a wide grin. "Highness, it means that every man who fought for you and with you today believes your golden spurs are missing, and, with your kind permission, these gentlemen will now rectify that situation before we ride on to Tonara."

After Nond and Moltai buckled on his swordbelt and spurs, Earl Caras himself touched Galan's shoulders with the sword and then gave him the traditional blow that sealed the ceremony, not to mention ringing Galan's ears.

"I wish your father had lived to see this," Earl Caras said weepily. "He would be the proudest man in the world."

"Aye, though even more I wish my brother had seen it," Galan said, and spoke the last part silently, for himself alone. *He would have split a gut laughing.*

The squires were properly knighted in turn, and then they all rode on toward Korsos for the final leg of the journey. As he rode, Galan wondered if any anticipation of the coming coronation at the splendid palace at Tonara could even begin to match that one small ceremony by the River Kor. A ceremony done, at least for the most part, because those whose right it was to judge deemed it the worthy thing to do.

"So much to do," Seb said, "especially with their own dead and wounded to see to. Yet they had time for this."

Seb and Tymon stood together on the ridge, looking down at the low mound of earth and single standing post that marked Molic's grave.

"That's Galan's hand showing, I wager," Tymon said. "There's a streak of kindness in him. I hope it doesn't interfere with his ability to reign."

"Kindness not being a virtue in a king?"

"For its own sake? No. More like an expensive luxury that ofttimes your subjects can ill afford. When properly seasoned with the right mix of self-interest and justice? A tool. No different from cruelty or praise or reward or punishment. All useful in their different ways to a king."

109

"And some who are not kings, Tymon? What was in that letter I brought to Duke Laras's nursery?"

Tymon sighed. "It was simply a promise, Seb, sworn on the infamy of my name and marked with a few sigils of tavern-trick magic in case there was doubt. A promise."

Seb waited, and finally Tymon scowled. "All right, Seb. I promised Duke Laras I would kill his wife and child in some horrible fashion if he didn't call off his hounds. The presence of the letter alone would make the threat credible and, yes, I damn well would have done it if need be." Seb just stared at the Magician for several long moments, and finally Tymon sighed. "You look like a carp when you do that. So. Has your opinion of me sunk even lower?"

"It's not that, Tymon. I'm just astonished that it worked. I mean. I would have thought someone who could plan the death of Prince Galan so easily would be made of something closer to stone than willow wood."

Tymon turned away from the grave and started back toward their horses, and Seb followed. "Laras has ambitions, Seb, but as far as I can winkle them out they are not of a dynastic nature. Witness his use of poor Molic as a puppet rather than taking the lead himself. Rather a refreshing change, given his family's history. His marriage, arranged as they all are, turned into a love match and he dotes on his daughter as much as any father ever did. You don't survive as a royal duke without a ruthless streak, but there's love in him as well. It made him vulnerable and I used that."

"You don't sound proud of it."

"I'm not, Seb. I pray I never would be proud of such a thing." Tymon mounted his gelding, and after a moment Seb followed onto his own horse.

"Still, we were much safer when you were thought dead. It's a shame to lose that."

"A necessary sacrifice, Seb," Tymon said. "Just one of many."

Seb urged his mount forward to stand beside Tymon's. "So. Where are we going?"

"Wylandia."

Seb sighed. "I hope your reason is a good one. You realize, of course, that everyone from the lowest pigherder to the highest duke knows your face there?"

Tymon nodded, even as he guided his mount toward the north. "My death, pleasant a respite though it was, could not last. We both knew that."

Seb nodded, looking unhappy. "Still . . . pity."

Galan's escort was nearly to Korsos before he asked the question that had begun to trouble him soon after the battle at the Kor. "There was more to my knighting than you've said, Tals."

The young man's expression didn't change. "Highness, how so?"

"Oh, I doubt not the sincerity of the earls, but the fact that I handled myself acceptably in one skirmish wouldn't have rated the accolade in and of itself."

Tals shrugged slightly. "Albon told me that, in almost any matter involving mortal humankind, there is the surface and there is what's beneath, and often what's beneath is buried so deep that even those involved most directly do not see it. If you wish, I will tell you what I see."

"Please," Galan encouraged.

"Well then," Tals said, keeping his voice low after a quick look to judge those within earshot, "first there is the matter of knighthood itself. Though it is nobler in theory than it ever manages in truth, at least the shared ideal creates a bond of sorts, even among enemies. So it is counted a good thing that one who commands knights should also be one. Not necessary, no, but a good thing."

"That's first. What's second?"

"Second, by knighting you themselves, the earls place you in some small way in their debt . . . well, not debt exactly. Say rather they create a special bond with you. Not that they were thinking of that solely, or even at all, but it is there."

"As by my accepting knighthood of them I have tied these earls even closer to the royal house, and to my considerable advantage under the present circumstances."

Tals smiled. "Spoken like a king. Though I presume to think this occurred to you after all was done. As I said, beneath the surface. Present but not uppermost in anyone's thoughts. You judged the honor a sincere one, Highness, and as your earls understand honor more than they ever will intrigue, I am inclined to agree. On that level it is enough to just accept it."

"I do. Yet can a king ever be content with the surface of things?"

If Tals had an answer to that he never got to give it. They were interrupted by a lone rider, one of the scouts sent on ahead in an attempt to avoid more surprises. "An armed body approaches from the south," the man told them. "The banner and livery is that of House Korsos."

Galan frowned. "So soon?"

"Our messenger would have reached him yesterday. If he's wise he'll be bringing force in arms as a show of support," Tals said.

"Surely we could expect no difficulty this close to Korsos?"

Tals shrugged. "Unlikely, but this show is solely for your benefit. Duke Molikan is demonstrating his loyalty in light of what's happened."

Galan looked puzzled. "No one has accused him of anything."

"No, but *he* doesn't know that. I also believe it is an embarrassment to him that the attack occurred as close to his territory as it did. He may try and make amends for that, and if so I think you should let him, Highness. It's possible he will misread any hesitation on your part as suspicion, and that's one wheel we don't want to start turning."

Galan thought about it. "I see your point. Albon chose you well."

Tals smiled wistfully. "I'll accept the compliment, since it's really a compliment to my mentor. That ambush didn't cost Borasur as much as it might have, for which we all give thanks, but the price was still very high."

"Indeed."

With Duke Molikan's escort they reached Korsos without incident. After his time on the road and in a succession of small manor houses, Galan's quarters in Duke Molikan's smallish castle felt almost decadently comfortable. He made sure his escort was billeted properly, but after that he indulged in the luxury of a hot bath and several hours uninterrupted sleep before letting events intrude on his attention again. He joined Duke Molikan for breakfast as Tals and two guards stood at a discreet distance.

"Any news?" Galan asked as he attacked a plate of bread and cheese.

"Not very much, Highness, I'm afraid," the duke replied. He was about Albon's age, graying but still vigorous, but there the resemblance ended. Galan looked into the man's face and could find not one trace of guile, try as he might.

The Powers witness, as I must and will have men like Tals around me, so will I not forget those like Molikan who do not look below appearances nor wish to. I need both.

"We found tracks on the eastern border, heading north, which from the number and direction might have been the horsemen you seek. As far as we can tell they have not returned the same way. We lost the trail near the Hossos River."

"It would make sense to take an alternate route on the

113

retreat," Galan said, and Molikan nodded.

"That was my thought as well, Highness. To do otherwise would freshen a cold trail and 'Caution is useful in retreat as well as advance,' as it is said."

Galan brightened. "You've read Koban's *Treatise on Tactics and Field Order*?"

Molikan smiled. "I'm afraid not, Highness; I'm no scholar. I learned that particular saying from my late father, who was a great friend of Sir Koban. It's possible Father got that wisdom from him. Or the other way 'round, as they often discussed the subject when Sir Koban visited us to use my father's library. Father built quite a collection, though I haven't the patience for reading that he did. There's an inscribed copy of Sir Koban's book in our archives, if you'd care to see it."

Galan smiled. "That I would. I'd be pleased if you'd show me—"

They were interrupted by a servant who entered the room hurriedly and whispered in Tals's ear. Galan could have sworn that Tals looked surprised; as his counselor approached the table, Galan was sure of it.

"Tals, what's happened?"

"It seems you have a visitor, Highness. A woman. She insists on seeing you now, and no doubt she will get her wish."

Galan sighed. "This isn't the best time for an audience, in light of the circumstances."

"I presume to think you might reconsider. It's Princess Ashesa of Morushe."

Tals presumed correctly. Soon Galan and Ashesa were together but not alone. Such a thing was close enough to impossible now as to make little difference. Tals and a member of Ashesa's escort kept a discreet distance in Duke Molikan's hall, but they were never out of sight nor allowed the royal couple to be either. Galan wondered how different things might be after they were married or if indeed they would ever be different at all.

"Protocol," Ashesa said. "I understand it, but I don't like it."

"I'm understanding more of it than I ever thought needful," Galan said. "But enough of that. I'm very happy to see you, Ashesa, and yet—"

"Puzzled, I fancy. Margy was too, when I told her what I planned. I spoke to some of your escort outside. I heard what happened at the Kor, Prince Galan, and I'm very happy to see you, too. Is the wound painful?"

Galan frowned, then glanced at the bandage on his arm, freshly changed after his bath. He'd almost forgotten about it. "Almost literally a scratch, Highness, and no sign of festering. I was luckier than many."

"To hear your escort tell it there was more than luck involved. That there was a hint of your brother about you that they had not seen before."

It could have been his imagination, but Galan thought there was an intensity to Ashesa's gaze that he found a bit unsettling. He also realized—with a little annoyance—that he was blushing, but there wasn't anything he could do about it. "Men believe what they will," he said, then smiled hesitantly. "I'm reliably informed that I didn't disgrace myself, for which I'm also grateful. Still, I know you didn't come to see me about the fight at the Kor."

She shook her head. "In truth I knew nothing of it until I arrived at Duke Molikan's castle. I came to tell you something, Galan. Something I think you should know before you make any public announcements about the marriage alliance." Galan barely had time to register his bewilderment before the words came rushing out of Ashesa. "The magician called Tymon the Black did not kill your brother."

He frowned. "He didn't? Then who . . . ?"

She didn't turn away from him, though he could see that she wanted to.

"I did," she said.

Chapter 8
"Settling Accounts on an Empty Purse"

Seb and Tymon spent just one night in the Kuldun monastery; it was the last stop before attempting the mountain pass that would take them to Wylandia. It was still early enough in the season that ice shouldn't be a threat, but this pass wasn't the main business artery between Wylandia and Morushe. Rather it was more of a smuggler's route known for its predators, human and otherwise, and wasn't called "The Serpent Pass" for nothing. It was still preferable to the main pass to the east; there the danger was that Tymon would be recognized, and Tymon and Seb agreed that this was more reason to worry than a few ragged highwaymen.

Tymon went off to pay his respects to the abbot. Seb waited in their quarters, grateful for a warm hearth and a bit of wine. By the time Tymon returned, Seb was feeling quite mellow.

"So. How is His Eminence?"

"Tolerable, for someone so close to death."

Seb blinked. "The abbot is ill? I'm sorry; I didn't know."

"I didn't say he was ill. I said he's close to death. That is to say, he's studying mortuary customs of the Kaleal. It's rather taking most of his focus right now and he's feeling too morbid for proper company. I do wish he'd chosen a cheerier subject, but scholarship has its own reasons."

Seb just shook his head and took another sip of wine. A big sip, truth be told, and then he changed the subject. "Speaking of which, how is young Koric doing?"

"Like a fish discovering water, the abbot says. It'll probably be safe for him to return home come spring, but I don't think he will. I suspect that this is his home now."

"He's turned into Brother Col. I warned you."

Tymon frowned. "That was a warning? Oh, I see. You think that's a bad thing."

Seb smiled. "Oh, not really, if scholarship is indeed his true calling. I'm all for everyone finding the work suited to them. Though I must say doing the same hasn't really made me happy. Or you, come to that."

Tymon sat on a cushioned stool near the window. Seb had lit the fire so he could open the shutters; beyond the weak glow of fire and candle the night sky over the mountains was alive with stars.

"It's not about happiness, Seb," he said. "I once thought that. Happiness, or at least satisfaction. Contentment. Now I don't know what finding one's work really means. I just know it has to be done. The alternative is worse."

"How so?"

"How not? A vague sense of life wasting away. Discontent for no reason. Unease for no reason. It's a shadowy sort of life, Seb. Hardly worth the bother."

Seb smiled grimly. "Whereas we sense, not ourselves, but time wasting away because there's never enough of it. Discontent because there's so much to do that it can never be done. Unease for good and sufficient reasons, but unease nevertheless. Isn't it exactly the same?"

Tymon looked at the stars. "It's all the difference in the world."

Galan and Ashesa were finally alone. There were guards at the door to the princess's new quarters, but they were out of both sight and hearing on the other side of two feet of tightly mortared stone. Ashesa sat primly in an ornate wooden chair and toyed with the needlework in her lap; Galan paced. Once he sat down for a moment on the edge of Ashesa's bed, suddenly seemed to realize just where he was, got up and began to pace again. Ashesa was the first to break the silence.

"What did you tell them?"

Galan kept pacing. "Just that you needed confinement for your own protection. Molikan had no reason to suspect anything else." Galan apparently thought of something, then. It made him stop pacing and stand in one place for a change. "You knew I didn't tell them the truth."

Ashesa shrugged. "No, I didn't know," she said, remembering something Tymon had said to her on their parting . . . when? It seemed like years and yet not nearly long enough. "I wondered. If you had told them, your options would suddenly be very limited."

"Meaning that once I had told Tals and Molikan and, well, anyone, what you told me, I'd have been within my rights to have you summarily executed?" The word seemed to pain him. Ashesa could have sworn that he'd actually winced when he'd said it.

He really is a dear, she thought, and wondered if that was good or bad.

Ashesa put the needlework down. "Meaning," she said, "that you'd have had to do something. Execution, the dungeon, torture, *something.* Honor demands it, and 'A king without honor is a king without a shield.' That is to say, he doesn't rule for long." She smiled a little sadly. "I'm sorry, Galan. Not for what I did, though I know that makes no sense to you. I'm sorry because of what my actions have done to you."

Galan's voice was full of anguish. "Ashesa, why did you tell me this?"

She met his gaze. "I had to. Lady Margate once told me that

there were good secrets and bad secrets. This was a bad one. For myself I could live with it; in truth I'd intended to. Except. . . ." She stopped.

"Except what?" Galan said, not sure he wanted to hear but unable not to listen. He felt numb.

"Except suddenly it was no longer just me. It was 'us.' And this secret would have been poison for us, Galan. I—I couldn't have borne it. I'll bear your hate, if that's all you have for me now. I couldn't have borne your love if you hadn't known, Galan. It would have crushed me."

The prince thought of something else. "Did your father know? Did he talk of alliance and all the while he . . . ?" Galan couldn't finish.

Ashesa reddened. "Of course not! Only you and I know."

"And Tymon the Black. And Tymon's associate." Galan sat down on the bed, since it was the only other place to sit, and this time he didn't get up. "What do I do now?" he said the words aloud, but he wasn't talking to anyone in particular.

Ashesa considered. Her voice sounded flat and lifeless, even to her own ears. "You can execute me, though if you choose that route I could demand a Judiciary Combat and champion and the delays would be substantial. You can slit my throat here and now and avoid all that if you're keen to." She paused, considering further. "You can throw me in the dungeon and take revenge for your brother with whatever instruments of torture appeal to you. You can denounce me and send me back to Father in disgrace."

"Any one of which leads to a state of hostility, if not outright war, with Morushe," Galan said. "Some more quickly than others."

Ashesa shrugged. "More than likely."

"You say it so calmly, Ashesa," Galan said numbly. "As if it were no more than moves on a chess board. This is your life

120

we're talking about! Doesn't it matter to you?"

She nodded. "Mine and, sadly, many others. So a more important question right now might be this: Does it still matter to you?"

"No. Yes . . . oh, damn all I don't know!" His hands clenched into fists.

She nodded sadly. "I suppose I should be grateful for your hesitation. That's something, I guess, so fair enough—come back when you've had a chance to think; there's still a little time before you have to depart for Tonara and your coronation. I'll be here, obviously." She picked up the needlework again, regarded it with some distaste. "Margy was always after me to learn these activities suitable to a princess. This may be my last chance."

Tals found Galan standing on the parapet of the highest tower in Molikan's castle. "You shouldn't be here alone, Highness," he said. "These are dangerous times."

Galan nodded. "I don't think I'd realized just how dangerous."

"You're not speaking of the Kor, Highness," Tals said, and waited.

Galan stared off into the distance. "Tals, you are probably the most discreet man I have ever met, and that includes your late master, rest his good soul. If there's something you want to ask me, ask."

"You've ordered the Princess of Morushe confined."

"Yes."

" 'For her own protection,' Molikan says. I don't understand; is the princess in some danger?"

Galan thought about it. "Yes, and more than a little."

"May I ask the cause?"

Galan looked back out over the parapet. "You may ask, but

I'm afraid this may be one matter I have to sort out on my own."

Tals looked unhappy. "Highness, I think you know my loyalty to your House. Your word is law to me."

Galan sighed. "And yet?"

Tals took a breath and overcame his hesitation. "And yet every act has consequences, and that of royalty more than most. King Macol will find out about this sooner or later and I am sure he will not be happy."

Galan nodded. "I've been thinking about that myself. Accepting on my word that the princess must remain confined for the moment and I have more than sufficient reason to do so, what can we do to contain the damage? In this I will welcome your help."

Was that relief Galan saw on the young man's face? More than likely, Galan thought, when he considered how his actions must appear to the counselor. More likely Tals's suspicions ranged from uncontrollable lust to pure madness, both extremes to which royalty seemed prone on occasion. Galan knew his actions in all other matters from then on had to be above reproach, if he was to keep Tals at his side.

Tals, for his part, seemed more at ease now with a scheme to occupy him. "From what members of Ashesa's escort have told me, Macol may be unhappy already. It seems the princess left Morushe without his knowledge or consent, adding a bit of plausibility to what you told Duke Molikan. So what if we send word to King Macol ourselves that Ashesa is safe and that you have taken her under your protection, say, to prevent any further rashness? Macol certainly knows her potential in that regard."

Galan smiled grimly. "He does indeed."

"We can word our communications so that he would infer that her confinement would only be until what time you can arrange for her proper return. Which, with the coronation so close at hand and other pressing matters, might be somewhat delayed." Tals raised an eyebrow. "Since our relations with Morushe are currently good, there's no reason for Macol to suspect otherwise. It might buy you some time to resolve whatever this problem is. I hope that's enough."

Galan nodded appreciatively. "It might at that. As for the rest, well, I hope so too."

"I'll have the letter prepared for your seal immediately." Tals turned to go, then hesitated. "One more thing, Highness."

"Yes?"

"Since there will be a delay, Macol might want to send one of Ashesa's maids or such to attend her. We should probably suggest as much ourselves."

Galan considered. "I hadn't thought of that. Yes, that might be a wise touch, showing concern for her comfort. See to it."

"As you will, Highness."

Tals bowed low and left Galan there. The prince knew his counselor's brain must be whirling with the possibilities and potential meanings of Galan's actions, but that could not be helped. The one thing on Galan's mind was and remained the problem of just what he was going to do about Ashesa. Galan knew he didn't have a great deal of time to solve that particular puzzle. Then again, he wasn't sure if all the time in Creation would be enough.

"How did he know?!"

Duke Laras sat on the parapet staring out over Deepwater Bay, but his attention came back to the same question over and again, like a vessel caught in a whirlpool. Vor saw the potential destruction ahead and tried to change the course.

"You're assuming someone betrayed you," he said.

Laras blinked. "Didn't you say as much? How else was that message delivered? My family, Vor! My own home!"

Vor sighed. "Well, then. I would guess the man you're looking for would be me."

Laras stopped. "If that was meant to be a joke, Vors, it was a damned poor one."

"I crave your pardon, but if what you say is correct then there is little alternative. There were three guards on the hallway at all times that day, in four watches, and all within sight of the others. I can see one guard being corrupted, but the entire watch? Plus the fact that Lytea's nurse was taken with the flux the day before and was either in her own bed or the garderobe all the while. It was I who took Lytea her meals when your lady was occupied elsewhere; it was I who told her a story and sang to her. And it was I who found the note. Besides yourself, only I and those I trust knew of our plans, which Tymon the Black discovered and expressly forbid us to carry out lest your wife and daughter's lives be the forfeit. What other conclusion is there?"

Laras didn't speak for several long moments. "Just one," he finally sighed. "I was mistaken."

Vor bowed. "I would not be the first to say so, Your Grace. I hoped that would be you. In either case, I thought the same when I said we were betrayed, but I realized that this was not possible. This magician clearly has other sources."

"If Tymon the Black really is in league with Galan, that means I've misjudged my royal cousin in more ways than one. Wasn't it Tymon himself who slew Galan's brother?" Laras asked.

"So it is told, Your Grace, and a good point, though Tymon was supposed to be dead, so our information is obviously incomplete. It's also quite possible that Tymon is backing House Kotara for his own ends, though why he would want to save Galan's crown is beyond me."

Laras chewed a fingernail, thoughtfully. "And me. Galan must be in league with the magician, Vor. It's the only reasonable conclusion."

"Yet regardless of whether Tymon is in Prince Galan's hire or not, if the magician had reason to tie our hands then he doubtless had magical means to gain the information he needed and to demonstrate his ability to strike at you," Vor said.

"I'm so used to seeing intrigue sometimes I think I've forgotten to stop. Even so, we face a dilemma."

"What is your wish, Your Grace?"

"My wish is that it had been a traitor—not you, Vor, but someone. Now I must confess myself at a loss. Tymon's warning was clear, and he has proven that he can strike my family at will. Even if Galan is allied with this dark magician, even if Galan *himself* ordered his own brother's death and I could prove all of this to the satisfaction of the Council of Nobles, I couldn't even *attempt* to do so without being prepared to risk the lives of my lady and my child. I am not so prepared, Vor."

"You could throw yourself on the mercy of House Kotara."

Laras smiled grimly. "I'm not prepared to do that, either."

Vor nodded. "Good, since it would serve only to humiliate you and force Galan to act sooner than he may intend, if indeed he intends to move against you at all."

Laras frowned. "If? How can he not?"

Vor shrugged. "Why should he? If you're right that Tymon is acting on Galan's orders, then the magician's threat to your family already puts you in Galan's power. You have to break that particular chain, and soon."

Laras rubbed his temples. "My head hurts, Vor. Be blunt. How?"

"Tymon the Black is the key. Remove him and you remove the threat. Whether he is acting on his own or is your royal cousin's hired dog, the result is the same. With him dead, you are free to act once more. It is the only way."

Laras looked grim. "You are right, of course, and I am ready.

We will leave immediately."

Vor shook his head. "Your Grace, your impulse does you credit, but you cannot play any direct part in this. Your absence so soon before the coronation would arouse immediate suspicion. You know you must send another."

Laras looked at him. "It would have to be you, Vor. You know there is no one else I could trust with this. Take whatever men and supplies you need. Do whatever you have to do."

Vor bowed. "I hoped for nothing else. It will be difficult, Your Grace, but I have a knack for doing what must be done."

"What can I do?"

"You must put your scruples aside and attend Prince Galan personally, summoned or no." Vor raised his hand to forestall whatever the duke meant to say. "And make all proper show and obeisance; give Galan no public excuse nor anyone else cause to question your loyalty. Not before we are ready."

"There is wisdom in that, of course. Do not concern yourself, Vor." The duke hesitated, then amended, "Friend. I will do what I must."

Vor bowed low. "As will I."

There always came a point in a king's reign when, despite armies or servants and subjects, knights and nobles, you had to take matters into your own hands. King Macol of Morushe knew that this was one of those times. There was no one he could send to do what he had to do now. He was still a little flushed from the long climb; the cell was in the highest tower of his palace. He dismissed the guards one by one as he passed them, until he came to the final short corridor and stood there alone. He unlocked the cell door with an ancient iron key, black and cold as the way he felt. He hesitated at the door and then knocked loudly.

"Come in, Your Majesty. The turning of the key was quite

herald enough."

Macol found Lady Margate sitting by the only window in her cell, calmly using the fading afternoon light to illumine a square of tapestry as she plied her needle. Macol stood by the door. Lady Margate stood up to curtsey, and the king waved her back to her seat.

If ever an artist wished to capture the essence of patience, he could do worse than paint Lady Margate sewing.

Her patience was only one of many things Macol admired about the Lady Margate, though sometimes he had to wonder if hers was the patience of the saint or the spider.

"How did you know it was me?"

"I heard you puffing. Most of your guards are more used to climbing the stairs." She paused. "Majesty, I feel awkward sitting in your presence. Perhaps you would care to sit? There's nothing but the one other stool, I'm afraid."

"It will do." Macol lowered himself carefully. The stool was adequate to his bulk, though only barely. "We are quite alone, Margy. I want to talk to you."

"I am my king's prisoner. You may do with me as you like."

Macol turned even redder, though that hardly seemed possible. "I'm not here as your king! I'm here as Ashesa's father. And it's your own fault, you know."

"That you are Ashesa's father?" she asked mildly. Her attention seemed to be focused on her sewing again, to Macol's considerable annoyance.

"You know my meaning perfectly well, Lady Margate. You put yourself in this tower as much as I did. If you hadn't helped my daughter slip away like that—"

"She'd have done it on her own, alone, and likely be in more trouble than she is already. I understand your anger, Majesty, but if I'd informed you of her plans maybe you would have caught her in time, maybe not. At best she'd be sitting where I am now, since if her mind was made up there'd be no other way to hold her."

Macol sighed. "I dare say," he stopped, as a new thought came to his attention. "What did you mean, 'more trouble'? You think there's more to this than foolish impulse?"

Lady Margate looked up from her sewing and met his gaze squarely. "Don't you?"

A look passed between them. Something of understanding and familiarity, of time and shared burdens. Macol put his head in his hands. "I wouldn't tell just anyone this, Margy, but Galan's message concerns me. I've written and received enough diplomatic meanderings to know when I'm being misdirected. I'd hoped his natural honesty would have lasted longer."

Lady Margate demurred. "The richest king in all creation could not afford that luxury. Galan has good advisors, no doubt. But to what end?"

Macol shook his head. "I don't know. There's a limit to how far I can press this without rattling protocol more than I care to . . . yet. I need more information, and for that I need your help, Margy."

Lady Margate went back to her sewing. "My help, Majesty?"

"Due to the delay, he says, Galan has invited me to send attendants to see to Ashesa's comfort. I want you to go. I know it's a long journey but, well, I think it should be you."

It could have been a command. It wasn't. Lady Margate smiled. "Oh, Macol. Of course I'll go."

If the king noticed the familiarity at all he said nothing of it. "Well then. It's settled. Take whatever attendants you require, anything you need. Look after my daughter, Margy."

Lady Margate put her sewing aside. "Always, Majesty."

The king rose and started to leave. He paused in the open

doorway. "And yourself, too," he added gruffly, and then he was gone.

Seb and Tymon were three days out of Kuldun. There had been no sight of another human being for the last two of those days as they picked their way on foot through the rocky pass to Wylandia. After one day on the trail it was clear enough to Seb why Tymon had directed them to leave their horses behind at the monastery; a few hours on these rocks and all their mounts would be lame or worse. With their travel packs and sturdy boots, Tymon and Seb were much better suited to it than any horse would be, save one that was part mountain goat.

"No wonder this pass isn't used much for legitimate commerce," Seb said.

Tymon nodded absently. "It could be improved, but with the eastern Pilgrim Pass open year 'round there's little need. That route has been a bone of contention between Wylandia and Morushe for years, but close to being settled, if rumor is true."

As Seb paused to shift his heavy pack he finally asked a question that was more of a mystery to him. "There's something bothering me."

"Always."

Seb glared at him. "I mean 'in particular.' Why do you support Galan for the throne of Borasur? You said yourself that House Dyrlos has the better claim."

Tymon climbed up a large boulder, stepping carefully. "For the same reason the Priests of Amatok preferred his ancestor, I fancy."

Seb frowned. "I thought they were bribed to favor House Kotara."

"I never said that."

"You said that it should have been House Dyrlos on the throne now."

"True, but I never said the priests were bribed. They did accept a large donation from House Kotara, but in truth it was somewhat smaller than the one House Dyrlos offered, if my sources are accurate. The priests no doubt considered the gold as little more than their due for being put in such a difficult position in the first place. I would be astonished if they based their decision on it."

"Then how did House Kotara steal the throne?"

Tymon reached the top of the boulder and sat down to rest. After a moment Seb clambered up to join him. They were near a rise. Below them the path fell away on a gradual slope, showing easier walking for a bit before the path rose again toward a narrow defile on the next crest. Overhead the sky was blue and almost cloudless. "I've been this way once or twice before, in my youth. Once we cross that we'll be within sight of Mount Whitetooth. If the weather holds we'll be in Wylandia tomorrow."

Seb nodded. "Marvelous. Don't change the subject."

"Hmmm? Oh, that. Perhaps 'steal' is the wrong word. I mean, House Kotara meant to have the throne whatever the correct genealogies told, and so it turned out. The same for House Dyrlos. If the issue was to be decided by royal kinship there was barely a drop's worth difference between them." He rose, and picked his way carefully down the boulder's side to the main path, such that it was. Seb followed.

"That," Tymon said, "was no doubt what settled the issue for the priests of Amatok. They judged the bloodlines for a solid month while the posturing of House Dyrlos got worse and worse. What they finally decided was that the minor difference in bloodlines between the Houses, although in Dyrlos's favor, just wasn't enough. They chose House Kotara."

"Then they overstepped their authority, didn't they?"

"Perhaps. Yet the Chief of House Dyrlos was a notorious

hothead with dreams of Empire. It didn't take the Long Look to see the path the kingdom would follow if they had chosen him. Greatness or ruin, but a good deal of death and suffering along the way. They decided the game wasn't worth the candle. They claimed 'the will of Amatok.' We have the hindsight of two centuries since of relative peace and prosperity for testament, so I tend to think they were right."

They were nearing the bottom of the path. Soon it would rise again. Seb wanted to save his breath for walking, but it was rare enough he found Tymon so talkative and he was loathe to waste it.

"That explains their reasoning. It doesn't explain yours. I know the Long Look has shown you some of this, but I also know those were early visions, the Long Look has been absent for a while, and the world has made more than a few turns since. Galan is little more than a boy with some natural gifts but no experience. I've no love for Duke Laras, but I can see the stuff of kings in him. Perhaps Borasur would be better off under House Dyrlos now."

"Yes. Perhaps now," Tymon said, affably.

"Yes? That's all you have to say?" Seb asked.

"What do you want me to say, Seb? That I'm making a choice on instinct and sentiment? Is that what you want to hear?"

Seb thought about it. "No, that is something I definitely do not want to hear."

Tymon reached the end of the downslope and started up again, using his staff for support. "I have done what I knew to do, Seb. That's all. I'm going to the Oracle to see if the Long Look can be regained. If so, perhaps then I can give you a better answer."

Seb's mouth felt suddenly dry. "If not?"

Tymon shrugged again. "If not, I'm going to find a quiet place in some obscure corner of the Twelve Kingdoms, like

Takren. Perhaps I'll grow apples, as Takren did. Perhaps something else. You'll be welcome to join me or not. In either case I'll no longer move in the affairs of the world and the name Tymon the Black will fade in memory. Houses Dyrlos and Kotara will just have to work this out on their own."

Seb blinked. The thought had come to him, and now he could not banish it. "Like Takren? How else like Takren?"

"I said he was my friend, and has been for a long time. That was true. I said his name was Takren. That is only partially true. He used to go by another name before he retired to farming. Perhaps you've heard it: Dommar the Beast."

Chapter 9
"Seek and Not Find, Find and Not Seek"

"That is certainly an oddity . . . Mones, was it?" Vor sat with a man he had just met in a tavern outside the city walls of Tonara. He signaled to the proprietor to refill his companion's ale yet again. "So what happened next?"

"That was odder still," Mones said blearily. "Aker meant nothing by what he said, 'struth. Well, other than to have a bit of fun with the dwarf, I reckon. He's like that, you know? Not actually mean except when he's really in his cups. The dwarf acted as if he hadn't heard, so Aker repeated it."

"Repeated what? You never did tell me exactly what Aker said to him."

Mones blinked. "I din'? Thought I did. After the fifth ale time and memory meld and flow so. That's what I like about ale the most."

"I dare say. Yet surely you do remember this?"

" 'Course I do. Such a trifle, really. He said 'Such a tiny man! I'll bet your mother scarce noticed your birth, else she'd have drowned you for a puppy.' Or words to that effect."

"Indelicate, to be sure," Vor admitted, "yet surely not the worse sort of insult a dwarf might hear in his life."

Mones nodded vigorously, then seemed to regret it as he turned a little pale. He belched once and a little color returned to his cheeks. "One would think so, wouldn't one? But no. He took a sip of whatever brew he was drinking, then climbed down from his stool—which in truth he had to do—stepped

133

away from the counter and stood toe-to-toe with Aker, who is scarce shorter than yon doorpost and nearly as broad. It was like a mouse staring down a barn cat, if you can imagine."

"I think I can." Vor took a drink from his own mug. "What happened then?"

"The dwarf said that if Aker was of a mind to discuss his mother, perhaps they'd best do it outside where the air was fresher. At least, that's the gist of it. It was ridiculous in the extreme."

"Did you laugh?"

Mones stared at his ale. "No. As I think on it now, I probably should have. And yet, well, at the time, you understand, I didn't want to make any sound at all. It was only after Aker had followed the dwarf out that I realized I'd been holding my breath, of all things."

"What happened then?"

"You won't believe me," Mones said. "You'll laugh."

Vor smiled reassurance. "My friend, you would be amazed at the things I believe."

Mones took one last drink of the good dark ale, sighed, and waved off Vor's offer of more. "You've been kind, friend, and I do wish I could reward you with a story of more of a dramatic twist, something not so expected, in the sort of tavern joke this may one day become. And yet, here's the thing: We didn't hear anything at all. After a moment or two the dwarf strolled back into the tavern as calm as could be, finished his ale, and then left. Naturally what few of us were present rushed outside to see what had happened to Aker."

"And what did you find?"

"Aker," the man said evenly, "flat on his back and out as cold as the summit of Whitetooth. His tunic had been neatly sliced open and the word 'fool' etched into his chest, apparently by a very sharp dagger. Not so deep as to kill him, you understand, but he'll bear that label for the rest of his life, I wager."

Aye, and in more ways than that one, was Vor's considered opinion. "That is indeed an amazing thing. Thank you for the information, Mones."

Mones looked at him. "You do believe me, don't you?" he said. He sounded a little surprised.

Vor nodded. "Oh yes." He lay a few coins on the counter for the tavern keeper. "You wouldn't happen to know which direction the dwarf was headed, do you?"

"I'd think he was best avoided," Mones said.

"I could avoid him better if I knew which way he went."

Mones apparently saw the wisdom in that. "You should be safe enough, then. I believe he was leaving Tonara. He was dressed for travel and, if I'm not mistaken, the tracks of his mount led north."

A sot you are, Mones, but no fool. Unlike your friend.

Vor took his leave of his new acquaintance and went to his own dun gelding, tied beside a smaller, darker mount whose arched neck spoke of eastern bloodlines. Another man came out of the bar, one that had sat close to Vor but had spoken not at all. He untied the dark horse and took the reins.

Vor nodded to him. "You heard, Aktos?"

"I did. Seb has several days' head start on us, which complicates matters. Still, if we find him, doubtless we find the magician as well."

Vor shrugged. "That's more insight than I would have had on my own, and a cold trail is better than none at all." Vor and Aktos rode out of Tonara together on the road leading north.

"This isn't cold. This is bracing," Tymon said.

Seb nodded. "Aye, and when I turned the bend in this ravine and caught the wind I was nearly braced all the way back to Kuldun."

The sky was still clear but the wind had picked up, to say the least. It blew straight out of the north and seemed to draw its character from every snowpeak and glacier it paced along the way. Seb could almost swear every crystal of ice on the wind was leaving tiny streaks of red across his face with every gust.

Seb and Tymon passed through one last narrow canyon and out onto a vast broad slope, still green with traces of summer that stretched out to a valley of sorts a few miles away. From there Seb could see more hills and more grassy plains, and more of the same all the way to the northern horizon, when suddenly there was what appeared to be one solid wall of mountain as far you could see to the east and west.

" 'Walk through the mountains. When you reach a place that's a little less rocky than a mountain, stop. That's Wylandia. If you reach mountains again you've gone too far.' Or so the proverb about traveling here goes. I can see the truth in it."

"It's lovely in its way," Tymon said, looking about.

"So's a snowpeak. It's still not my favorite haunt. I'm also surprised there's no watchtower here. You could bring an army through that pass in time, as long it was on foot."

"And do what once you had?" Tymon asked. "No one here but a few scattered shepherds and herdsmen, taking advantage of the last of the summer grass. Most of the main grazing is to the east. That leaves an army with nothing to eat but what they've brought—on foot—and a long march to Toldon. And there are patrols; Aldair's mounted rangers would have sent word ahead and be prickling their flanks within a day. By the time it came to open battle the soldiers would be frost-bit and starving, if the lot hadn't deserted before then."

"I didn't know you were interested in tactics," Seb said.

"I'm interested in everything, Seb. And you did know that."

"About those patrols." Seb began, scanning the horizon. "Best we're away from here before they make the rounds."

"I'm more concerned about running into any of the herdsmen, since they're more likely to recognize us in the first place. Common knowledge sometimes travels faster than any other kind. You're right, though—we should be going. It's still a long walk to the Spring of Yanasha and I don't know how much time is left."

"For what?"

"For the Oracle. They don't last long in any case, and the turning of the year is particularly hard on them."

Seb frowned. "Why?"

"Because it's getting cold, of course. Especially at night. So in their weakened condition—"

"Weakened condition?" asked Seb, feeling more and more confused.

"Starving, Seb. If they last as long as this, the first really cold night generally kills them."

When she arrived at Molikan's duchy on the evening of the seventh day, Lady Margate asked to see Princess Ashesa right away. She was not the least bit surprised when, instead, she was first shown to her rooms and all but forced to bathe and rest, then hours later brought to the quarters of someone else entirely.

"Greetings, Sir Tals. Something told me I was seeing Lord Albon's hand in all this, though I knew that to be impossible. Nevertheless, I wasn't too far wrong."

Tals smiled warmly as he rose to greet her. He waved to the other chair at the room's one small table. "Hello, Lady Margate; I'm pleased you remember me. Will you join me for some wine?"

"I would not protest overmuch," she said, and Tals poured the drink from an earthenware jug as Lady Margate lowered herself into the chair. The seat had a thick cushion, for which she was grateful. Travel by horseback would never be her favorite activity. *Next time I ask for a wagon. I don't care how much it rattles the bones.*

Tals handed her a glass chalice filled with a deep purple liquid. "Nowas port. Not the finest vintage in the Twelve, but an honest one."

Lady Margate sniffed the glass and took a sip, then decided she agreed with his assessment. She wondered if she would be able to continue doing so. "You were behind the letter, then? Or rather the part concerning me?"

Tals's grin broadened. "Lord Albon spoke of you with reverence, nor was he mistaken. You saw yourself in what was not said. Yes, I suggested that bit, because I wanted to speak to you about this . . . situation. I couldn't name you specifically—that would have been more than odd—but I had little doubt that you would be the one Macol sent."

Lady Margate took a good long drink before she replied. "I am the Princess Ashesa's humble Lady-in-Waiting. Before that I was her nurse, after my own child died of the plague the same day as my husband, and Ashesa's sainted mother, rest them all. It was good work for a poor widow to have. So, as much as I admired and respected your late master, I confess myself puzzled. Who else would Macol send?"

Tals sighed, and took a long sip of the wine himself. "Both our Houses are well nigh afire, M'Lady. Would you rather hide the well or fetch a bucket?"

Now Lady Margate allowed herself a smile, as she took her measure of the young man before her and approved of what she saw there. "That depends," she said. "First pour me a bit more of that charming Nowas port. Then tell me about this fire my lamb Ashesa's started."

Tals told Lady Margate what he knew, which was at once very little and yet, perhaps, more than he realized. Lady Margate was able to fill in a little of the tale in the spaces he'd left, though she decided to keep silent about that for the moment. She'd liked Tals instantly and she respected both Lord Albon and his judgment, but there was too much at stake to forego caution. She merely nodded to him as he finished relating the events before Ashesa's confinement.

"You heard nothing of what was said between them, I suppose?"

"I was too far away, except one time. I distinctly heard Prince Galan say 'Daras' at one point, when he raised his voice a bit. He seemed agitated, though he controlled it well."

"But not perfectly. Still, it's curious," Lady Margate said musingly.

"Now then," Tals said, "I don't suppose you can shed any more light on this?"

"I'm afraid not, sir. Though I confess I was involved in arranging for Ashesa's initial escort. Beyond that she told me nothing. She's a very intelligent girl . . . young woman, rather. Yet she has a mind like a mountain once it's made up. There's no shifting it."

"I must speak frankly, Lady Margate," Tals said. "I've tried to ferret out the root of all this but I've failed, and Prince Galan will not speak of it. Worse, the more I press the less he says, and I dare no more. That was why I arranged for you to come. I think perhaps Ashesa will tell you what my prince will not tell me."

Lady Margate shrugged. "Perhaps. Though I wouldn't count my life against it. Nor will I guarantee to share what I have learned. Your pardon, sir, but I feel you have been honest with me and I must return the favor. My first loyalty is to Morushe and its royal house, of course, but what I feel for Ashesa is beyond loyalty. I'll do nothing to harm her, whatever purpose it serves. Do I make myself clear?"

Tals nodded. "I expected no less, and I seek no more. Yet I

know you realize the situation as it stands serves no one, save enemies of both Morushe and Borasur. One way or another, it must be resolved."

"We don't even know what 'it' may be."

Tals went back to the wine. "All the more reason, and this is the nut of it so far as I'm concerned. How can you defend against a danger if you don't know what it is?"

How indeed?

Lady Margate put her glass aside. "Well, then—take me to see Ashesa."

Seb and Tymon wrapped themselves tightly in their cloaks and set out at a quick pace, and for a long time Seb rationed his breath for walking. When they finally stopped to rest in the lee of a small hillock, Seb still remained silent. Tymon began to look concerned.

"You can ask me, you know. I know you want to."

Seb stared at the grass. "Ask what, Tymon? Where would I begin? Where would this improbably twisting loop of your life ever reach a point that I could point to and say: here. This is where I should concentrate my feeble energies for a better understanding. Hah, and again I say: hah. Is there such a place, Tymon? I'm beginning to doubt it very much indeed."

"I can tell you one thing for certain: don't sulk. That's a waste of energy if there ever was."

"All right—let's begin with 'Dommar the Beast,' also known as Takren, a gentle farmer whom I can personally attest wouldn't harm a mosquito even if it was in the act of biting him."

"Did you think the Long Look was something unique to me, Seb? That the Powers' interest in the world began with you and me and our pitiful hardships?"

"Now that you ask—no. Our own difficulties have proved quite sufficient, thank you very much."

Tymon smiled. "Fair enough. But it's true, as I've told you."

If Seb was short on empathy, he could still muster a bit of curiosity. "Was he as bad as they say?"

"Are we?" Tymon asked. He paused to kick over a stone and look beneath it with mild interest while Seb mulled that one over.

"Usually I don't think so," Seb said finally. "Sometimes I'm not sure," he said. "I suppose it was much the same for Takren."

Tymon nodded. "He was by nature a gentle man. When the Long Look was lifted from him he put as much distance between himself and what the Long Look had made of him as he could manage. Given the opportunity, I'll do the same."

Tymon started walking again and Seb hurried to catch up. Seb could still feel a cold edge in the wind, but now he could feel the sun, too. Traveling would have been almost pleasant now except when Tymon was in a mood to ponder he walked with the same sort of focused intensity that he brought to whatever else had his interest at the moment. It was hard to keep up with him and Seb hated to remind Tymon that there was a reason for a more stately pace when they walked together. Tymon tended to forget the height difference, which Seb didn't mind most of the time. Now, however. . . .

"Slow down," Seb demanded. "I'll wager a hill giant couldn't keep pace with you when you're like this, and I'm only a dwarf."

"Hmmmm? Oh, sorry. I was thinking. Or rather, I wasn't."

"You mean you were thinking about something else entirely. What, may I ask?"

"Something I said."

"Some people feel it's best to think about what you say before you say it," Seb said dryly.

"This kind of thought can only come after the words, Seb. It's the nature of the beast. That is, I just told myself something I didn't realize that I knew, and so almost didn't notice."

Seb rolled his eyes. "Once more, in the language of our birth?"

"I said, speaking of Takren, that 'the Long Look was lifted from him.' And so it was, else Dommar could not become Takren. But who lifted it, I wonder? Were the Powers done with him?"

"One would presume so; who else could remove that curse once it's laid on?"

Tymon said. "It's not a curse, strictly speaking, as I've told you before. I hope you never get to learn the difference firsthand. No. Perhaps the Powers, or one of them, did finally relieve Takren of the burden. Yet I know for a certainty that this is not true in my case."

"How do you know?"

"Because an old acquaintance, of sorts, told me so, though it took me some time to realize it."

Seb shook his head. "I repeat: if the Long Look is bestowed by a Power, who else is powerful enough to remove it?"

Tymon looked thoughtful. "Who indeed?"

Seb changed the subject. "This path is too well-traveled," he said. "We should have kept to the ridges."

At first after they left the pass there had been no trails at all, then a few old cattle paths with no sign of recent use. This was no cattle path. They'd come to it as a downslope turned into the entrance to a green valley and Tymon had started down it without a word. Seb had followed, feeling more and more uncomfortable.

"This is the way to the Spring of Yanasha," Tymon said. "And we're unlikely to be the only supplicants, even at this time of year. If we keep to the ridges we'll only draw more attention when we finally do join the path."

Seb wasn't convinced, but he didn't argue; Tymon knew more about the business of oracles than he did, certainly. But Seb remained alert for trouble. What actually happened was something else.

They came across the man and his son on the other side of a small stand of pine, one of many along the path at the valley floor. The man had the sunburnt look of a farmer about him; his clothes were rough-made but clean and well tended. They had clearly sat down to rest on a solitary stone. Or at least the father had. The boy was about ten and tended to fidget with the kind of pent-up energy that Seb remembered with a twinge of envy.

The man's glance lingered on Seb for a moment or two, but to Seb's considerable relief the man didn't gawk. "Greetings, friends. Are going to the Oracle too?"

"That we are," Tymon replied. "My name is Jakan; this is my friend Paka. We've come from Morushe."

Well, at least now I know who I'm supposed to be, Seb thought. He returned the greeting himself, but otherwise let Tymon take the lead.

"I'm Hoba, this young rascal is my son, Tuls. Our farm is to the east of here, but not so far as Morushe. That's quite a ways to travel, so late in the year. I hope you've not come for nothing."

Tymon smiled. " 'One can only truly judge a distance by the journey,' " he said, quoting the familiar proverb, "and I'm sure you must begrudge the time away from your work."

Hoba nodded. "Aye, that's so. Tuls, I think I saw a spring back a ways." He handed the boy a half-full waterskin. "Fill this up before we go on, there's a good lad." The boy hurried off to his task, and his father watched him go. "There's my reason, though I'll not be talking about him in his presence as if he were deaf as well as afflicted. Thus the errand."

Seb's respect for the man grew considerably. "What's wrong with your son?"

"Nothing that I can see. He's 'strong as an ox and quick as a fox,' as the saying goes. The problem started when we lost his mother last spring."

"We're very sorry for your loss," Tymon said. "That must have been hard."

Hoba shrugged. "Thank you for that, friend. Yes, she was a good lass and I'll not see her like again in this life, I wager. But it was harder on the boy, you understand. He's not spoken a single word since the burial, and that was months ago. I've come to ask the Oracle how to restore his voice. Or rather his will to use it, which is the heart of the matter. And you?"

Tymon told the man a story of missing family and increased desperation. It was convincingly told but Seb wasn't really listening; he watched the path for more travelers and was relieved that only Tuls came through the wood, carrying the dripping bottle.

"Safety in numbers," Hoba said, rising. "Though there should be no trouble this close to Yanasha's sacred place. Still, shall we walk the way together?"

"That's very kind of you," Tymon said, ignoring Seb's signal of protest. "We would be pleased."

They set out together and set a good pace. When they paused to rest again, Seb managed to get Tymon's attention while Hoba and his son were attending to nature some distance away. "I don't think this is a good idea. What if they recognize us?"

"Seb, 'a tall man in the company of a dwarf' is a pretty unique description throughout most of the Farlands, so if they haven't recognized us already they're not likely to. And if they do know who we are—which I doubt—much better to stay close where we can keep an eye on them, don't you think?"

"Well. . . ." Seb still didn't like it, but there was wisdom in what Tymon said. "I guess, then, we're a little less likely to be spotted as two tall men, a boy and a dwarf?"

"Breaks the pattern," replied Tymon cheerfully. "Besides,

we're almost there. We should reach the shrine by nightfall."

"The sooner the better," Seb said. "Though from what little you've told me of the Oracle of Yanasha, I can't say I'm looking forward to it."

"Child, who do you think you're deluding?"

It wasn't much of a greeting, but Ashesa put down her sewing and threw her arms around Lady Margate and hugged her fiercely just the same. "Margy! How did you know? Did Father send you? Oh, never mind all that. I'm so happy to see you!"

"I fancy you'd be happy to see anyone other than those rather nervous men outside. You do remember them, don't you, Highness? The ones with the spears?"

"Well, under the circumstances, I wasn't expecting anyone." Ashesa shrugged.

"Circumstances. Indeed."

Lady Margate sat down without being asked, and after a moment or two Ashesa sat down too. She reached for her sewing again. "Margy, there's a rather difficult stitch that goes with this tapestry and it just eludes me. Do you think you could show me how you—"

"Stop it, child. And I do mean now."

Ashesa reddened. "Margy, don't think I'll let you take that tone with me, despite our friendship. I am a Princess of the Blood!"

Lady Margate smiled sweetly. "Are you now? Last time I checked, princesses of the Royal House of Morushe did not live in cages."

"This isn't a cage!"

"Delighted to hear that. So let's leave it for a while, shall we? I've just spent three days in a very hard saddle and my bum's one solid bruise. I think I fancy a walk. Will you come with me?"

Ashesa shook her head. "You know I can't, Margy. All right—maybe this is a cage. Maybe I'm not worthy to be a Princess of Morushe. Maybe I'm right where I should be, and, well, that's all," she finished, looking miserable.

Lady Margate smiled faintly. "All? Not even close. Suppose you did try to leave, Highness. With me. What do you think would happen?"

"I-I don't know."

"Then let me tell you: Not one blessed thing."

Ashesa blinked. "But those guards—"

"—are veteran men, hand-picked soldiers of greater or lesser intelligence, but I'll wager you there's not one complete and utter fool in the bunch; you don't live long in their profession by being so. And only a complete and utter fool would lay a hand on or otherwise harm a Princess of the Blood Royal, prisoner or no. Galan knows that as well as I do, else he's not the man I judged him to be. Those men and their spears are for show, just as the door to this cushioned cell is. Or next you'll be telling me you didn't know the door wasn't locked?"

Ashesa wouldn't look Lady Margate in the eye. "I knew," Ashesa said softly.

"Then the only reason I can fathom for your continued presence here is that you want to be here. Is that what you want, Ashesa? Sewing, of all things. You hate sewing! You, me, and every other living soul in your father's palace besides knows that."

Ashesa stared at the needlework for a long moment and finally put it aside. "Yes."

Lady Margate nodded grimly. "I wanted to ask what Galan is punishing you for. I think a better question might be: what are you punishing yourself for?"

Ashesa looked up. There were tears in her eyes and they were coming harder and faster. "Margy. . . ."

"I'm right here, child."

Ashesa threw her arms around Lady Margate again, and this time she did not let go for a long, long time.

"Margy, I've done something terrible."

Lady Margate held her hard, bracing against her sobs like a ship preparing for a storm. "Cry now. Let the poison of it out if you can. After that you're going to tell me everything, and I do mean everything. It's long overdue. Perhaps then we can discover what's to be done."

It wasn't strictly by chance that Koric wasn't seen, but almost. If this had been an ordinary day he'd have been in one archive or another, either assisting the curate in charge or busy with his own burgeoning studies. As it was he'd just come out of the Lasandic Archive on an errand to the abbot when he saw the two men in the courtyard, their mounts being led off by another lay brother to be tended. Koric took two quick steps backward, almost slamming into the doorpost as he did, and barely missed a collision with the curate.

"Koric, what's gotten into you?"

"I know one of those men, the ones who just arrived. I must speak to the abbot at once."

The curate, a cheerful old monk with the patience of stone and about as much hair, barely shrugged. "Your errand is with the abbot. I dare say you can speak to him then."

"But the visitors are being taken to the abbot! I saw them walking toward his rooms."

"I gather this is a problem? Are you in some kind of trouble, Koric?"

"Yes, if you consider having a hired assassin within arm's reach 'trouble.' " Koric quickly related some of the story of how he came to be at Kuldun in the first place. It wasn't a complete version by any means, but the curate got the gist of it easily enough.

"You think he's followed you here? Why would anyone go to such bother for you?"

"I wish I knew," Koric said, "but until I'm sure of his errand I'm taking no chances. I must speak to the abbot alone, as soon as possible, but I can't let the visitors see me. Could the abbot be brought here on some pretext?"

The curate considered. "It barely needs a pretext to get the abbot into the archives. I'll see what I can do. Wait here."

Koric waited, fighting the urge to bite his nails or hide in the rafters. He was eyeing the rafters with more than casual interest when Brother Lons returned, the abbot in tow.

"Brother Koric, what's this about? Are you saying one of today's visitors is not who he claims to be?"

"I'm saying he's a murderer for hire because I know it to be true. As for the other, I cannot say, Lord Abbot. I do not know what he claims to be."

The abbot looked annoyed, but only for a moment. "Well. That's certainly true, and I apologize for the oversight. These men claim to be simple travelers, looking for a friend who they believe passed this way."

Koric glanced around as if seeking the best avenue of escape. "Did they describe who they were looking for? Did you believe them?"

The abbot sighed. "Slow down, lad. For the first, yes, and for the second, no." He turned to the curate. "Convey my apologies to our guests and tell them I've been detained. Offer hospitality as is our custom; doubtless they will wish to stay the night at least. See that they're comfortably housed."

Koric started to protest, but the abbot silenced him. "We can't very well refuse without a good reason, and the best reason I can think of at the moment is one we don't want to share with them." He turned back to the curate. "See to it, Brother Lons. I don't think we need fear them so long as we behave as expected."

Lons hurried away, and the abbot watched him go. "Now that Lons is gone, I can tell you—our guests are not looking for you. The man they've described is clearly Tymon, your benefactor. Naturally I was noncommital about his whereabouts; it's reasonable enough since so many folk visit us."

Koric allowed himself to enjoy the relief for a moment, then moved on to a new fear. "They'll ask questions, Lord Abbot. Not everyone here is so discreet. I would not like to see Seb or Tymon harmed."

The abbot smiled at that, then grew thoughtful. "Well spoken, and I'm afraid you're right about the questions part. I can't very well forbid all here to talk to our guests without raising even more questions, which defeats the purpose in any case. I think it quite likely they'll discover what they want to know within a day or so and be on the trail of our friends soon after."

"Then what do we do?"

"The only thing possible. We must send someone to warn Tymon. Tonight."

"I'll go," Koric said. "I don't want to. I don't want to leave my studies, for one thing. I don't want to give this assassin another chance at me, for another. But if I remain here there's a chance I'll be seen anyway."

The abbot nodded. "Sensible. Now then, let's see about getting you provisioned and away while our guests are resting from their journey. With luck and a little prevarication we can get you off with a day or two head start."

"That should be enough," Koric said, though he wished it might be much more.

"Let us hope," said the abbot, "because my most optimistic assessment says that's all you're going to get."

Chapter 10
"A Wonderful Capacity for Surprise"

Seb wasn't prepared. How could he be? Nothing Tymon had said or the stories he had heard could prepare him for the sight of the Oracle of Yanasha in all her glory. The shrine itself gave little hint of what awaited them; it was a simple stone structure beside a rushing stream. There was one basin for offerings, one statue of the Goddess Yanasha, her arms raised in benediction, a statue earnestly but naively carved by some long-vanished priest. Tymon made his offering right after the farmer did, gold following bronze, but there was no price set that Seb could discern.

"Does the value of the offering matter?" Seb whispered.

"Not to Yanasha, supposedly. I imagine the priest who lives on the offerings or the Temple at Kodna which takes the rest might be concerned; their vestments are rather threadbare these days, I hear. As it is, the goddess does not value the offering at all. The theory is that the supplicant does so, for the cost can only be weighed against the means. The goddess—through the Oracle—judges their sincerity accordingly."

"Do you believe all that?" Seb asked.

"Believe? No. I accept it, as I would a rule in chess, and make my moves within those constraints."

"How can you value omens and pronouncements from a goddess you have no faith in? Why did we walk so far to get here?"

Tymon shrugged. "I believe in very little, all in all, and as the years go by I find I believe in less and less all the time. It's not such an obstacle; you'd be surprised how few wonders of the universe require our faith to manifest. Simple acceptance of those wonders, on the other hand, is a much rare commodity. That's the real coin I bring, Seb. The gold is for the priest."

Seb let it go, since he had no argument to offer. Their offerings made, they traveled past the portal at the rear of the stone shrine and out to the Oracle itself.

They stood near the end of a dead-end valley. It was a sheltered spot; here the grass was still green, albeit beginning to turn in the growing cold. A swift mountain spring rushed down the rock face some fifty yards away to gather in a stone basin for a moment before flowing outward in two separate streams. The two streams flowed around a small grassy island before meeting again near the back of a small garden in back of the shrine and flowing on past, making the stream they had seen upon first arrival. The Oracle lived on the island.

Living, Seb thought, *might be a bit of an exaggeration.*

It was a weak sort of witticism, unspoken and quickly shamed into oblivion. Seb considered himself a hard man; by necessity, certainly, and he had reason enough, but a hard man nonetheless. He wondered if it were possible to be so hard that what he saw now could not touch him.

The Oracle of Yanasha was a girl. Seb guessed her to be about nine or ten, but it was hard to be sure. She was thin past gauntness; her hair was a tangle of weeds and filth. She sat in a little ragged heap near the center of the little islet, rocking very slowly, whimpering to herself in her madness.

"Sweet Yanasha. . . ." That was Hoba, but he didn't say anything else. He just stared at the wretched bundle.

The attendant priest was a youngish man with a furrowed brow and cold blue eyes. "You knew what to expect, good pilgrim."

Hoba shook his head. "I know the locusts may come in summer and devour everything I own. Seeing it happen is something else again. Is there nothing . . . ?"

The priest didn't let him finish. "No. There is nothing we can do for her."

"She's hungry," Seb said, because he could clearly see that it was so.

"And thirsty, I dare say," the priest admitted, "though she has been known to sip from the stream now and then. She doesn't often manage, and now she is almost too weak to try. If you have a question, I would ask it soon. I doubt she'll live the night."

Seb studied the priest. Why does he look so angry? He's not the one being treated like an animal. Or worse than one, by the look of things. "I'd feed a stray dog if I had a scrap to spare," Seb said mildly. "Surely the Priests of Yanasha can do that much for one who enriches their sect so greatly?"

The priest just looked at him for a moment. "You don't understand," he said.

"Aye, and he's not alone." That was Hoba.

"It's really very simple," said Tymon.

They all looked at him; for a moment Seb had forgotten that he was even there. He and the mute boy Tuls had just been standing by the stream's edge, looking at the Oracle, both saying nothing. Now Tymon spoke. The boy just kept staring.

" 'When the spirit of Yanasha moves across the land, it reaches the one who would be her vessel. Be it man in arms or woman in childbed, in matters not. That one chosen is taken by the spirit, and invested with a portion of that spirit. That one will journey to the shrine of Yanasha in Wylandia. That one shall speak with Yanasha's Voice until death or the Goddess release them.' Or so it is written," Tymon said. He turned to the young man. "Have I gotten the gist of it, Guardian?"

"Gist? More like word for word, from *The Book of Time*," the priest said. "Of which only three copies are known to exist. Are you a theologian?"

"I try to be whatever is needed as the need arises," Tymon said. "Today I am simply a pilgrim."

Seb, sensing danger, tried to steer the conversation away from Tymon's profession. "So a person is possessed in some fashion and compelled to come here and become the Oracle," Seb said. He pointed accusingly at the island. "That doesn't explain this."

"Oh, but it does," the priest said, warming to the subject. "Think about it."

"I will not," Seb said.

"That's your good fortune, sir," the priest replied. "I've been able to do little else for the past few weeks."

Something in the man's voice got Seb's attention. "You didn't choose this task, did you?"

The priest sighed. "Only a monster would choose this mission. There are surprisingly few monsters in the Priesthood of Yanasha, despite what you may think."

"Are you being punished?" Hoba asked.

"In a manner of speaking," the priest replied. "Or tested, rather. The Guardianship of the Oracle of Yanasha is a heavy burden. We have had individuals leave the Temple rather than bear it."

Seb put his hands on his hips. "How heavy? You neither feed her nor clothe her nor house her. All you do is watch!"

If Seb was hoping to move the priest to anger he was disappointed. The man merely nodded, looking glum. "Aye, just that. We watch. Every day until the end. That is what we do. That is all we are allowed to do."

Hoba looked away from the wretched girl and glared at the priest. Tuls did not move, nor look away. He watched the girl with an awful, fixed expression that Seb had noted but didn't want to try and read. Hoba, for his part, spoke his mind plainly.

"As I said, Priest: one thing to know, another to see. I know the stories; I grew up in a household dedicated to Yanasha! Yet as I see this . . . everything I once knew to be true could be a lie. It would take the weight of a feather to turn the scale now."

Seb sighed. "You may all know the reasons, but I am neither a scholar nor one of the faithful. I would be grateful to have it explained."

"They have to be certain," Tymon said, "that the one who comes to the shrine is actually the Blessed of Yanasha."

Blessed? Seb could barely form the thought without feeling ill.

The priest nodded. "That's the heart of the matter: for food and lodging and a gentle life there are many who would feign madness quite convincingly. They would come into the shrine upon the death of the former Oracle and take their place on the Islet of Time. And they would lie, false prophesies, false oracles, and no way for us to tell true coin from false. It could happen—nay, it *did* happen on several occasions according to our chronicles, and there was a great deal of damage done. Our forebearers had to find a way to be sure that the Oracle was genuine."

"And they chose this," Seb said.

Another shrug. "The Oracles eat whatever they can scrounge. They wear whatever they bring with them. They die quickly. Sometimes the shrine is vacant for months. Sometimes years. But never in the last three centuries has a false Oracle sat on the Islet of Time. The forebearers were wise," the priest said, then repeated, softly, "wise indeed."

"Speak the word three times, Priest," Seb said, "Try and make it true."

The priest didn't seem to hear. "Time is growing short," the priest said. "Do you wish an oracle or not?"

Hoba glanced at Tuls, then at the Oracle again, then at nothing in particular. "Aye," he said.

The priest nodded. He stepped across a small wooden bridge to the island and kneeled before the Oracle. She did not react at first. Finally she raised her head a little and looked at him without any sign of comprehension as he whispered to her. He could have been a courtier before a queen for all the deference in his posture and attitude, and not one plain-robed priest before a mad, dying girl. After a moment the girl's head slumped forward again and she did not move. The priest waited for several long moments then reached out and touched her neck and wrist. He held his hands there for several long moments, then finally rose again and crossed the bridge.

"I'm sorry, but there can be no oracle today."

"Is she dead?" Tymon asked, but the priest shook his head.

"No, but almost. I do not think there will be any more oracles for some time. I'm sorry," he repeated.

"Say it again," Seb said, trying to give his anger somewhere to go.

The priest met his gaze squarely. "I'm sorry."

Seb was still angry, though now he felt a little ashamed as well, and he didn't know why. The priest turned away and started toward the shrine, his shoulders hunched, his face turned toward the ground. He stopped only a few paces away, and turned to look at the Oracle. Everyone else was doing the same, or rather looking at Tuls, standing where he had stood from the first, gazing across at the Oracle.

Tuls was singing.

Seb did not know the song; he thought it was a hymn of some kind, but he had only heard a very few in his life and could not say for sure. There seemed to be little of faith, glory, or even joy in what words Seb could make out; that didn't seem to matter. Nor was Tuls's voice anything special; indeed the first stirrings of adolescence seem to be playing merry hob with his pitch. That didn't seem to matter either. Tuls looked at the

Oracle with his eyes full of tears, and he sang. No one else said a word. Even Hoba seemed stunned with joy as if he had taken Tuls's muteness into himself.

The Oracle looked up. She didn't revive, exactly. There seemed precious little left of her that could be revived. Yet, like the others, she listened to Tuls's simple song.

Did she . . . smile?

Seb wasn't certain, and whether it was a smile or a grimace of lunacy or pain, it faded as the song ended. In a moment Hoba was at his son's side.

"Father, I'm so sorry. . . ."

"You are answered."

The voice was strong and clear; that of a young girl and yet born and carried by something far older, like a lost rose drifting in on the tide. With that the girl's eyes closed and she slumped over on her left side. The priest took a step toward the bridge, but there was no need. They could all see her stir fitfully, see the slow rise and fall of her chest.

"She's asleep, or fainted. Probably not much difference now," the priest said.

Tymon went to the farmer. "I'm very happy for your son," he said.

Hoba thanked Tymon and Seb and the priest and the Oracle and Yanasha, and everything else within thought or hearing, and then he led his son back through the shrine and out toward the path home. Tymon watched them go.

"That was fortunate, though unexpected," the priest said. Tymon nodded, but that was all. The priest went on. "I wish I could say the same would happen again, but I'm afraid there's not much chance. I am surprised she had that much strength, but it's gone now, as you can see."

Tymon looked at the sleeping girl. "Guardian, with your permission we'd like to camp just beyond the grounds on the off chance the Oracle revives in the morning. If not, we will be on our way."

"As you will. May Yanasha smile on you." The priest clearly thought it was futile, but no harm in trying. Tymon's face was unreadable.

"Let's make camp, Seb. I'm tired."

When night came it was very cold. Not freezing the breath in your body and the blood in your bones cold, but chilly enough. Seb got tired of lying awake. The stars were bright in a cloudless sky but, try as he might, Seb could see nothing in them but cold, distant points of light. The campfire embers were fading; Tymon's huddled form was barely visible some distance away, wrapped in his bedroll, silent and still.

At least one of us can sleep.

Seb gave up. Moving quietly so as not to wake his sleeping companion, he laced on his boots and wrapped himself in his cloak. He hesitated only a moment, then took one of the blankets from his bedding and a few biscuits and sweetmeats from his pouch and slipped away toward the shrine. The door was not locked, as he had expected. He eased it open; there was an alcove of sorts near the back where the priest slept; a curtain was drawn across it, but Seb waited until he heard the man's snores, then moved like a moonshadow past the altar and out toward the Oracle. In a moment he was standing on the bridge to the Islet of Time.

"I wondered if you'd be along."

Seb, casting backward glances at the shrine, had not been paying as much attention to the Oracle as perhaps he should have. Thus he did not see the figure kneeling before the Oracle of Yanasha until it was too late.

"T-Tymon? What are you doing here?" Seb had enough presence of mind to keep his voice to a whisper, but only just.

"I could ask you the same thing, if I didn't already know,"

Tymon said. He neither moved nor turned around. "Did you think you could make that much difference with one little blanket and a few scraps of food?"

Seb looked grim. "A small difference is better than none. It might at least help a little."

"Perhaps. But help whom, I wonder?"

"Don't go cryptic on me. I suppose that business about waiting until the morning was just a ruse?"

"Until I could sneak in here under the Guardian's nose and get my oracle before the wretched girl dies? Of course. What else?"

"Tymon, have I told you lately what a bastard you can be?"

Tymon still didn't turn around. "No," he said. "You've been rather remiss."

Seb could barely get the words out. "How can you joke about that? Even you?"

" 'Even me' isn't joking. I am a bastard, because serving the Will of the Powers requires it more often that not, and it was my choice to do that. My own, albeit reluctant, choice. I need to be reminded in case I forget. Unlikely, but why take the chance?"

Tymon stood up. Behind him was the huddled form of the Oracle, covered in Tymon's blanket.

Seb shook his head. "I suppose next you'll tell me that you brought the blanket just to help keep her alive long enough for the oracle to be given?"

Tymon looked puzzled. "You mean you think there might be some other explanation?"

"It's possible," Seb said, then nodded. "Yes. You came to help her too, didn't you?"

"No." As if to emphasize that point, Tymon reached down and pulled the blanket away.

It took Seb a few moments to understand what he was seeing. "First you bring a blanket, now you take it. What do you think you're doing?!"

"I think I'm looking for an answer." Tymon walked past him, dragging the blanket behind him like an afterthought. "I'm taking the blanket because if the Guardian finds it in the morning he'll be doing purification rituals for a bloody month, and—strangely enough—I don't think he deserves that. Besides," he said, and sighed, "she doesn't need it anymore."

It only took Seb a few moments to confirm what Tymon had told him. The Oracle of Yanasha was dead.

In the morning Seb and Tymon helped the priest place the girl's wasted body in a stone mausoleum. Seb had noted the smooth stone structure the day before but hadn't made the connection; he'd thought it some kind of storeroom. Which, as he looked about at the pitiful bones of Oracles past, wasn't too far wrong. There was no grand ritual; only a simple prayer which the priest made as they swung the bronze door shut. Soon after, the priest himself started to pack his few belongings and the remaining shrine offerings onto the back of a stout donkey.

"Your mission then is done, I take it?" Tymon asked.

" 'One is a test. Two is torture,' as my old teacher used to say. I'll return to the Temple at Kodna and my abbot. There are devotees of Yanasha among the herders here; when a new Oracle appears at the shrine they will send word."

"And a new Guardian will be appointed."

"That is the custom." The priest hesitated, then added, "For now."

Tymon smiled. "You stated the argument for the rules very well yesterday."

The priest shrugged. "I'd heard them often enough."

"Yet you still think those rules regarding the Oracle are wrong."

The priest smiled a grim smile. "Don't you?"

Tymon ignored the question. "And as you advance in the hierarchy of the Temple you will try to change them. I doubt you will succeed, and you will make enemies. You'd be better off to leave the Temple."

"Yes," the priest said. "I would. Like that farmer, I came within a feather's touch of losing my faith and leaving the Temple. In fact, until yesterday I had resolved to do just that."

"What changed your mind?" Tymon asked.

The priest looked almost embarrassed. "The boy. His song. When he had nothing else to offer, he found that much. I looked at my own faith compared to his and was ashamed. I don't know Yanasha's will where the Oracle is concerned; no one does. I don't understand the harshness of her Blessing. Yet I do believe there is something worth preserving here. I still want to leave; now I can't."

"Who's preventing you?" Seb asked.

"I am. Because then nothing would ever change. More souls lost to the Temple for the wrong reasons. The Temple continues to decline under the burden of guilt; Yanasha will still send the Oracle to this little canyon to die. Leaving would be a brief balm to my conscience, and that's all. When I return to Kodna one of the first things I'll do is have an argument with my abbot. It will be a long argument. Years, perhaps, but as I study and dispute perhaps I'll learn what I need to convince him, and where he goes others will follow. Perhaps. One has to start somewhere."

"That," Tymon said, "one does. Good fortune, Guardian."

The priest raised a hand in blessing. "Thank you for your help, good sirs, and your attention for my rambling. Go with Yanasha," he said, and led the donkey down the path to the south. Seb watched him go.

"Dogma puts most mountains to shame for implacability. He

doesn't stand a chance."

Tymon nodded. "Probably not. Then again, maybe that's not the point."

"You're being cryptic again."

"Yes," Tymon said. He looked at the now-empty shrine. "We'd best be going ourselves."

"Where?"

"At the moment? Anywhere but here."

Galan granted an audience to Lady Margate only after she made it perfectly clear that she wasn't going to go away, but it was Tals who finally tipped the scale.

"Tell her I'm busy. I don't want to see anyone right now."

Tals bowed. "Highness, I am at my tether's end. I tell her you're busy. She tells me you're not. I tell her you have much on your mind. She says you have only one thing on your mind, and there's the problem. I don't understand her meaning, Highness, but she is rather insistent."

It was Galan's considered opinion that Tals knew Lady Margate's meaning only too well, but there was nothing to be gained by saying so. He reluctantly granted her request. At the appointed time Lady Margate didn't so much arrive at Galan's quarters as invade, flags flying and with the glint of spears in her eyes. Within a few moments Galan was beginning to see what Tals had been up against.

Lady Margate curtseyed with surprising grace for her size, then dismissed the guards with such force of command that they left before they quite had time to wonder if they should. She waited only until she and Galan were alone and got right down to business. "Honestly, Highness, how can you be such a fool?"

Galan sat, stunned. "Lady Margate, are you mad? Don't you know who I am?"

"Prince Galan of House Kotara, Crown Prince of Borasur, Protector of the Shrine of Charada, Duke of Colna, Earl of Seleb, recently Knight of the Order of the Ocean Star. Shall I go on? I fancy I know your titles better than you do."

Galan's face went bright red. "I'm new at this, Lady Margate, so I have to ask: should I execute you now?"

"You can do what you want, up to a point," Lady Margate said. "And if you do take my poor head I hope you have a better story than the one you gave King Macol. Even he only believed it because it was expedient to do so."

Galan just looked at her. "If you know what I assume you do, then you know why I have done what I have done."

"For someone 'new to this,' as you say, you've certainly mastered the art of pronouncing words while avoiding meaning. If you're talking about your unfortunate brother then, yes, I do know what really happened to him. I didn't dismiss the guards merely for the privilege of chastising you, Highness," Lady Margate said, and then smiled. "That was merely fortunate happenstance."

Galan imagined a shark would smile thus. "So now you know? How soon before the knowledge is common to every keep and hovel in all the Twelve Kingdoms? Lady Margate, how can I refuse to act when that happens? My brother, a Prince of the Blood, was murdered!"

"Your brother was indeed murdered, Prince, but there's a distinction here that you are missing: Ashesa killed your brother, she's admitted such to you and me both. That doesn't mean she was responsible for his death."

Prince Galan sighed deeply. "You're right, My Lady. The distinction eludes me."

"Oh? Then why is my dear child's head still on her shoulders? You had the power to take it on the first day, legalities be damned."

"I had—have, the right. There would have been consequences, right or not. I don't want a war with Morushe. Or anyone, come to that."

"Do you hear the excuse in your voice? I do. If 'justice' is what you really want and war is the price, well then you'll pay it, and I think you realize that as well as anyone. Yet you've been trying to find some other way out of this. Do you deny it?"

Galan just stared at her for a moment of two before he found his voice again. "No, of course I don't deny it!"

"Why? The truth, Highness. You want another option and I think I can give it to you. But before I do anything, or you decide to haul me away to an adjoining cell and call the headsman, I want to know."

"Because I'm still in love with Ashesa!"

The words came out. It wasn't what he had meant to say. He was no longer sure what he meant to say. But once the words were spoken, Galan knew them for truth. "She killed my brother. I should not love her. Yet I do. Martok forgive me."

Lady Margate nodded. "No doubt, but it's not Martok you should be asking. You punish yourself as much as you punish Ashesa. As she accepts her confinement with—let's both be truthful here—uncharacteristic meekness due to her own very considerable remorse. She wished your brother no ill, Galan. She even tried to warn him about Tymon's trap. But he had some very strange ideas about what being a hero meant, one of which prodded him to demand something of Ashesa that she could not give him."

"That didn't give her the right—" His voice cut off as if someone had interrupted, but Lady Margate had said nothing. When he remained silent, she went on.

"Highness, I don't pretend to know where those notions came from. You were his brother, so perhaps you know more, but it simply does not matter now. What does matter is this—Ashesa *defended* herself. Yes, she killed your brother, Highness, and in her place I would have done the same! But she did not murder him. Tymon the Black bears that crime."

Galan looked as if he was in pain. "Even . . . even if I can accept what you say, that still leaves the matter where it was before—what must I do?"

She raised one eyebrow and looked at him like a parent regarding a stubbornly thick child. "Do? You must make up your mind. Here it is, Prince: You can forgive Ashesa, and you can help her forgive herself. You can learn to live with what she's done, just as she must. Or call the headsman now and let's get this over with. You're late for your coronation already. Whether you're also late for a war or a wedding is entirely up to you."

"My brother—"

"—Was marked for death by the sorcerer known as Tymon the Black for reasons we may never understand. That is the way history will remember it, Your Highness. Are you strong enough to do the same?"

Galan looked at her, all anger gone. "I don't know."

"Then I suggest you find out, but do it soon. Right now Ashesa is very confused and hesitant, but she won't stay that way."

Galan smiled then. It was a faint sort of smile, but a smile nonetheless. "That I do know."

"Then you know that she won't wait in that comfortable cage forever, not for you or a legion better. There's still time to sort this out, mind, but not a wealth of it. Make your decision as a brother, a lover, or a king, or all three. But make it soon."

With neither leave nor curtsey, Lady Margate withdrew and left Galan to battle his demons alone.

After their first day in the mountain pass to Wylandia, Aktos paused on the trail for a long time. "Someone else is following them," Aktos said.

"Following Seb and his sorcerer? Are you sure?" Vor asked.

Aktos nodded. "I'm not the greatest tracker in the Twelve Kingdoms, and this rocky ground doesn't help. But the only tracks through here in some weeks have been those two sets, and now this one which I'd noticed but didn't pay proper heed before. I thought it was coincidence."

Vor grunted. "This pass isn't used often but neither is it abandoned, nor is it very wide. How do you know this person, whoever it is, isn't just going the same way?"

"Because they follow too closely. You can see here," Aktos pointed to one of the few muddy spots among the rocks and frost, "where he loses the track and then casts back and forth several times until he finds and follows it again." Aktos showed the tracks leading away, and Vor could follow them himself for a short while until they moved into the rockfield again and grew too tenuous for his untrained eye to see.

"You're right. He's following, not merely going in the same direction." Vor looked thoughtful. "What could this mean? A bandit?"

Aktos shrugged. "Possible," he said, in a tone that did not sound optimistic. "Yet the habit of bandits is to go to a likely spot and wait for their prey to come to them. It's also not their habit to attack a larger party unless they're very sure of themselves, and the prize is worth the risk. In this instance my instincts say no."

"Which leaves?"

"Well, it may be my imagination, but don't you think the abbot was just a bit, say, jovial to the pair of us? They're used to visitors. It's not so rare or remarkable."

"He was very helpful," Vor said.

"But not very quick in that help. It's my considered opinion that everything, from answers to provisioning, took just a mite longer than necessary. Or so it seemed to me at the time, but it was such a small thing I convinced myself I was mistaken."

Vor stopped. "They knew our errand," he said. "They've sent someone ahead to warn Seb and that bastard magician!"

"Possible," Aktos said. He didn't sound the least bit uncertain.

"Well, then. We can't reach Tymon before he does. We can, however, stop him from reaching Tymon at all."

Aktos bowed. "I can travel faster alone, sir. If you think speed is needed."

Vor barely hesitated. "Speed is needed. I have an appointment to keep within seven days, whether our current business is concluded or not."

Aktos frowned. "A meeting? You didn't tell me anything of this."

"Because it doesn't concern you. Right now that messenger does, so go on ahead and kill him. Then stay for me. I want no action taken on Tymon and Seb without my presence, even if the opportunity arises."

"Are you certain? I trust my skill and would hope that you do as well, albeit those are two very challenging targets."

Vor sighed. "Your skills are not in question, but that devil has risen from the dead once already. I'm going to be there to make sure it doesn't happen again."

Chapter 11
"Monsters and Heroes and Everyone Else"

"They've been in there for some time," Tals said.

Lady Margate, intent on her needlework, barely nodded. "Hmmm."

They were in the corridor outside Princess Ashesa's cell, and had been for what seemed like hours, at least to Tals. Lady Margate, on the other hand, could have given a stone lessons in patience and taught a milch cow a thing or two about serenity, so far as Tals was concerned. She merely sat, plying her needle, taking advantage of the last of the good western light from a row of high windows lining the walkway to the tower. Tals had tried sitting for a while, but now all he could do was pace the length of the corridor, over and over.

Say, rather, most of the length of the corridor. When the voices within Ashesa's cell had risen to an almost intelligible pitch, Tals had tried to use the cover of his perambulations to get an ear closer to the cell door. All he heard was a distinct rumble of disapproval from the "inattentive" Lady Margate. He'd sighed deeply and gone, chastised, back to his pacing.

Tals finally stopped in front of her. "I gather you know more about this than I do," he said, which only brought another "Hmm" from Lady Margate. Tals tried again. "Lady Margate, do you know what they're talking about or not?"

Lady Margate finally looked up. "Of course I know what they're talking about, and so do you. They're discussing their future and trying to decide if they have one, and their respective kingdoms' say in the matter be hanged. That's all we know and all we need to know."

"Dynastic marriages should not turn on the whim of the people involved," Tals said.

Lady Margate paused to replenish her needle with blue thread. "Ideally? No. Yet surely you will concede that this situation is a little unusual?"

"Aye, that I will. Though exactly how unusual continues to elude me."

She smiled at him. "One doesn't need to know all the details, Sir Tals; indeed, in the future that knowledge could be an absolute inconvenience. It is the results that concern both me and you now, and those are currently out of our hands. Do sit down. You hover like a vulture."

"I'm sorry, but I can't help it. How long must we wait?"

Lady Margate raised an eyebrow. "I gather that's a rhetorical question?"

Tals sighed and sat back down. "Your pardon, Lady. I just wish there was something I could do."

Lady Margate shrugged. "We've done all we can do except wait and pray, so that's what we're going to do. The rest is up to them. I find needlework very soothing in this sort of situation."

"I'm a knight," he said. "If I touch a needle other than to sew up a wound I'll never be able to show my face in the field again."

"Then go hit someone in the practice yard. Or read a book. Do whatever you must do, but do not touch that door. There's too much at stake."

Tals leaned closer. He looked at what Lady Margate was doing for some moments, then asked, "Could you show me how you do that?"

"Why?"

Tals looked unhappy. "The altar of my curiosity," he said, "demands a sacrifice."

"Have you ever wondered about Wylandia, Seb?"

Seb dropped another piece of dried cow dung on the campfire. "What do you mean?"

"I mean it is less than it should be, as a kingdom, as a place in the world. The valleys are rich, the grazing is good, the temperature relatively mild considering how far north we are. The hills have ores and gems in abundance. And yet. . . ."

Seb finished the thought. "And yet it remains a pariah among the Twelve Kingdoms. Neither their mineral wealth nor their prized horses are traded as extensively as they should be. Too restrained by the passes that bottle it up here, and yet still making the occasional raid—with provocation always claimed—just as in ancient times. Any of that?"

Tymon nodded. "Yes. All of it. Aldair is a good man, for a king. Even his enemies say so. Yet it doesn't seem to make any difference. This year he negotiates with Morushe to advantage; the next he'll lead a quick slash-and-burn raid over some imagined slight or other and undo all. It's a land of bad choices; the method of validating the Oracle is just one example. I want to think about this, as time permits."

"Fine. Just stop stalling on the current problem."

"I don't understand," Tymon said.

"There's something you're not telling me. And before you get cryptic, let me be more specific: there's something about the Oracle of Yanasha you're not telling me."

Tymon stared at the fire. "You're right."

Seb looked at him. "You did receive an oracle, didn't you? She died, but she spoke to you before she did. Is that what happened?"

"Yes, Seb."

Seb blinked. "I suspected as much. Yet I did not expect you to be so straightforward about it."

Tymon shrugged. "I'm never deliberately obtuse, and even if I chose to be so, this 'oracle' would be cryptic enough without any help from me. Frankly, I'm baffled."

"What did she say?"

"It was after I wrapped her in the blanket. She looked at me for a moment, and said, 'You are answered.' Then she died. She closed her eyes and she just . . . stopped."

The flicker of emotion on Tymon's face apparently worried Seb. " 'You are answered'? That's exactly what she said to Hoba."

Tymon chewed on a ragged thumbnail. "Yes."

Seb sat down by the fire. "She was the Oracle of Yanasha, but she was also a mad, starving little girl. Perhaps she was babbling."

Tymon nodded. "Perhaps."

Seb poured himself a mug of the strong bitterbush tea, though he couldn't quite tell if the full pungency was from the tea or the smoke from their fire. "You don't believe that, I take it."

Tymon looked away from the fire now; this time his gaze was fixed on the sky full of stars above them. "When she said the same thing to Hoba it was nothing less than the truth. And, as with Hoba, the voice was not entirely that of a little girl. Especially not one so near death as she was."

"You keep mentioning her condition."

Tymon shivered, and pulled his blanket closer about him. "Do I? I didn't realize."

"Deny it if you want. I'm just telling you what I see."

"I know the reason the Oracle is treated as it is."

"That's not the same thing. You don't agree with it, any more than that guilt-wracked priest does."

"I never said otherwise."

Seb conceded the point. "You wrapped her with the blanket before she spoke, that and nothing more?"

"Nothing. I didn't speak to her at all."

"Neither did Hoba. Tuls sang, which wasn't exactly a question. . . ." Seb's voice trailed off. He frowned in confusion for a moment, then smiled. "She did not answer Hoba. She said that he was answered, that an answer had come. And it had. She said the same thing to you, and there you have it."

Tymon kept his gaze on the stars. "Now who's being cryptic?"

"Not at all. I just mean that there was something in your actions that forms the answer to your question. The fact that you never asked it apparently does not matter."

"I'm not a total fool, Seb. That occurred to me, too. But what did I do? I just brought a blanket. It was not a courageous thing, since I fear no priests and suspect that Yanasha cares even less about her sect's dogma than I do. I simply didn't want the waif to die before I'd received her oracle. It was selfishness."

"So you keep saying."

Tymon sounded almost desperate. "But what else? And what does it have to do with the Long Look in either case?"

"I think you keep asking yourself that, and I think you keep getting the wrong answer. We're tired. Let's sleep on it, and maybe we'll both be thinking clearer in the morning."

Seb banked the fire while Tymon found a decent sleeping spot nearby. After he had lain there a while looking at the stars, Tymon realized it wasn't sleep he needed as such. Rather it was the open doorway that sleep could sometimes bring, when you asked it the right way. He set his sight on a distant goal and closed his eyes.

The understanding took time, but Tymon hadn't realized just how distant the goal was. He had been walking for what he thought was a long time, though granted it was hard to be certain in that place. Time wasn't as straightforward a notion there as it pretended to be in the conscious world. Here the masks were missing, save the ones you brought along yourself.

Tymon stopped, and took a long look around at nothing. "I think I'm lost."

"You are worse than lost. You are thick. Even for a mortal."

Tymon still saw nothing and no one. "Amaet?"

"More and more thick. Why are you calling for that one? She is not the one you seek. I am."

"Who are you?"

"You are wasting time, and you mortals have so little."

"I need to ask her a question!"

"No, you need to listen to the answer you've already been given."

Tymon sighed. "Riddles. What is it about the Powers that loves riddles?"

"What is it about mortals that seeks pebbles while ignoring mountains?"

Tymon kept looking, but he still saw no one, no image of a willow tree, no shaded cool place by dark waters. Nothing. "If by that you mean I don't understand, you're right. What I received from the Oracle was not an answer. It was merely the statement that an answer existed!"

There was a low, thrumming sound that might have been laughter. If, that is, thunder could be said to laugh. "True, but changes nothing. The answer is there; what you really seek is an explanation."

Tymon thought about it. "Yes."

"Then find it."

Now Tymon did see something, if only a lessening of the darkness in one direction. He thought of it as north, if such terms had any meaning there, but that didn't really matter. It was a path, and he followed it until he came to a familiar place.

"This is the Shrine of the Oracle of Yanasha. Or at least appears so."

More laughter. "Very good. Since the shrine is a place in the mortal sphere, which this is not, then it cannot be the shrine of which you speak, can it?"

"Then why does it look like the shrine?" Tymon asked.

"A better question might be: why do you see it as such?"

Tymon sighed. To his own way of thinking he'd long since given up on the idea of getting a straight answer—or one he knew as such—from any Power. Still, there was something in him that persisted in choosing hope over experience. Try as he might, he could not rid himself of the impulse entirely. For the moment he tried to suppress it, and save his attention for what he saw there, trying to understand what it meant.

He came to the door of the shrine and passed through. The priest was there at the offering bowl, sorting the offering coins into little piles by type—gold, silver, copper—and eating them. He glanced at Tymon, said, "You've paid already," and went back to eating coins. They snapped and crunched under his teeth like little sugar wafers; the priest smacked his lips with pleasure. Tymon shuddered delicately and moved past him, out to the back of the shrine and through the small arched door that led outside to the Oracle.

She was waiting for him, as somehow Tymon had known she would be, huddled alone and miserable in her madness on the little island of dirt, rock, and willows.

"Don't forget the blanket."

Tymon shook his head. "It was a useless gesture."

"Yet you made that gesture."

Tymon had the blanket in his hands. He held it up, looked at it. It was the same one. Then, because he didn't know what else to do, Tymon crossed the bridge. It wasn't exactly the same, this time. This time the Oracle looked at him as he approached, and reached out for the blanket when he offered it.

"Thank you," she said, and wrapped herself up snug and warm. Tymon recognized the voice, even though the only sound was in his head.

So there you are, he thought. "It wasn't like this," he said aloud.

"That's not a question."

"All right, then: why have I lost the Long Look?"

"Silly man. You didn't 'lost' it, and that's the wrong question besides. My patience is not without limits, Tymon. I'll give you one more chance, but that is all."

Tymon thought about it. He hoped this time his understanding was better. "Why did I bring that blanket?"

"Because," said the Oracle, "you didn't want that wretched little girl to freeze."

Tymon frowned. "Just that?"

"You can lie to yourself all you please, but you cannot lie to me. You had other considerations, of course. You always do. Yet you strip this one to its core, and that is what you find. That's what it meant, and that's all it was."

The Oracle looked at him then, the way she had looked at him that night. There was no madness in her eyes, but rather something far more terrible. She said the same thing, in a voice that was not quite her own. "You are answered."

"Yes," Tymon agreed, "I believe I finally am."

Tymon returned to darkness, the Oracle and the shrine were at first hidden and then, Tymon realized, gone. He looked around him, this time to the west where a lightness began and then grew to become brighter and brighter until it almost blinded him. Almost. And then he could see very well indeed.

The Long Look had returned.

Seb dreamed about a boat on a quiet river. It was summer; he was warm. The banks of the river were firm and covered with soft grass and willows. Ahead there was an island, where many friends he did not have gathered for a picnic, waiting for him. They called out and waved to him, and he happily paddled in their direction.

The river changed from placid to raging in the space of a heartbeat. The boat shuddered violently, rocking side to side and finally turning completely over. Seb fell down in the cold darkness where someone or something grabbed him, shook him, held him, drowned him—

"—Seb wake up!"

Seb woke, blinking in the very early morning light, or rather what there was of it. The hands shaking him were Tymon's. Seb yawned. "If anyone would rock my boat, it would have to be you."

Tymon stopped, but only for a moment. "Hurry. There's work to do and almost no time to do it."

Seb sat up, yawning and scratching. "What are you talking about?"

"I need twine, and I need wood. Real wood, not this dried cow flop we've been using for fuel. Sticks, twigs, saplings . . . and clay. I think I saw a bank of it near that stream we passed on the way to the Oracle, as well as a small grove of aspen. We shouldn't be far from it now."

Seb struggled against the cobwebs in his head. "What's happened?"

"Nothing yet, but something will if we don't move quickly. Get your ax."

Now Seb was fully awake. He threw the blankets off and reached for his boots. "You've seen something, haven't you?"

Tymon didn't even look up as he shoved equipment into his pack willy-nilly. "Yes."

Seb finally understood. "It's the Long Look. It's back."

It wasn't a question, so Tymon didn't answer it. There was no need. Seb scrambled to his feet and rolled up his blankets as quickly as he could, while dreams of retirement and friends and picnics and afternoons on lazy rivers died on the cold morning frost.

It only took an hour or so to find what Tymon required. Seb cut several small saplings to length, found a chunk of spalted deadfall for the torso. Tymon took the wood and twine then whittled and tied and knotted until a wooden approximation of a man with stick arms and legs and a molded clay head lay on the dead grass. Tymon carved two glyphs on its chest and knocked once on the body like someone trying to open a door, and it was done.

The stick golem sat up.

Seb shivered. No matter how many times he had seen this done, it still raised the hairs on the back of his neck. Seb's discomfort grew when the creature bent its jointed arms and held its twiggy fingers before its face. It seemed to be looking at its hands, though it was hard to tell since the creature had no eyes. Nor proper hands, either. Seb did not know how the creature saw. He did not know how it stood or walked and seemed to be alive either, but that was all part of the mystery.

Tymon rummaged about in his pack until he found a soiled tunic and this he slipped over the creature's head, then a spare blanket wrapped and hid the rest of the body and made a deep cowl for the head. When Tymon finished dressing his creation he spoke to it. "I know you're just now come to being and that's a stressful thing, but there's no time to contemplate your existence. I have a job for you."

Seb listened along with the golem as the creature got its marching orders. The very last thing Tymon did was to present the creature with the knife he had used to create it. Then the creature set off on the path back toward the northern pass, slowly at first on its sapling legs, then faster and faster as it got its balance and some more coordination in its body. Soon it was out of sight.

Tymon watched as the golem disappeared. "We'll follow, but it can travel much faster than we can, for all that it's a rushed job and not very strong. Either it will be in time or it won't. Either it will be enough or it won't."

"The Long Look didn't tell you?"

"Even under the best of conditions—which this is not—the Long Look only tells me what's going to happen without intervention. It never tells me what to do about it, nor often either if I should do anything. That part's always been up to me. Which," he said, and sighed, "was precisely the problem."

Seb nodded, and began to finish his packing while Tymon did the same. "I wondered if you'd get around to telling me. So what happened? What was the problem with the Long Look?"

"Nothing. The problem was me."

Seb hoisted his pack. "I don't understand."

"Neither did I, until some Power nearly hit me over the head with it. You've said before that you believe the Long Look is a curse, and I'd pretty much come to agree with you, but we were wrong. It's not a curse, at least not strictly speaking. It is something within me, something I was born with. I think I was aware of it at some level even as a child, but it was only during my later studies that it really manifested its full power."

Seb trudged along gamely, though Tymon, carried away with his eloquence again, was walking too fast. "First, slow down. Second, tell me what that has to do with the Long Look going away."

"Don't you see? The Powers neither gave nor removed the Long Look; they *use* it just as they use me, and I confess I've been a willing tool for the most part. But when it failed it was only because I, so deep down that I wasn't aware of it, wanted it to fail."

Seb frowned for a moment, but the cloud on his brow soon lifted. "Ah, I see. Without the Long Look you'd be freed of the responsibility."

Tymon shrugged slightly. "Well, there is that. But it wasn't the main thing."

Seb, feeling a little proud of himself for his insight, was somewhat let down. "It wasn't? Then what was?"

"I was afraid of the same thing Takren was afraid of. That we were going to become monsters. Just as dark and just as evil and twisted as everyone believed."

Seb laughed. When he finally stopped he said, "Tymon, you are a monster. Ask anyone!"

Tymon shook his head. "I'm not talking about anyone's opinion, Seb; I'm talking about my own."

Seb's good humor left him. "Oh."

"I know what people say of me, Seb. I know there are good reasons that all good folk in the Twelve Kingdoms think of me as they do; we've even added to rumor when the possibility arose. Yet, when I tote up the balance of the things I've actually done, it's still not very pretty. I know there are reasons for that, too. My deeds have always bothered me. I was afraid that they weren't bothering me enough."

Seb almost smiled again, but he resisted. "Then, it seems, I was right. If you were afraid of what the Long Look was making you become, the obvious solution was to get rid of it."

Tymon sighed. "Or bury it so deep that the difference wasn't worth mentioning."

"So what dug it up?"

"The Oracle of Yanasha, when I brought her that blanket."

"For reasons you explained."

"I was lying. As much to myself as to you. I brought her the blanket because she was cold," Tymon said. "I-I didn't want her to be cold." Tymon looked at him. "I'll have much to answer for in the final tally, no doubt, but I'm no monster."

"No, you're not, Tymon," Seb said. "I always knew that, even if you didn't."

Tymon smiled. "Thank you for that."

Seb cleared his throat and then looked at the path ahead. "So, where to now? Back to the pass as quickly as we can?"

"Yes. And then, well, we'll see. A lot has happened in my temporary blindness. There's no guarantee that we can set it all to rights."

"Is there ever?"

"No. One thing I can guarantee, however."

"And this is?"

Tymon smiled. "Only that, as before, for some matters the people involved are just going to have to straighten things out on their own."

Koric looked at the first few white flakes as they fell. He held out his hand and let one cold wet flake settle there. It turned to water almost instantly. "Is that snow?"

It almost never snowed near the coast and, other than a few white-capped mountains near the monastery, Koric had never even seen it. He was uncertain what to do. The temperature was falling as night approached and while time was important so was not freezing to death. He looked around; there wasn't much in the way of firewood, and he didn't think the situation would improve much further on.

I think the best I can do is look for shelter.

There didn't seem to be much in the way of that, either. He thought about going further; maybe his luck would be better farther along the trail.

I need to get out of sight.

Koric blinked. Where had that notion come from? Out of sight? There was no one else around to be out of sight of. He started off again, and again the thought returned, stronger. Koric tried to take another step and stopped in a near panic.

"What is happening?" he asked, softly.

There was no answer, and no real alternative to obeying the impulse. Koric looked around and finally spotted a crevice in the west wall of the pass. He tested it with his staff. It wasn't more than four feet deep, but it was large enough to wedge himself inside, and a fallen boulder shielded at least part of it from view. Koric pushed his travel pack in as far as it would go, then wrapped himself in a dark blanket and followed, holding his staff in front of him as he wedged himself in.

The snowflakes were getting thicker as he settled in to watch, and wait, for what he did not know. When his breathing slowed and he was finally free of his own footsteps, he heard a new sound, distant but not very. A slow *crunch crunch* rhythm on the falling snow. It stopped often and then began again. Slowly, carefully. Koric was neither a hunter nor a tracker, but he had sense enough to know when he was being stalked. Bandits? It seemed more than likely. Koric waited, shivering, hoping the snow would hurry up and cover his trail and knowing it was too late as the footsteps got closer and closer.

"Hello, Koric. I must say I never thought it would be you."

Koric pushed backward, hoping against hope to find a deeper crevice than the one he knew was there, but there was no place to hide.

"Aktos," he said.

The assassin nodded, and the dagger was already in his hand. "Apparently it is your fate to be killed by me."

Koric took a tighter grip on his staff, though there was no room to use it, and Aktos blocked the only way out. "Will you at least tell me why?"

"Why? Next I suppose you'll be telling me that you aren't here to warn Tymon of our coming? Ah, no. It's written in your expression as plain as any text. That is why you are here. And that is why I must kill—ah!"

Something flashed by the crevice behind Aktos. The assassin spun quickly, and Koric saw a splotch of red on his tunic before he slipped out of sight. Koric inched his way out of the crevice to find Aktos confronting a nightmare.

"Well now," Aktos said, "what are you?"

His voice was calm enough but Koric could see the fear in his eyes. Koric shared it. The thing facing the assassin in the snow, a short single-bladed knife in its twiggy fingers, was not a human being. It was hardly taller than Seb, a simulacrum of wood and clay, dressed in a tattered shirt. It balanced itself on two little stumps of wood, leaving round holes in the snow wherever it stepped. It circled Aktos, then struck again with such great speed that a new line of red appeared on the back of Aktos's right hand.

The assassin glanced back at Koric now free of the crevice. "You'll run if you've a brain in your head, but I'll catch you once I've attended to this thing."

Koric could barely croak out the words. "Maybe it will attend to you. Maybe there are more of them."

Koric could see that Aktos wanted to look around then, perhaps expecting mannequin assassins to appear behind ever boulder and bush. "No," he said. "I've heard of these things. Tymon's work. But rather shoddy, hasty. The twine at the joints is near to giving way. I wager this is the only one."

"Tymon did this?"

Aktos spared him another glance. "Surely you don't think the man's reputation is entirely idle talk, do you?" The mannequin danced forward again; Aktos barely eluded it.

Koric took a better grip on his staff. "That thing's faster than you are."

Aktos conceded the point. "But I have better reach." He drew his rapier with one smooth motion and struck in almost the same wile. A piece of clay exploded from the side of the creature's head, but it did not falter.

"Ah, silly me. I know better than that—" Aktos struck again and, though the mannequin parried, Aktos still managed to slice one of the cords at its left hip; the cord wasn't completely severed and the creature stumbled, recovered, then favored the damaged hip as it changed the direction of its circling. Aktos smiled. He was still wary, but the fear was gone.

"See? It can be hurt. It can be destroyed. In the last century Toman of Calyt destroyed a magic guardian of brass and steel to kill the Duke of the Isles. I can do as much to this piece of wood. Rather a feather in my cap, I think."

Aktos struck again. This time the creature parried and almost managed to run up his guard. Almost. With its blade on Aktos's sword that left its body undefended. Aktos kicked it solidly and the thing spun end over end across the snow before it clattered into a boulder. It started to rise again but Aktos was there, striking once, twice, three and four times at the twine of its joints. Koric fancied he could almost see the spark or life or animation or whatever passed for living in the mannequin fade out. It collapsed, a puppet with all its strings completely cut, and lay scattered and still in the snow.

Aktos grinned in triumph. "Done. Now, where were we—"

"Here," Koric said. His staff *whooshed* through the air as he swung it with all his strength against the back of Aktos's skull.

"Careless," Tymon said as he looked at Aktos's body. "No good to slay the dragon if you ignore the wolf."

Koric shivered miserably. "I'm not a wolf," he said.

"It was a metaphor. He talks that way, often as not. You get used to it." Seb took the blanket that the golem had dropped before its attack on Aktos and wrapped Koric in it. "Sit down. You look nigh to keeling over."

Koric sat down on a boulder. His eyes had not left Aktos's still form. "I killed him," he said.

Tymon nodded. "Yes. I'm sorry it came to that, but I was working under very short notice and didn't realize your danger until it was almost too late."

Koric shuddered. "You made that thing for me? Well . . . thank you."

"You're welcome. And it was the least we could do, since I gather you were trying to warn us about Aktos and his companion?"

"Yes. They came to Kuldun looking for you. The abbot sent me on ahead, but I guess they discovered what we were up to. And there's another one," Koric said, almost as an afterthought. "He'll be along soon, I'm sure."

"So am I," Tymon said. "I'm expecting him. I don't think he's the tracker that Aktos was; he may need a bit of help. And we do have a funeral to see to, so that works out nicely."

It turned out that it wasn't Aktos Tymon was referring to. Oh, they covered his body with a cairn of stones, but then there was no more said of it. Instead Tymon found a flat piece of rock and carefully gathered up the pieces of his broken golem and set flint and steel to them, its own body serving as the fuel for the pyre.

Tymon gave a wistful sigh as he watched the flames catch and grow. "A shame to be called so soon to life, even of a sort, and to leave again so soon. Hardly time to get used to the idea, then back to the void with you. It deserved better."

Koric watched the flames. "That thing was alive? Animated, I thought, and marvel enough. Alive?"

"It had a spirit," Tymon said. "Of what or who I couldn't say. The part of the technique that animates dead wood is to create a temporary home for some wandering soul and make that home known. Only at great need would you attempt to summon a specific spirit."

"What if a demon or worse answered the summons?" Seb asked. "Now that we're on the subject, I always wanted to ask you that."

"It doesn't work that way. A demon is corporate in its own realm; it cannot abandon its true body without great risk, nor inhabit such a lowly vessel without destroying it on the spot. Plus, there are safeguards built into the summons. They usually find the right spirit for the work."

"Comforting," Seb said.

Koric didn't seem to be listening. "Could I learn to do that?"

"Perhaps," Tymon said, then he glanced at Seb, who nodded. Apparently it was a signal. "We'll discuss it later. Right now we have a guest."

Tymon turned and addressed the darkness toward the south. "You may as well show yourself, Lord Vor. We know you're here. I gather you have business with me? Come out and let's discuss it."

"I'd like that," said the darkness and then Vor of House Dyrlos, sword in hand, stalked into the firelight. He barely paused, just long enough to judge the distance to Tymon and then he lunged. Tymon wasn't there. And just off Vor's path stood Seb, patiently waiting. He struck as Vor passed. His weapon, one booted foot. Vor stumbled and went down headlong, his sword slipping from his grasp to clatter on the stones. Koric had the presence of mind to scoop it up as it slid toward him. He prepared to strike, then hesitated.

"No, Koric. To me."

Koric gave the sword to Tymon gratefully. Tymon pointed it

at Vor's throat as the man glared up at him. "This boy warned you I was coming, but how could you be so sure I'd try for you?"

"Despite the fact that it's three to one and you hadn't a chance of surviving, even if you killed me? It was obvious."

"More damn sorcery!"

"Not even a little, I'm afraid."

Vor, prepared to die, willing to die, apparently insisted on an answer he could understand. "Then how?"

Tymon shrugged. "Because," he said, "you're that kind of damned fool."

"Margy, wake up."

Lady Margate was aware of someone shaking her gently as she climbed out of the depths of a nap. Ashesa stood in front of her, smiling a tentative smile, Galan standing a discreet distance behind her. Lady Margate yawned and stretched demurely. "Just resting my eyes, Highness. So. What's it to be? Wedding or execution?"

"A wedding," said Princess Ashesa, looking pale and tired but happy. "As soon as. . . ." She hesitated, and Galan stepped forward.

"As soon as some unfortunate business is concluded and, I hope and pray, soon. I've been a fool, Lady Margate. Thank you for pointing that out."

"I would not presume, Highness," Lady Margate said. "Though I am glad to hear it just the same."

"Rhsmmmzzit. . . ."

They looked at the other form, stretched out on a bench. Sir Tals, snoring peacefully.

"I suppose I should give him the news," Galan said.

Lady Margate smiled impishly. "Later, if you please, Your

Highness. He's had such a long day. Perhaps we should just let him sleep."

CHAPTER 12
"MONSTERS IN TRAINING"

"You'll have to kill me, you know," Vor said. "So why delay the inevitable?"

Tymon sighed. "Lord Vor, you are hardly in a position to tell me what I must do."

Vor's position indeed seemed very uncomfortable; a boulder for a stool, his arms tied behind him firmly, and Seb holding a small arbalest ever so casually pointing in the general but really very exact direction of Vor's heart.

Vor shrugged. "I merely point out the realities of the situation. You knew I was coming so you must know I'm sworn to kill you. Killing me first is the only way to save yourself."

Seb nodded. "He's right, you know."

Tymon just sighed. "As much as I like to see any of us agreeing on anything, in this I must beg to differ." He turned to Vor. "Lord Vor, why are you stalking me?"

Vor laughed harshly. "You can kill me, but you can't make me play your game, whatever it might be. You know the answer as well as I."

"I assume it was because I threatened Duke Laras's family, yes?"

"What else?"

"What else? Why at all? All he need do to insure his family's safety is to forego his planned treachery."

Vor's expression went stone cold. "What you call treachery others call justice, and the righting of an old wrong. Now that you've joined Galan's party you've made yourself an obstacle to that justice."

Tymon's expression matched Vor's and bested it by a few degrees. Koric, watching the exchange with silent bewilderment, shivered.

"If you think I'm in Prince Galan's employ," Tymon said. "You are mistaken."

Vor shook his head. "It doesn't matter if you support Galan for gold or a whim. I won't dispute with you, Sorcerer, nor plead for my life. There's no point. I don't believe you and you'd be more than a fool to believe anything I might say to save my skin. All you can believe of me is this: you are an obstacle and a danger to House Dyrlos. Kill me if you want to live a little longer. There will be others following me."

"If you say so then I suppose it must be true," Tymon conceded. "But not just yet. Come, let's get moving."

Seb frowned. "Where to?"

"To where Lord Vor will be staying for a while. What it lacks in comfort it makes up for in isolation."

"The grave," Vor said grimly.

Tymon sighed. "I must remind you again that I am in charge here, Lord Vor. Your life is mine to do with as I will, and you will die when it is convenient for me and not one instant sooner. Do we understand one another?"

"Arrogant bastard!" Vor spit at Tymon, missed.

"Apparently the gentleman does not." Seb motioned Vor to his feet. "I doubt that you can appreciate this, but Tymon's really a very amiable fellow," he said, "once you get to know him." He turned to Tymon. "Is the boy coming with us now? Wouldn't it be safer to send him back to the abbot?"

"It would appear so," Tymon conceded, "but for the moment I think he'll have to stay with us. You don't mind, do you, lad?"

Koric shook his head. "I'd rather stay. I won't be in the way."

Seb sighed deeply. "He doesn't have as much sense as I thought."

Tymon smiled. "By that I assume you mean: more sense than yourself?"

"Yes," Seb said wryly. "That's it exactly."

After they had been busy for some hours Tymon spoke to Koric again. "Once more you are caught up in matters beyond your control or comprehension. I think I should apologize."

Koric wiped a bead of sweat from his brow, and rested from his labors for a few moments. "I'm still alive, and more, discovering an entire world that has nothing to do with milking or weeding or hauling fodder."

"I think you would have discovered that sooner or later without my help," Tymon said. "As for the other, one day you may look back at hauling fodder as a nobler use of a life, by comparison."

Koric shrugged. "Who can say? But in the meantime, could you show me that glyph again?"

Tymon and Koric kneeled near the entrance to a small dead-end canyon adjoining the pass, working on another stick golem while Seb kept an eye on Lord Vor. Lord Vor, in turn, was keeping all his attention on Tymon and Koric; his increasing puzzlement was apparent. Tymon finally called a halt, satisfied with their handiwork on the assembly.

"What are you doing?" Vor asked.

"Constructing your jailer," said Tymon. He turned back to Koric. "Now, watch carefully."

Tymon demonstrated the tracings of the glyph again, then went through the step-by-step procedure for carving it legibly into the prepared space on the trunk of the golem. "All this is preparation, you understand. It's the final step that does it, and that I will not show you just yet," Tymon saw Koric about to protest, and held up a hand to silence it. "I would no more give that knowledge to you at your current understanding than your mother would hand a toddler a sharpened ax, and for much the same reason. Be patient, Koric. Time is not the plodding thing you may think."

"It is at his age," Seb said dryly.

"Even so. Now be quiet, all of you."

Tymon closed his eyes. In a moment the golem sat up, with a creak of rope under tension and the almost musical tones of wood on stone. It was much larger than the one Tymon had sent ahead to intercept Aktos, nearly half a head taller than Tymon himself. Its construction, while still crude, was much more solid than the earlier mannequin. It rose very unsteadily to its stump feet, but in a few moments of experimentation it was moving very easily. It thumped its way to just inside the entrance to the canyon. Vor regarded it contemptuously.

"And just what is the purpose of this thing?"

"To keep you here, of course," Tymon said. "Didn't I already mention that?"

"How? What makes you think I won't find a way to destroy this thing?"

"You're welcome to try," Tymon said softly.

Vor smiled and sprang into motion. He scooped up a rock almost the size of his own head and rushed the creature, the stone held aloft in both hands to smash the clumsy-looking stick figure. He brought it down with all his strength.

The golem caught the rock.

Twiggy fingers cradled the stone as Vor pushed against it to no avail. Then he suddenly released the stone and tried to slip past. A swat from the thing's left arm sent him sprawling, whereupon it reached down, picked him up by the back of his breeks and dropped him back in the canyon, then resumed its post, still holding the stone it had taken. It dropped it just as Vor charged it again. Vor tried twice more with much the same result. He finally stopped, out of breath and battered.

"I'll find a way," he said. "You don't dare leave me here alive."

Tymon shrugged. "Well, I'm sure you'll come up with something. But in case you're thinking about climbing the canyon walls. . . ."

Tymon nodded at the golem, which picked up the last stone it had taken away from Lord Vor. The creature read his intent in ways that no one else there could fathom. Tymon pointed at a small dead bush about thirty feet up on the canyon's sheer back wall.

"Hit it."

The golem hurled the rock. Its branches creaked and groaned like a catapult and the stone flew through the air almost as fast as an arrow and more accurately. It smashed the dried-out bush to kindling; Vor was forced to cover his head as the rain of shattered stone and wood rained down. "I'll also note," Tymon said dryly, "that it neither eats nor sleeps. It does not get cold, it does not get tired. If you try to leave this canyon it will stop you. If you try too hard, it will kill you."

"I'll find a way," Vor said, though he seemed to be telling himself as much as Tymon.

"Assuming you don't." Tymon picked up Vor's pack. "Did you check it, Seb?"

Seb shrugged. "Of course. There were a few items of lethal potential. I've removed them. The rest is food and bedding."

Tymon swung the pack underhand and it clattered to a stop at Vor's feet. "I'd suggest you ration yourself, Lord Vor. Otherwise you may starve before we return. Unless, of course, you do manage to escape. Come along."

The last bit was addressed to Seb and Koric, who had already gathered their things together and were ready to follow.

They turned south. Koric fell into step with the two men. "You won't let him starve, will you?" he asked, once they were out of earshot of the canyon.

"He was going to kill you," Seb said dryly.

Koric blushed. "I know. I'd kill him if I had to, to defend myself, but I wouldn't let anyone starve for no reason."

"What if there was a reason?" Tymon asked.

Koric thought about it. "I can't imagine a reason good enough for that."

"Neither can I—at the moment. The distinction is more important than you might believe now." Tymon paused, and smiled. "Oh, don't worry. Lord Vor won't enjoy his stay but he will survive it. A week or so at most, and he has food enough for that. Just long enough that he won't be an obstacle to us."

"If he gets out he'll come after you again," Koric said.

"More than likely."

"You think he can escape?" Seb said. "I watched what you were doing. That's a first-class piece of work, despite its rough appearance and middling construction materials. Vor won't get away from it easily."

"Until the proper time comes for his escape," Tymon said, "he won't get away from it at all."

"So. Prince Galan is still being a fool. Just on a different matter."

Lady Margate sat with Ashesa in the princess's chambers, though in truth her prison cell was only a little less sumptuous by comparison. Ashesa poured herself another cup of warm spiced wine from an earthen crock. "He is a dear in many ways," she said. "In others, I can see his brother in him and it both saddens and frightens me."

"You're in love with him, aren't you?"

Ashesa took a good sip of the warm wine. "I suppose I am. I've never been in love before, Margy. I didn't realize it would be such a damn nuisance. I can't think clearly where he is concerned, and sometimes I think he's the same regarding me. Pity. A little hardheaded consideration on both our parts might put a stop to this mess."

"Clarity of thought is not one of love's attendant virtues; that's why it plays little part in political marriages most of the time." Lady Margate sighed deeply. "So. I gather this course isn't being forced on Galan for political reasons?"

Ashesa shook her head. "Now that he knows Tymon is alive, Galan wants revenge for his brother. I suppose I should be grateful; it made him able to transfer his anger from me to Tymon the Black. Now he wants the magician's head on a pike at the city gates before the wedding can proceed."

Lady Margate considered. "Would that be such a terrible thing? Tymon's reputation certainly warrants it."

"If we were executing his reputation," Ashesa said dryly, "I might agree."

"He kidnapped you, worried your father and me half to death, and put you in a situation where the best way out was to knife your fiancé. I don't think you have reason to regard his safety overmuch."

Ashesa contemplated her wine. "No, on the face of it you are absolutely right."

"You don't sound convinced."

"Because I'm not. There's more to this magician, Margy; even more than Galan knows or, I'm afraid, would be willing to understand. I think it's time I told someone. I think that someone should be you."

Lady Margate looked to heaven. "I seemed destined to hear that phrase a lot. It must be my too-amiable disposition." She paused to pour a cup of the steaming wine for herself. "All right. Let's hear the rest of it." Lady Margate sat back to listen.

Ashesa related the rest of the story. Now that the circumstances of Daras's demise were out of the way, if not forgotten,

Ashesa concentrated on what she had learned of Tymon and Seb in their brief time together. At times Lady Margate seemed to be more interested in her wine than what the princess told her, but Ashesa wasn't fooled. Margy had that distant look she got sometimes when she began to reflect on some facts before she had heard everything, but Ashesa knew her nurse had missed nothing. When Ashesa was done, Lady Margate did not speak for several long moments.

"Well," she said finally.

Ashesa frowned. "That's all you have to say?"

Lady Margate nodded. "At the moment, Highness. I must say you've given me a great deal to think about."

"You do. . . ." Ashesa hesitated, began again. "You do believe me, don't you, Margy?"

"Heavens, child, of course I do. I'm just not sure yet how well you—or I, come to that—understand what it means. As I said, something to ponder. Quickly, to be blunt. We don't know what Galan plans to do or how soon."

"You don't think he might even delay his coronation for this? Would he be so foolish?"

"You apparently think so," Margy said dryly, "or you wouldn't have mentioned it. And you know Prince Galan better than I."

Ashesa blushed slightly but she did not look away. "It's a fear, that's all. We still don't know who tried to kill him at the Kor River. The longer he delays the coronation the more vulnerable he becomes."

"I wondered if you understood that. You've a fine mind, Highness. When you choose to use it."

Ashesa sighed. "That's what Tymon said. Margy, if you don't mind my saying, you remind me of him in some ways. Except for the murderous reputation, of course."

Margy shrugged. "Such a reputation doubtless serves him better than it would me. Still, say what else you want about him, he's a good judge of people. Now then, Highness, with your permission I'll take my leave. There's a lot to consider and I'd better get to it."

"Do you have any idea what we should do?"

"Not until I know what needs doing. And to that end I think I should go talk to Sir Tals."

"Tals? Ah, yes. Has he forgiven you yet?"

Now Margy smiled. "Not really. But he'll be able to put that aside to the greater good, once he sees it."

The princess finished her wine. "You're a good judge of people too."

"Another way I compare well to a known fiend." Lady Margate sighed. "Highness, you do compliment in a unique manner."

Duke Molikan had not exaggerated the extent of House Korsos's library. It was, even by Prince Galan's standards, enormous, taking up the entire lowest level of the castle's largest tower. It just as clearly had not been used in quite some time, save for Galan's visits. He had found himself retreating to the bottom level of the tower as often as time allowed during his stay. It was a monastic sanctuary compared to the noise and bustle of the rest of the castle. If he ever wanted to be alone, as he did now, it was the one place where he knew solitude awaited him, and Galan found it almost impossible to comprehend why Duke Molikan himself did not make more extensive use of it.

This was a puzzle with more than one part. After a while in Molikan's castle, Galan realized that it wasn't so much that the duke ignored the library, but rather he seemed to be actively avoiding it. So distinct was this impression that, after about a week, Galan was compelled to ask Molikan about it.

"It's rather strange," the duke said then. "I know I mentioned that I don't have the patience for books these days, but I used to. There was a time when this archive was my favorite place in the castle. Yet I seldom come here now."

"Why? What triggered this change, if I may ask?"

"You certainly may, though I'm not sure I can answer. New books were constantly being added as Father tracked down items of interest, and I never thought anything of it. He spent a good deal of time there and I never thought much of *that,* either. Then one morning he was found dead, sitting at that very table," Molikan said, pointing at a large trestle table of the sort often used to support heavier tomes.

"You need not explain further, Your Grace," Galan said. "Such an association would have soured me on our own library, if my father had died thus."

Molikan shook his head. "That's the strange part. My father's death as such did not turn me from this place immediately. It took time for me to realize that, whenever I touched anything, I always put it back where I had found it even if that was not where it belonged. I could change nothing, affect nothing. That, for some reason I cannot fathom, I no longer *mattered* to this place. I started to look at my time spent there not as a joy but rather an ordeal. That, in some strange way, the books *did not want me here.* I know that all sounds like nonsense. If I could explain it better, Highness, I would."

Prince Galan found himself mulling over that conversation with Molikan from time to time, but it hadn't made a great deal of sense to him then or now. He had come across many strange books, both in his late father's own royal library and in the libraries of Morushe. Galan considered books very fine things, but he knew that there was nothing inherently "alive" about them. Some were better than others, *truer* than others, more fun to read or less, but they were never more than what the scholars, poets, or copyists had made of them. He had never known of a book that *wanted* anything.

"Rubbish. What sort of book would not want to be read?"

The moment he phrased the question, Galan thought of an answer. Both thought and answer were a bit nebulous at first; Galan almost felt as if both deliberately wished to elude him, which was as insane a notion as Molikan's belief that his father's library had somehow turned against him. Yet now Galan was very aware of being alone, down in that great silent room where the dust made him sneeze whenever he opened a book and the flickering lamps never quite gave enough light, even during the days when the sunlight through high windows should have flooded the entire room. Galan wouldn't call what he had just felt "fear." He could find other names that fit as well: nervousness, worry, unease. He would not be afraid. Perhaps he felt what Duke Molikan had felt before he abandoned the place entirely. Galan would not do the same. Acting on an impulse he could not name, he told the books as much.

"Duke Molikan used to come here for solace. So did I, but that's not why I'm here now," he said aloud.

He felt foolish then, but not very much. Not, he reasoned, as much as he should have. Galan knew he had a problem, and that problem was Tymon the Black. He could accept that Ashesha had felt forced to act as she did, but only if someone else bore the true guilt for that act. That someone was Tymon the Black. A legendary dark magician had caused his brother's death, and Galan owed his brother vengeance. But how was he to get it? Send an army? Where? Lay a trap? Again, where? Find another magician, a more powerful one? By all accounts, there were none. What options did that leave him?

Just one, Galan knew. Perhaps one day he would be a passable king, a passable commander, a passable husband. He hoped to be better than passable at all those things, in time, but right now he had only one skill above all others, one he had often used for his own and his brother's amusement, and it was simply this: if a book existed on a subject he was interested in, he could find it. He had done it that day, which now seemed ages past, when he had found Borelane's *Tales of the Red King* in Macol's library. When he had last seen his brother alive. Call it a talent or a strange sort of natural magic, Galan knew he could always find what he needed. Now he intended to do that again, except now he was going to find a book that would tell him how to kill Tymon the Black.

"I know you're here," he said aloud. "You can't hide from me."

Galan was well aware that anyone listening now would think he had gone mad. Yet the only ones listening were the books, and they could take no notice. He had to announce his intention. It was important, though he could not have said why. Galan started to search, but after no more than a few moments he stopped, and walked back to the table, back to where Duke Molikan's father had left this earth more than twenty years earlier. The library had hardly been touched in all that time. Molikan said as much himself. And that meant that, whatever Molikan's father had been reading when he died was still present.

There was one book on the table.

"It's you, isn't it? You're the one I'm looking for."

If the idea hadn't been ludicrous, Galan would have sworn that the book was *glaring* at him. It seemed angry. Just as he was angry. Vicious. Just as he needed to be vicious. Just as he needed to be whatever his brother's shade required. He leaned closer. The book was bound in a leather he did not recognize, but the iron fittings were in good condition despite the book's obvious age. The lettering on the cover was faint, but still legible. Galan traced a letter, then another, and recognized the Sistaran dialect of Old Wylan. Possibly the most obscure written language in the Twelve Kingdoms, if not the entire world. Duke

Molikan's father was one of the very few in recent memory who could still read it.

Galan was another.

If he paused to consider the matter at all, Galan might have thought it an interesting coincidence that one of his major interests was the northern folk literature recorded mostly in Old Wylan. He did not pause. He was certain that he had found what he needed, and all that remained was to sort out how to use it. The iron hinges groaned and protested as he opened the book, but he ignored that just as he ignored everything else for a very long time.

"I thought I was to stay with you?" Koric said.

"You are," Tymon said. "Only, at the moment, 'with me' means going back to Kuldun for a little while. Not long, since I don't think we have that much time, but there's some information I need. I hope it's to be found there. Don't worry; I'll explain matters to the abbot."

Winter was still well on its way, but today there was sunshine, weak though it was. Tymon, Seb, and Koric made good time through the pass, despite Seb's grumbling. "You do realize I have to move my legs twice as fast to cover the same distance?"

Tymon sighed. "You do realize that you only remind me of your condition when it's convenient for you?"

"That's as may be, but it doesn't change the first point. Besides, it'll be dark soon."

"It's not that late, is it?"

"Days are getting shorter. Sun's lower in the sky. Evening comes early. Stop me if any of this sounds familiar." Seb didn't wait for an answer. He'd been scouting a campsite for the last hour as they walked, and now he'd found one. It was in the lee of some large boulders in case the wind turned nasty. There was a flat stone for a campfire, though with the fuel available it would have to be a small one. "Here," Seb said, and dropped his pack to indicate that was the end of the matter.

Tymon and Koric didn't argue. They set down their burdens gratefully. Koric helped Seb scrounge for wood; when they returned Tymon was rummaging through his pack for no particular reason that Seb could see. He dropped a small arm-load of kindling on the rock. "What are you looking for?"

"My knife. Ah, here it is." Tymon held up the small, single-edged carving knife he'd used on the golems earlier. Koric brightened but Seb shook his head.

"You're not going to make another one now, are you? We've barely enough wood as it is."

"I just need one bitty piece." Tymon pulled one short, thick stave out of the pile and went to sit on a nearby rock. He went to work without another word, whittling intently on the hard stub of wood. Soon he had a fair pile of shavings accumulating beside the rock. Seb scooped up a few for fire starter but otherwise didn't comment. Koric assisted with the meal, but his attention came back again and again to Tymon, sitting by himself, carving. Seb stirred the broth. The smell was starting to drift around the camp, and Koric remembered how hungry he was, but it still couldn't drag all his attention away from Tymon.

"What's he doing?"

"I don't know. Ask him."

Koric frowned. "Aren't you even curious?"

Seb just shrugged. "I used to be. Then I discovered that, whatever notion had entered his head at that time, sooner or later it meant trouble for us both and more work for me. Now I just let him tell me when the matter is settled. Best for both our nerves. Oh, go see. You're dying to, and nothing will help this broth but time."

Koric needed no more encouragement. He stood a discreet distance away at first, but that distance proved to be too great;

the wooden figure was half-obscured by Tymon's hands, and Tymon took no notice of him. Koric stepped closer, and cleared his throat.

"I didn't know you were a woodcarver, Master Tymon."

Tymon sighed. "I'm not. If I were, this image might be a little easier to recognize."

Koric inched closed. "What is it?"

"I don't know. I don't recognize it," Tymon said, a little impatiently.

It occurred to Koric that perhaps here was another reason Seb's curiosity had withered. "You mean you don't know what you're trying to carve?"

"That's it, neatly tied," Tymon said. He sighed. "I'd hoped I would by now, but no luck."

Koric considered this, and came up with the only reply he had. "I don't understand."

"It would be a wonder of the world if you did." Tymon said. He held the thing up in his two hands, looked at it speculatively. Now that Koric could see it better the mystery wasn't much clearer. Tymon nodded, noting his stare. "It might be a person, it might be a spirit. It might be the larvae of some obscure stink beetle. I just don't know."

Koric considered a while longer. "I'd better go help Seb with the fire," he said finally. Tymon just nodded. Koric went back to the campfire. Seb just stirred the broth, patient as a stone, but Koric was pretty sure he'd been smiling a moment before. There was still a ghost of it around his lips. "So. What did you learn?"

Koric let out a sigh. "Practically nothing."

"He gets like that sometimes."

Koric glanced back at Tymon, still calmly whittling on the unknown, and asked the question he really wanted to ask. "Seb, is Tymon mad?"

Seb shrugged. "Probably a little. I think you have to be. That doesn't mean that what he's doing is mad, just because it doesn't make any sense to you, me, or even him. As I said, I've seen this before. He's working on something. As yet, he knows no more than you or I. You can bet that, when he solves the riddle, we'll know. Probably to our regret, as I've said before."

When the broth was finally ready, Seb had Koric fetch Tymon to the fire. By then the light was failing rapidly. Tymon had put the carving away and was simply staring off into space. Koric, warned of the Long Look by Seb, thought that perhaps Tymon was in its grasp, but as Koric approached he merely looked up. "Dinner is served?"

"Such that it is," Koric says. "Though it smells good."

Tymon rose slowly, stretching out his muscles and yawning. "Seb does wonders with travel fare. I sometimes think he'd have made a master cook, if the circumstances of his life had not dictated otherwise."

"Have you told him that?"

Tymon blinked. "Hmm? Oh, no. I've complimented him on his cooking, but that's all. The last thing Seb needs from me is a new regret."

"I hadn't thought of it like that," Koric said, as they walked to the campfire.

When all was done and the last of the bread either eaten or donated to the birds, they scouted out spots for their blankets and attended to nature. No one believed the fire could last for long; they wound up wrapped in their bedding some distance away from the dying fire, close to a sheer rock wall and out of what wind there was.

"Why are we going to Kuldun? Why?" Seb asked.

Tymon yawned. "I need to find some information on Wylandia. Something about the murder of two royal princes in a cave several hundred years ago. It may just be a legend, but I need a few particulars."

"I repeat: why?" Apparently Seb had not lost all curiosity.

"Maybe just a whim," Tymon said. "It's too soon to know. Still."

Koric turned away from the stars. "Are you talking about the Vanishing Princes of the Blackpits?"

Tymon frowned. "You've heard it? Apparently the legend isn't as obscure as I'd thought."

Koric shook his head. "My father—or rather the man my mother named as such—was from Wylandia. He visited us on the farm on several occasions when I was younger. He was a trader, I think. He always told me stories, until one season when he didn't come back. Later my mother said he'd died."

"Probably true," Seb said. "Lone travelers are often at risk. So. What about this misplaced prince?"

"Princes. Twins. Caral and Kydren, born in the reign of Iono the Seventh."

"It must have been quite a story, to leave its details so firmly impressed," Seb said dryly.

Koric blushed. "Well, he did that. He was quite a storyteller. I think that's how mother and he . . . well, never mind."

"Regardless, if he's right, that was about seven hundred years ago." Tymon put his hands behind his head and looked skyward. "Tell us the story as your father did, Koric. It'll be good to hear a story to sleep on."

Koric blushed. "I'm not much of a storyteller."

"And it may or may not be much of a story. Still, I'd like to hear it. If you would be so kind?"

Koric gathered his thoughts and what he could of his memories, and began: "Ionos of Wylandia had three sons before his queen died. The first two were born on the same day, the twins Caral and Kydren. They were young boys, fair and tall before their brother Yakaran came into the world. Yakaran was as dark as his brothers were fair. While they grew tall and broad-shouldered, Yakaran was lithe, stealthy cat to their hound."

Seb broke in. "If he was so dark, why was he referred to as Yakaran the Red? He wasn't known for being bloody, except possibly where his brothers were concerned."

"You're getting ahead of the story, Seb," Tymon scolded. "I know you've heard it before but I want to know how Koric tells it. Go on, lad."

Koric frowned. "Let's see . . . oh, right. Almost forgot. It was Yakaran's birth that ended Iono's queen's life. Some say he blamed the boy for it. Others that he just favored the twins because of their natural gifts. Whatever the reason, when talk turned to the future, it was Caral or Kydren's names he spoke. Never Yakaran. Imagine how he felt. Think of what resentments he nurtured and cherished as the years passed—"

"That would be your father talking, I wager," Seb mused. "A way of drawing the listeners in. I wonder. . . ."

Tymon shushed him. "Telling first. Critique later. Otherwise, neither works."

Seb sighed. "I'll be quiet, I promise."

"There really isn't a lot more to it," Koric said apologetically. "Yakaran knew all the natural gifts and virtues with which his brothers were blessed. He also knew their one real vice, as his father did not: greed. One day he came to them both when they were alone and produced a map of that part of the White Mountains that do not fit the name, and thus were given another: the Blackpits. He told a tale of bandit princes and hidden treasure, and for proof produced two ancient trinkets that he had acquired from a traveling merchant. He soon had the lust for gold burning in their breasts. 'We shall take porters and soldiers to carry it out,' Caral said. Yakaran just smiled and said that there was too much to carry in one trip or hundreds, and who could they trust to keep silent? So it was agreed the princes would go themselves to bring back what they could, and keep the rest hidden. To that end they left the palace by separate means to reduce comment, and met again at the Blackpits. There they entered a great cavern, and went farther and farther into the blackness. 'Where is the treasure?' the twins asked and always Yakaran replied, 'A little farther,' until he pointed at the entrance to a great underground room and said it was there. The twins rushed forward into the narrow opening, saw nothing but blackness, heard nothing but the drip of water from the ceiling. What treasure? They cried. Where? To which Yakaran replied, from his place of safety in the passageway, 'The Kingdom of Wylandia!' and sprung his trap. The loose rocks piled over the entranceway came down, and Yakaran left his foolish brothers to die in the darkness."

When Koric was done Seb glanced at Tymon, then said, "An interesting incident. But not a story."

Koric blinked. "It's not? Why not?"

"Because it's not finished," Seb said. "He played a trick and it worked. Yakaran ascended the throne. Where's the moral consequence? Where's the. . . ." Seb groped for a word, found one. "The completion? What happens after Yakaran took the throne?"

Koric shrugged. "He ruled for a few years, then died. He won. The villain won."

"Then it's not a story," Seb said.

"Why?" Tymon asked. "Because in the end a murderer takes the throne?"

Seb grunted. "With most royal houses, I take that as a given. It just isn't, that's all. Besides, it's not true. If there were no witnesses, how did they know what happened?"

Koric sounded defensive. "According to Father's version they didn't, though everyone suspected his hand in it. The particulars didn't appear until soon after his passing. The rumor was he confessed to the matter on his deathbed, but the ghosts of the murdered princes still howl at night in the mountains. People shun the place now."

"People shunned the place then, I'll wager," Seb said. "Tymon and I were there once before. It's dangerous and, worse, it's worthless. No grazing to speak of, little water and that sulphurous and steaming."

"Still," Tymon said thoughtfully, "Yakaran the First did not have a happy reign. Doubtless he was cursed for his crime."

"Then the story should have said that. Otherwise it's mere coincidence," Seb said. "And the gods' hand in this must have been shown sooner. As it is, they're not even present."

"More than likely," Tymon conceded. "Even so."

Seb let out a gusty sigh. "Tymon, you're up to something. I know the signs."

Tymon shook his head, then pulled his blankets firmly up around his chin. "Not yet," he said. "But, I fervently hope, soon. We don't have a lot of time, but fortunately young Koric here has just saved us a trip back to Kuldun. I knew there was a reason I asked him along."

Morning found Lady Margate outside Sir Tals's rooms, waiting for admittance. In fact, she waited so long that she regretted not bringing some needlework with her. At first she thought it was just for spite, but while she was there several couriers came, were admitted, and left almost as quickly. By the time she was admitted Lady Margate had discarded her original plan and went with an alternate.

She smiled at him. "So. Now it seems you know something I do not."

Tals rose to take her hand. "And good morning to you too, My Lady. Sorry to keep you waiting."

"No you're not."

Tals smiled in mock surrender. "That's twice you've been

right already this morning. That still doesn't mean I had a choice. Please sit down."

Lady Margate complied gratefully. "My Lord, what's going on?"

"Kingdom business, I'm afraid," he said, but Lady Margate wasn't to be thwarted so easily.

"Sir Tals, you know as well as I that, since early yesterday morning, 'kingdom business' concerns both Borasur and Morushe."

Tals sighed. "Not officially until after the wedding. Not even then until His Majesty Macol names his daughter his successor and passes from this world or abdicates in her favor. . . ." Tals saw the look in Lady Margate's eye and decided to return to discreet silence where the legalities were concerned. "Nevertheless, I see your point."

"Prince Galan is trying to track down Tymon the Black. What I need to know is what he plans to do and why."

Tals looked a little crestfallen. "Seems there's less I know that you don't than I thought. All right, that is what's happening. Do? Separate his head from his shoulders. Why? For justice, of course. Prince Daras's murderer must be punished."

Lady Margate raised an eyebrow. "Now?"

Sir Tals nodded, looking extremely unhappy. "So it seems. Prince Galan is delaying his entry into Tonara, the bloody coronation, the wedding, all of it. And before you ask, no, I do not think that is wise. I do not think so at all, and told His Highness as much as clearly as I knew how. He listened serenely to every word and then told me to give the couriers their instructions. That's what I've been doing all this morning."

"Which are?"

"Some are to hire certain . . . soldiers of fortune, shall we say, to help search for Tymon the Black. Others to gather information from Borasur's vassals and allies. The dukes of

Houses Dyrlos, Makara, and Kodan have been summoned here for consultation. They'll come, if they know what's good for them."

"So it's all true," Lady Margate said, almost to herself. Then she said, "I hope they tell him to get his royal rear end to Tonara."

"So do I," Tals said. "Though I'm not optimistic. You see, it gets worse."

"Worse?"

"He was reading a book."

"I'm given to understand that's long been his habit," Lady Margate said dryly. "I do it myself now and again, when I can find the time."

Tals shook his head. "I don't mean 'a book.' I mean . . . I don't quite know how to explain it, Lady Margate. I'm not so old, but I've seen a lot and done a lot in my time. I've been in danger more than once, and I've certainly felt fear more times than I can recall."

"No doubt. Yet I fail to see—"

"Lady Margate, this is the first time in my life a book frightened me."

Sir Tals had Lady Margate's complete attention. "What was it about?"

"I don't know. There was writing on the cover, but it was nothing I recognized, and I've got all my letters, not to mention Old Lyrsan and a fair bit of Islish to boot. Yet I couldn't read a word of it. I may not be the scholar Prince Galan is but even he seemed to be struggling."

Lady Margate nodded. "You suspect sorcery."

"I won't say so. I won't deny it either."

Lady Margate sighed. "No need. Well. I think we have a problem. Just how great of one remains to be seen."

"I'd appreciate any help you can give."

"I've none to offer, I'm afraid. Still, do you think you can reproduce some of the symbols you saw on that book? An entire word or even a phrase would be best."

"I-I think so. But why? You said you couldn't help."

"I can't," Lady Margate said. "But I know someone who might."

CHAPTER 13
"SPIRITS, LOST AND FOUND"

The events of the next morning were a little hazy, as far as Koric was concerned. He had woken just after dawn to find Seb gone, and Tymon quickly breaking camp.

"There's biscuit and hot tea by the fire," Tymon said. "You won't have time for anything else, I'm afraid."

Koric saved his breath for eating while Tymon rolled up their bedding and got the travel packs together. When Koric was finished with his meager breakfast, Tymon put the pot away without a word and set off back up the pass towards Wylandia. Koric picked up his bundle and hurried after.

"Where are we going?"

"Where? To the Blackpits, of course."

Of course? There was nothing about it so obvious as that so far as Koric could see. He thought of Seb's example where Tymon was concerned and decided not to press the matter just yet. He then thought of Seb the man and had to ask. "Where is Seb?"

"He's on a different errand. I didn't want to separate, but after last night I see we have even less time than I thought. No help for it."

Koric couldn't resist. "Time for what? Why are we going to the Blackpits?"

"To save a kingdom or destroy it. To do great harm or great good. I haven't quite worked out which is which yet."

After that Koric just concentrated on walking. It seemed the safest thing to do.

When the summons came, Duke Laras thought about taking his wife and daughter and taking ship to the Isles. It would be a temporary solution at best, he knew. Just until Prince Galan and the Duke of the Isles could settle on the price of Laras's head. Still, it didn't make sense to put his family at peril; Laras was pretty sure Galan would be content with the one execution, if that was his reason for the summons.

How could it have all gone so wrong?

Tymon the Black. That was the answer. And still no word from Vor; Laras suspected the worst.

There was nothing for it, Laras decided, but to play the game out to the end. He had his long-unused parade armor made ready and sent couriers to gather his escort. It could not be too large, but as a duke of the kingdom he was entitled to more than a handful. He knew that if it came to a fight they would not be half enough but better to have them than not. He also decided that, short of fleeing to the Isles, there was one more precaution he could take. When preparations were well under way and he could delay it no longer, Laras went to see his lady.

Mero is not going to like this.

This proved an understatement. When he broke the news, Mero was braiding Lytea's hair in their private rooms. She immediately gave the child to her nurse and had the servant carry her out despite Lytea's protests, crying, and long blond braids unraveling as she went.

"Mero, what—?"

Mero stood up. She only reached to his chin but Laras certainly felt as if she were meeting him eye to eye. "My Lord, what is all this about?"

Laras frowned. "I've been summoned to appear before Prince

Galan. Under the circumstances—"

"Yes. The circumstances. I'm afraid that's the part I do not understand. If I am to drag myself and your daughter to what can only be described as the middle of nothing—with all due respect to our eastern possessions, including the aptly named Seagull Keep—then Lytea is going to want to know why. What shall I tell her?"

"Why . . . tell her it's an outing. An adventure. She'll accept that."

"No doubt. Yet must I accept it as well?"

Laras rubbed his eyes. He was suddenly very, very tired. "My Lady . . . Mero, please don't make this any more difficult than it already is. Just accept that I have good reasons for all that I do."

She sighed. "You are my lord. Your will is mine in all things. It is for that reason if no other I must ask if this is your will or Lord Vor's. He is often to be found if trouble is nearby."

Laras was more than a little taken aback. He had never known Mero to take such an interest in ducal business or to question anything he'd ever done. He fumbled for a response that wouldn't feed the gathering storm he saw in Mero's eyes, even as he tried to understand why it was there in the first place.

"That's because Vor serves me in difficult matters," Laras said, stiffly. "What has this to do with Vor?"

"Nothing, as far as I know, and so knowing only that I had to ask. It's a sensible question. Surely you have noticed his ambition?"

Now Laras's own confusion leaned a bit toward anger. "What are you saying? I'd trust Vor with my life, even," he added, "yours. Or Lytea's. In fact, I have done so more than once. He's never given me reason to doubt him!"

"Nor I, in matters concerning an outside threat to your House, and that is my point. Don't mistake me, Husband—I am very fond of Vor. When I say he is ambitious I mean only that his ambition is for you, and the House of Dyrlos. Sometimes I think it excessive."

Laras's anger turned as quickly to confusion. "Excessive? That he champions House Dyrlos's place in the world? You seem to feel this a problem?"

Mero looked grim. "If it has not become so, then why are you so concerned about this summons? Not annoyed, not inconvenienced, not curious. You are afraid." Laras started to protest, but Mero headed it off. "I have eyes to see, ears to hear, and a mind to think, and I know you. I am your wife, Laras, whatever else I may be. You're worried and I want to know why. I want to know what you fear so I can face it with you, not hidden away on some Amatok-blighted rock on the borders."

Laras shook his head. "Mero, you will go where I ask, reluctantly or no, but I would rather you trusted me."

She smiled then, in a way that almost broke Laras's heart. "I do trust you. Very well; if I am to be left in the dark I'll need candles. And a good many blankets. I hear Seagull Keep gets very chilly this time of year."

Mero proceeded to summon servants and give instructions, and she continued to do so with the singleness of purpose of a cold mountain stream flowing downslope. Laras waited, he wasn't sure for what reason, until it was clear there was no reason. He left without another word.

In only a very short time, Koric came to appreciate why the Blackpits was an area generally and best avoided.

It's as if the lands under the sun were being invaded by the underworld!

That was the best interpretation Koric could put on it. He and Tymon walked through a landscape of nightmare. Vegetation was sparse, mostly stunted trees and lichen. As they approached the mountains it got worse. Mud stained with sulphur bubbled to the surface along their path; steaming pools of yellow-crusted water made breathing difficult.

Now I know why Tymon brought wood with him.

Tymon shifted his bundle and looked up the slope thoughtfully. "I think most of the vents are along here; farther up we should get a little relief. Let's go."

Tymon was right, but only barely. They left the sulphur pits behind as the land rose beneath them; instead they passed steam vents and small mud flows, and spring-fed pools of hot water.

"Much better," said Tymon.

Koric nodded. "At least breathing's easier."

"I was speaking of the hot pools. That one we just passed looks perfect for a bath."

Koric frowned. "What are you talking about?"

Tymon raised an eyebrow. "You do bathe, don't you? I didn't notice before; we were all a little busy and travel grimed. But if you're going to be in our company for any extended period, well, I really must insist."

Koric blushed. "Of course I bathe! It's just that the water looked hot enough to boil me."

"Speak of that after you've experienced it," Tymon said, and smiled. "Ah, well. Later. We've work to do."

They came to a shelf of rock about twenty yards wide before a sheer rock face that seemed to reach to the sky. Tymon dropped the bundle and pulled out his twine and carving blade, and now Koric was pleased to see he was wrong about the wood. Not a campfire—a golem. Koric watched closely and did what he was told. Soon there was a small wooden mannequin lying on the rock. Tymon carved the glyph himself this time, and the animation of the golem seemed to take longer than Koric remembered. A look of intense concentration came to Tymon's face, and Koric didn't feel it wise to speak until the golem stirred and sat up, then looked around it with an eyeless face made of sulphurous mud.

"Welcome," Tymon said. "You took a bit of finding."

There was a movement from the golem, a twitching in what passed for its shoulders. Koric wondered if that was the golem equivalent of a shrug, but he tried not to wonder very much. The thing slowly stood on its spindly legs, fought for balance, found it. Even though Koric had seen this before, it still gave him a chill to the pit of his stomach to see inanimate wood and twine come to life. It wasn't just movement; Koric sensed to the core of his being that, somehow, the simulacrum was alive, and that was the biggest chill of all.

Koric glanced at Tymon and realized something he hadn't before, something that was probably true the first time Koric had seen Tymon create a golem. The magician was watching the creature intently, with a trace of that same awe that Koric felt clearly visible.

Maybe you never really get used to it, he thought. *At least not completely.*

Tymon addressed the creature. "You know the terms. If you've accepted, then there's no time to lose."

The creature turned and set off along the eastern face of the shelf, its little stick legs click-clicking along the stone. Tymon followed without a word; Koric quickly hoisted his pack and followed.

"Where are we going?" Koric asked as he caught up.

"Hmmm? Oh, didn't I explain that part? We're here to find the two lost princes of Wylandia."

Koric frowned. "This thing knows the way?"

"Of course. Who better?"

"Who . . . ?"

Tymon sighed. "I didn't explain that part either, did I? And I suppose there are niceties, such as a bow when you're introduced . . . a moment, Your Majesty."

The golem hesitated, turned to face them with what passed for its face. "Your Majesty, may I present Koric of Borasur?"

Koric just stared. "Majesty? That golem—"

"That golem, lad," Tymon said, "is the former King Yakaran I of Wylandia."

Not having a better idea, Koric bowed. The introductions out of the way, they continued, with the golem moving rapidly and Koric and Tymon close behind. He followed when the golem led them into the deepest, blackest cave that Koric had ever seen. They paused only long enough to light a torch, and they quickly moved down into the mountain.

Koric shivered. Nothing in his experience had prepared him for this, not even his time at Kuldun. Within the space of a month he had gone from a reluctant farmhand to would-be scholar to . . . well, he wasn't quite sure about that part yet. All he knew was that now he followed close behind a man rumored to be the wickedest creature on earth, who in turn followed a former king who was now a mannequin of wood and clay down into the depths of hell. Koric would have laughed, if he hadn't been too afraid that the sound would make the cavern roof crash down on his head.

They moved through near-darkness. Tymon held a torch, which was all the light they had. The golem made a spindly shadow as it tap-tapped down a smooth corridor ahead; Tymon in turn cast his own shadow back on Koric, so that the boy walked in darkness much of the time. At first the cave was like Koric expected a cave to be: cold and damp. Later it got much warmer. In places fire showed through rents in the wall and cracks in the floor and the air was sulphurous and stifling. He stepped carefully over a small river of lava and was relieved to find the ground beneath his feet sloping upward, and the air turning cooler. There was a freshening of the atmosphere as well; almost a breeze, and Koric knew there had to be an air shaft nearby. Even the light was better. . . .

Why is the light better?

Of course. Koric finally noticed one more thing that he hadn't before: the golem was on fire.

"Ah, Master Tymon—"

"I know. His Late Majesty walked across that last lava flow like a water-strider across a pond. I guess when you've been a spirit long enough certain physical realities tend to be forgotten."

"Shouldn't we extinguish him?"

"A grand idea. I'm open to suggestions."

Koric, cursing himself for a slow-wit, finally saw the extent of the problem. They'd set off so quickly from their camp that even their travel cloaks had been left behind. They had no water, and nothing to smother the flames. The golem, for his part, stumped along with even more determination but not much more speed. Both its legs were well engulfed and the flames were licking about its trunk and, even more ominous, the cords that bound its legs and trunk together.

"I don't think it's much farther," Tymon said. "We can only hope the mystery gives way before His Majesty's limbs do the same."

They almost made it. Koric saw the cords fray and begin to part just as they came to a widening of the cavern. Another halting step and the cords snapped. The golem, now burning throughout, fell into a heap like a pile of kindling and burned down to embers almost as fast. The clay of its face hissed as its moisture steamed away and it began to crumble. Its right arm, now a blackened cinder, stretched out ahead of the glowing remains.

"Well blast. . . . Yet it's clear enough that he was pointing straight ahead," Tymon said. "Let's go on."

The cavern continued to widen; now Koric heard the sound of dripping water and the nature of their surroundings was changing as they walked. Koric thought they were ascending slightly but it was hard to be sure. "The cave seems a little different here," he observed.

"That's because it is a cave, finally," Tymon said. "I think up until now we've been traveling through a lava tube that was only partly dormant. I think the vulcanism here in the Blackpits is much more recent than the age of the original cave system suggests. Look here. . . ." Tymon pointed to a fissure in the wall where the passage they traveled opened out into darkness. "The lava path actually touched one of the water-created caverns. Probably only in the last thousand years or so."

Koric blinked. *Last thousand?* "Doesn't sound very recent to me," he said.

Tymon smiled. "Could be wrong; it's a guess. Still, it makes sense that a lava flow takes much less time than hewing out a cave with drops of water. I'm guessing we're only now reaching the mountain cave system proper; a lava tube would have been part of a layer created by a later eruption."

Koric sighed. "I don't understand any of that."

"Ask the curate next time you're in Kuldun. The references are there. So. What's this?"

Tymon held his torch in the opening. The way was blocked by a huge pile of broken stones, apparently where part of the roof some thirty feet overhead had fallen in.

Koric looked it over. "This at least fits the description of the incident. What do we do now?"

"Now we go in and see if his late majesty was full of beans or no."

Koric blinked. "The passage is sealed, Master Tymon. Even with some of your golems to help, it will take days to clear."

Tymon smiled. "I try to reserve golems for the more appropriate uses. Besides, the entrance is not completely sealed. Look at the torch."

Koric looked at the flame and was a little startled to see that it was leaning toward the opening as if being pulled there. Koric took a step closer and could now feel the same breeze that Tymon and the torch felt. Tymon nodded. "Rubble might have been more of a problem. Large stones don't pack very well; there are always instabilities. It probably wouldn't take as much to shift them as you might think. Stand back a bit."

Koric was more than happy to oblige, retreating back into the darkness as far as he dared, while keeping his eyes fixed on the light cast by Tymon's torch. Koric wasn't sure what to expect but was pretty sure that Tymon, standing in front of the rockfall and doing absolutely nothing that Koric could see, wasn't it. When the minutes had stretched beyond counting and Koric now shifted from one foot to the other and stretched periodically to keep from falling asleep, Tymon finally did something. Koric still wasn't quite sure what. As far as he could see, Tymon had simply reached out with his walking staff and poked one massive boulder the size of a small cottage. Whatever the cause, Koric saw the result immediately. A stone larger than Koric near the top of the pile shifted, then tumbled down end over end, taking several other large stones with it as it crashed to the cavern floor below.

Koric closed his eyes against the cloud of dust and debris that rolled up from the rockslide, and for a moment after he opened his eyes he could still see nothing. "Tymon!"

"Right here, lad." Tymon stood beside Koric, his torch still lit, himself not even bruised and barely dusty.

"What did you do?" Koric asked, still not quite ready to believe what he'd seen.

"I very politely asked the stones if they would move. Only

one did, but then we only needed one. Let's go see."

There was still a large tumble of rocks blocking the entrance-way, only now the stones did not quite reach the cavern ceiling. Tymon slowly climbed the tumulus, Koric close behind. When they reached the top they stood in a hole in the barrier just a little taller than themselves. Tymon lowered the torch to keep the backwash of flames off their cloaks and slipped inside. After a moment's hesitation Koric followed, stepping down carefully behind the will-o'-the-wisp of Tymon's torch as the magician climbed down the opposite side of the rockfall, and farther down than the floor of the cave on the opposite side.

This room is much larger.

It was only when he stood with Tymon again on the cavern floor did he realize just how much larger. Even in the weak torchlight it was obvious that the room was enormous. The roof was barely visible as a faint glimmer high overhead. They stood, as best Koric could tell, near one end of the long, vast space. Spires of stone reached up around them like a forest; the torchlight caught bright reflections in rock crystal and moist stone.

Everywhere Koric heard the sound of water. Dripping onto the ends of the spires of stone from the barely visible ceiling, gurgling slowly as it flowed past them in a small river near the center of the room. Koric shivered in the damp.

"We'd better cross here," Tymon said. "From the shape of the room I'm guessing there'll be a pool or a natural cistern of some kind near the other end."

Even though the stream was closer to brook than river where they stood, it was still too wide to jump across. Tymon waded slowly into the water, feeling ahead with one foot for drop-offs. Koric stepped in behind him and the shock of cold water on his legs made his teeth chatter. In a moment they were through it and dripped their way along the riverside toward the front of the cavern.

Koric kept casting worried glances at the torch. "Master Tymon, the torch won't last too much longer."

"Hmm."

Koric wasn't sure if that meant agreement or just unconcern. Tymon finally came to a place where the bank sloped up sharply for a few feet and climbed it, holding the torch high. Toward the end of the cave there was another rise in the cavern floor, forming a shelf several feet wide along the far wall, where it disappeared into a side passage.

Tymon nodded in that direction. "It probably doesn't go very far, though that might be corrected, if necessary."

Koric started to say something, realized that Tymon wasn't really talking to him at all. He simply waited until Tymon finally nodded and turned, smiling.

"It's perfect," he said. "Almost like a stage. I couldn't have arranged it better if I'd hired a master draftsman."

Koric just stared for a moment, before deciding he could talk again. "Perfect? I don't understand. Are the princes here or not?"

Tymon frowned. "Of course they're here. Didn't you see them? They're down by the pool . . . well, lake, really."

Koric looked down to a place where dark water turned the floor of the cavern into an underground lake. By the shore he saw two forms, still easily and quickly recognizable once he'd had them pointed out to him. Bones. Human bones, still holding their shape where they fell.

"His Late Majesty had no real reason to lie, so I expected no less. No scavengers or predators to disperse the remains. I'd expect mummification if the air had been a little drier here. As it is. . . ." Tymon had a new thought. "Come with me."

He went down to the side of the lake and Koric followed. "I

thought the point was to find the princes?"

Tymon stopped for a moment, then turned to look back at the natural theater he had found. "No, Koric. There is something about the legend that may yet fit into all this, but that wasn't why we came. We were here to find a place like this. That is where it is, and what it is, well, that's just fortunate. It will help."

Koric felt totally lost. It wasn't the first time since entering the Blackpits he had felt that way. "Help what?"

"Create the lie. A really grand one. Perhaps my best. We'll see."

"Why do we have to lie?"

"To get to the truth, of course. What better reason is there?"

Koric had to admit he didn't know, since he didn't understand the answer. He started to ask about it but Tymon had already turned back toward the natural theater he'd found there under the earth, deep in thought. Koric glanced back toward the shore of the lake, then away, then back when something faint, nearly indiscernible, caught his attention.

"Did you hear that, Master Tymon?"

Silence.

"Tymon?"

Koric didn't get an answer. He realized with a growing sense of unease that he wasn't sure if he'd spoken aloud or not. He also wasn't sure if Tymon—or anyone—was there to hear. There was a distance surrounding him, separating him from everything he had taken for granted as a part of his "here" and "now." Koric found himself walking toward the one thing that remained—the shore of the lake itself. He saw, but did not know how he saw. There was no light as such, but rather a sort of yielding darkness that flowed around him, always parting as he walked toward it, like a fog.

This isn't the cave.

It was and it wasn't. Koric still felt that sense of distance, dreamlike and frightening. He also heard voices, faint but getting louder. Shouts. Screams. Silence. Soon he wasn't just hearing, he was feeling. A rush of confused emotions like a wave of nausea swept over him, almost overpowering even fragmented as they were. Koric felt rage, despair, darkness, silence. Finally he felt himself dying, but that wasn't the worst of it.

Koric felt that he had died, and still the rage, the despair and the silence remained. He looked down at the bones of the princes of Wylandia. From the marks on nearby rock he could see that the direction and flow of the currents in the pool and the feeder streams had changed now and again over the years. The spot was dry now, but in times past water had flowed over the bones repeatedly, leaving a thin casing of rock crystal and minerals in its wake. In the light that was not light Koric saw the bones glimmer and sparkle.

Beautiful.

"Yes. Aren't they?"

She came out of the fog of distance, clothed in rainbows. Her hair was a tumble of storm clouds and her voice a boom of thunder that shook the bowels of the earth.

"So. Whose little boy are you?"

CHAPTER 14
"THE HUMOR OF THE GODS"

"Well, Highness," Lady Margate said, "here we are again."

There was a note of weary resignation in her voice.

Princess Ashesa was in her not-very-good squire disguise again, only this time Lady Margate found her before she'd reached the stables. She did this mainly by entering the princess's chambers in a hurry and unannounced.

Ashesa glared. "Do you have spies everywhere or are you just some minor goddess with omniscience and time to waste? Frankly I'm beginning to wonder."

"Highness, I thought you might do something like this sooner or later. You certainly don't expect me to be surprised, do you?"

Ashesa's anger didn't last. She sighed. "Margy, I can't just sit here and do nothing. You know that."

"You were planning to warn Tymon, weren't you?"

"Certainly not . . . and what if I were?" Ashesa asked.

"I can think of several things that apply, you back in your cell in the tower being the least of them. Let that be, since I'm not here to stop you as such. You're aware of what Galan's up to, aren't you?"

Ashesa looked grim. "I have heard rumors, yes."

"Then you should realize that it is this that needs attention, not your former kidnapper. How did you plan to find him, by the way? Assuming he doesn't wish to be found, which is no doubt usually the case."

Ashesa blushed. "I hadn't worked that part out completely."

Which was mostly true, though she did have a strong hunch.

"If it's action and purpose you must have, then I propose an alternative." She handed a parchment scroll to the princess. "Look at this."

Ashesa unrolled the scroll, stared at the glyphs for a moment then quickly rolled it back up. "What is this? Oh. Galan's book."

"You've seen it?"

"Once, when he didn't know I'd come into the room. He put the book away then. Hid it, more like. I-I didn't like it."

"That seems to be the consensus, to anyone not ridden by obsession. If you want a mission, Highness, I propose this one: take these samples to the monastery at Kuldun. Maybe one of the brothers there can tell us what they mean, or at least what they are. For Galan's sake. Perhaps for everyone."

Ashesa's smile put the candles to shame. This was a bit of luck that might suit her plans very well. "That's why you came here in such a hurry?"

Lady Margate nodded, looking unhappy. "I was going to ask if you'd brought your squire's disguise. If it doesn't really conceal your sex, at least it may hide your identity. I don't like this in the least, Highness, but who else could we trust with this?"

"I'll leave immediately."

Lady Margate went to the door and called out to someone Ashesa couldn't see. Ashesa heard loud footsteps. Two armed and armored men came in the door and bowed respectfully. "A slight correction, Highness," Lady Margate said. "You and your escort will leave immediately."

Ashesa put her hands on her hips. "Margy—"

"Oh, come now, Highness. Did you really think I'd forget?"

Tymon sat down on the stone bench, looking weary. "Amaet, did you have to frighten the poor lad out of his wits?"

"Are you questioning me, mortal?"

Amaet stood by the shore of that quiet place in Tymon's dreams. Shining waters flowed around their island. Sometimes Tymon imagined he saw something breaking the surface of the water here and there, though whether trout or leviathan he didn't want to guess.

He sighed. "I'm asking. It's not quite the same."

"Then I answer: Yes. And it was fun."

Tymon raised an eyebrow. "Just 'fun'?"

"There was one more thing: I revealed myself in my power and he was afraid. That is the sign of a man with more wit than willow in his skull. I consider that worth knowing, Magician. Don't you?"

Tymon thought about it. "Yes. Considering."

"Considering what you share. He has the Long Look, does he not?"

"You know he does in at least some measure. Else he would never have found you," Tymon said.

"You only recently rediscovered your own talent. How long have you known about Koric?"

"I didn't know, until it came upon him in the cave. Now I know how Seb feels. No matter. I strongly suspected after he managed to avoid that assassin in the pass. I knew I was too late even as I saw the vision; by rights he should have died on Aktos's knife. He received a warning that didn't come from me," he finished, "nor, I gather, from you."

"You might be surprised at how few mortals impinge upon our consciousness, Magician."

"Unlikely. Nor at how seldom that counts as a blessing when it happens," Tymon said, too weary for tact.

Amaet just smiled. "More wit than willow in your skull, too. Fortunate, since you're about to need it very much indeed."

Tymon sighed again. "I know of what you speak, so I will not ask of that. I do want to know the answer to one other question, if you will grant me such."

Amaet was not so easily readable as most humans were, but Tymon was fairly certain he saw curiosity there.

"Ask," she said.

"Was that you at the Oracle of Yanasha?"

"Your question is very imprecise. I was there, if that's what you mean."

Tymon nodded. "As I suspected. You are Yanasha."

Amaet was smiling again, and Tymon sensed that she was very close to laughter. "No, Tymon."

"Then why were you at the Oracle? I sensed you, even if you never identified yourself to me."

"We were all there, mortal."

Tymon frowned. "All? You mean all the Powers? Why?"

"We are all Yanasha."

"Sir Tals, how much longer will our attendance be required?"

Duke Laras had finally cornered Tals as he was about on one of numerous errands. Tals had been dreading this, since he had just the one answer to give. "Your Grace, Prince Galan is very concerned with bringing this sorcerer to justice. As such he's called on all his allies and servants to give what assistance they can."

"Which I am more than willing to give," Laras said, though the words kept trying to stick in his throat, "and have told His Highness as much. Yet I have business elsewhere before the coronation—as, indeed, do most of the other peers twiddling their thumbs here. Surely he understands that?"

"All I can say is what I've told you, Your Grace. You're of course welcome to take it up with His Highness when his . . . meditations are complete."

"And when will that be?"

"Your Grace, I wish I knew. Now, I really must take my leave."
Tals bowed and then turned away. Laras watched him go.
Laras didn't understand what was going on around the prince.
It was certainly nothing he had expected, but Laras knew that
whatever it was, it was dangerous. Sir Tals was afraid, and he
wasn't alone. Laras, for want of a good alternative, had come
with little escort, half-expecting to be thrown in irons the moment he entered the council chambers. To his considerable
surprise, Galan had greeted him warmly and with all courtesy.
Then he had asked what he knew of Tymon the Black, his activities, if any, within Laras's sphere of control, or just for good
rumors. Laras told what he knew—minus the incident with the
cradle—but mostly he kept his own worries and expectations
under control as he sized up Prince Galan. It took a surprisingly short amount of time.

*He's telling the truth. He may be concealing all else, but he does
not know Tymon the Black.*

Laras, who had played the game of Court and Diplomacy
almost since he could talk, looked into Galan's open gaze and,
try though he might, could not avoid that one simple fact. Laras
felt no relief, however. If Tymon the Black was not in Galan's
employ, then he served the Royal House of Borasur for his own
reasons, and he knew all there was to know, it seemed, of Laras's
attempted treachery. Tymon had to die, and soon, or House
Dyrlos could never be safe. Laras did not think that Tymon was
dead, no matter how much Laras wished it true. As for Vor,
there had been no word, none at all. Laras did not know what
to do.

Damn all, Vor! Where are you?

"I've been giving some thought to your predicament."
Vor had made his meeting, though not in the way he had
expected. After three days Kyre, personal advisor to King Aldair

of Wylandia, had come walking—alone—through the pass near Kuldun, and found an increasingly agitated Vor still suffering under the eyeless gaze of Tymon's golem. Kyre was surprised, to say the least. Now he sat on his haunches a safe distance away from the entrance to the ravine, considering. He was a little older than Vor, and heavier, but anyone who mistook bulk for corpulence would have gotten a rude shock upon pressing the issue.

"No more than I," said Vor dryly. "I welcome your opinion on the matter."

Kyre smiled. Vor had met the Wylandian only once before, but his one impression at the time did not change now: he did not like it when Kyre smiled. There was a nasty edge to the man's humor that made Vor uneasy.

"All in good time," Kyre said. "First, I need to know why you requested a meeting with me."

"To discuss matters of mutual benefit between your lord and mine. Which we can still do, if you'll help get me free of this thing."

Now Kyre chuckled, which was even worse. "Lord Vor, I'm afraid you're going to have to do better than that. I've walked a long way to find you in an odd predicament that, even to the uninitiated, smacks of sorcery. More to the point, it doesn't speak well of your worth to me or my master. I'm afraid you need to convince me I'm not wasting my time."

Vor eyed the golem. "You seem to have me at a disadvantage," he said.

Kyre shrugged. "You can look at it that way. Or you can decide that even a dog deserves a bone now and then, if it soothes your wounded pride. I care little either way."

Vor took a deep breath, and let it out. He kept his voice absolutely calm. "We have reason to believe that Galan of Borasur is in league with Tymon the Black."

"Reason? Proof would be better."

"What we have is damning enough. Or would be, if presented well."

"Which I'm sure you can do. Why haven't you?"

Vor considered his words carefully. "Because the sword we hold cuts both ways, and I'd not have my master harmed in Galan's downfall."

"Well said, but beside the matter: what is it to Wylandia who rules in Borasur?"

"Are you telling me Wylandia could not benefit from trading alliances with Borasur? Ports to ship your grain and ore and horses and wool without interference?"

"Morushe is halfway between Wylandia and Borasur," Kyre pointed out, "and, come to that, we're halfway to agreement with Morushe as it is."

"With hefty tariffs to pay, I wager. No, Lord. Morushe is a walnut between two stones," replied Vor. "Or would be. Do you still think I have nothing to offer?"

Kyre considered. "Possibilities only. Still, worth considering. His Majesty must have matters cast in the proper light, of course," Kyre said.

"King Aldair's distrust of both diplomacy and intrigue is well known," Vor said. "Yet I believe we could persuade him. I believe we could use that very distrust to persuade him. Are you interested or no?"

Kyre made his decision. "I am. Now, as to your situation. Surely you noticed that section of loose rock to the right of and above your jailor? I think it could be persuaded as well, don't you?"

Vor glared. "Of course! Yet if I so much as picked up a pebble to throw my jailor would splatter me all along the side of this wall!"

Kyre picked up a large stone. "Well, then. Fortunate for us both that I'm not you."

"How are you feeling?" Tymon asked.

They were back in their camp on one of the slopes of the Blackpits, where Tymon had carried Koric after his collapse. Since then he had kept watch over the sleeping young man for the better part of a day. It was very later in the afternoon when Koric finally sat up on his blankets and took the mug of spiced cider that Tymon offered. "I feel terrible," he said.

Tymon had no reason to doubt it. Koric looked as if he'd been pummeled by experts, and his gaze had a slightly unfocused aspect to it that worried Tymon. After a few stiff sips of the potent cider, Koric's world apparently came into better focus. He shivered.

"Are you cold?" Tymon asked.

Koric shook his head, though he wrapped the blankets around himself. "I . . . I went away, I think. I saw something." Koric shivered again.

"So I gathered," Tymon said. "Exactly what did you see?"

The question seemed to confuse the boy. "I don't know. A woman . . . a goddess? It wasn't the way I'd imagined such a thing to be." He reddened, then finished, "If I had imagined such, that is."

"If you haven't you're a rare creature indeed," Tymon said dryly. "That it wasn't what you expected, well, few things are. Yet you survived, and that's something."

"Did I?" Koric didn't look convinced. What he looked mostly was lost. "What happened to me, Master Tymon?"

"That's a little hard to explain."

"I'd appreciate the effort," Koric said, draining the mug and holding it out for more. Tymon poured the last of Takren's cider and then set the jug aside.

Tymon considered. "There have been times in your life when you've known things you shouldn't have known, yes?" he said.

"Like discovering your mother has a lover?" Koric asked, then immediately blushed again.

Tymon smiled. "Well, I was thinking more in terms of realizing there's a viper under that fireberry bush before you reach for a berry. Or knowing a stranger is coming to visit the farm the day before they arrive. That sort of thing."

Koric frowned. "Sure. Hunches and such. Everyone has them. What's that to do with this?"

"I'm getting to that," Tymon said. "And what you say is true enough, but not everyone is right as often as you are."

The look on Koric's face was admission enough. "How did you know that about me?"

"Because, at a certain point in my life, I could have been you. Most of the time it's just hunches and intuition, right sometimes, wrong far more often. And sometimes those hunches are the first glimmering of what Seb calls 'the Long Look,' and for want of a better description, so do I. The Long Look is a talent, a curse, and a doorway all at once. You will see things, things that are true and things that might be true unless headed off. In time, you may even be able to tell the difference."

Koric seemed to consider this. "So. She was real."

"If you're referring to Amaet, then the answer is yes. Very real. I suppose I was lucky in some ways, as were you. The manifestation of a talent like the Long Look always attracts attention. There are far worse entities that might have come calling."

The young man shuddered again. "I don't see how. She was more than I can get my wit around and hold on. She was like a raging fire, beautiful and terrible all at once. I was afraid her mere presence would destroy me, and afraid again that I would die if she left me."

"Wrong on both counts," Tymon said kindly, "but understandable; she has that effect when the mood strikes her. I remember my first time very well."

"Master Tymon, is she a goddess?" Koric blurted out.

Tymon sighed. "Of all the questions you've asked, I think that's the hardest to answer. What do you think a goddess is?"

"Why, a goddess—" Koric thought about it a moment longer. "I'm not sure."

Tymon spread his hands. "Now you see the problem. Amaet is a powerful entity, that's obvious. Is she a goddess? I've never heard her call herself such, nor do I worship her. For me, the answer is likely no, she isn't. What she is to you is a decision you'll have to make for yourself."

Koric rubbed his eyelids. "An even more pressing question might be 'what am I to her?' "

Tymon smiled again. "Don't worry about that. When the time comes she will doubtless let you know."

Lady Mero looked deeply concerned. "You're not going to write about this, are you?" she asked.

Seb looked up from his journal, surprised. "Heavens no. No one would believe it, anyway." He held the journal open to the current page for her inspection. "See? This will merely show that I succeeded in kidnapping the Lady Mero and her child, in furtherance of my master's fiendish aims. The fact that she came willingly, nay even slipped away from her guards at Tymon's request, is simply too incredible."

"I'd have thought discretion was a better reason to keep silent on that point," the duchess said dryly. "Why is it plausibility that concerns you?"

"Because, if Tymon's—and my—story is to be told properly, people must believe it. My considered opinion is that no one would believe this."

They were camped now some thirty miles from Seagull Keep, inland near where the course of the Kor River turned more west than north, on the border between Borasur and Nols. It had been simple enough to get Tymon's note into Duchess Mero's hands, but Seb had been more than a little surprised when Mero had later slipped away from her servants to join him, as Tymon said she would do. A few days' travel would see them to their rendezvous with Tymon at the Blackpits.

"I'm not sure I believe it myself," Lady Mero said. "I know Tymon's reputation as well as yours, yet I cannot discount the service you did my father. He never spoke of it after, but I know. I made a point of knowing."

"Your father was a good man," Seb said simply. "And I think Tymon was genuinely happy to be of service to him in that matter. That it served his own ends as well was no doubt the point, though, as I'm sure you understand."

She looked grim. "Even so, a debt is a debt. My father cannot repay it now, so I am honor bound to serve in his stead. I think you'll agree that I am more than making an effort."

"You've delivered yourself and your daughter into our hands with no more coercion than that debt. I can fault neither your sense of obligation nor honor."

She smiled faintly. "Just my judgment, then. Well, even that entered into the matter, just as honor dictated my compliance."

Seb raised an eyebrow. "Oh? How so?"

"Master Seb, would it surprise you that I have an idea what this is all about?"

Seb didn't even blink. "I've known you for only a little while," he said, "but it wouldn't surprise me at all."

"My lord is into this up to his dear, foolish neck, isn't he?"

"Your Grace does have the right of it," Seb conceded.

She looked at Seb intently. "I'm here because I have to be, Master Seb, but understand me—there are limits to what I am prepared to do, even for a debt of honor. I will not let you harm my husband or my daughter. I recommend that you do not try."

Seb considered his words carefully. "Your Grace, I cannot say for certain just what my master has planned. Yet I pray it never comes to that," Seb said with conviction, "for the last thing on earth I would desire is to have you for an enemy."

"Momma?"

Lytea sat up on her blankets, looking about frantically. Mero picked her up and smoothed her hair. "What is it, my heart?"

The little girl snuggled into her mother's arms. "Had a dream. There were rocks in it."

"Probably under your blanket," Mero said. "They're under mine, too. I'll move them."

Lytea looked at Seb. "You're little," she said.

Seb smiled. "So are you. You'll grow, though. Soon you'll be as tall as your mother, I wager."

Lytea shook her head fiercely. "Like being little. Need to be little to ride my pony!"

"You have a pony?"

"She does not," Mero said. "Yet. Maybe when all this is over. . . ."

"A pony. With a fish tail," said Lytea happily.

CHAPTER 15
"FOR WANT OF A WORD"

Whoever wrote this was being difficult by design.

That understanding wasn't as discouraging as Galan might have expected. He stared at the page of the book. He looked away for a while, then looked back. He turned the page a little one way, then another. The changed perspective didn't really help. He lit more candles, trimmed the wick in his lamp, even looked at the offending word with a special glass lens that made it larger but didn't do a thing to make the word plainer.

Galan finally sat back in his chair, at least temporarily confounded, but his mind raced on to new possibilities. This was a profound but simple challenge of the sort that Galan knew very well. Removed from diplomacy and the tricks of the human heart that he was forced to deal with as Crown Prince. Difficult, yes, but uncomplicated by politics and events beyond his control. Self-contained, needing only the book, and Galan's own skills, plus the aid of an unknown scribe, long dead, who had copied an even older script into what was now known as the Sisaran dialect of Old Wylan. No surprise either that such a thing had been forgotten; there couldn't have been more than a few dozen people in all the Twelve Kingdoms who could still read Old Wylan, and fewer still who could translate the Sisaran dialect. Galan was proud to count himself one of those few.

Or would have been, if he could figure out why the one word did not translate.

K'kara lo magata.

He repeated the phrase for what seemed the thousandth time. The script was clear enough: "Lo" was the possessive tag, though in this case it probably meant "of" rather than "belonging to." "Magata" was just an archaic form of "maga" which meant "Power." Either one of the Seven, or an entity of considerable strength in its own right. The rest of the script referred to a summons, and conditions for controlling the maga so summoned.

Sorcery. How else to combat sorcery? Galan had hesitated only a little while, once the idea had taken hold, and the book's text had done the same. From what Galan had gleaned from the text, this was the perfect way to fight magic with magic, and put an end to Tymon the Black's villainy forever. But first he had to finish the translation. "K'kara." That was the stumbler. There was nothing in his sources that compared to it.

It would help if I knew exactly who I'm summoning. . . .

Galan blinked.

Of course! Why didn't he think of that before? What if "K'kara" was simply a name? Most proper names were derived from older sources, so it was quite likely that there wouldn't be a translation as such, at least not in the language in which the book was composed. More like this was simply a phonetic rendering of a word that had no analogue in Old Wylan. It fit. But was it right?

There was one quick way to find out. There might be other ways, but none of them would be quick. Galan put aside the book and reached for a reed pen to make out the list of supplies he would need for the summoning.

"I wish I had more time," Ashesa said to no one in particular.

She waited for the abbot in the library at Kuldun. She had never seen so many books together in one place. By comparison the Royal Library at Morushe was one parchment notice tacked to a tree.

"Is there something you'd like to see in particular?" the balding curate asked.

Ashesa considered. "I've heard rumors of a book detailing the known histories of several infamous people. Dommar the Beast, the pirate Deaken Krail, Duke Thakrel of Lyrsa. . . ."

"That could be Olpan's *History of Blood*. Rather melodramatic, but compelling reading in spite all. We have three editions—"

"—I'd recommend the recent translation by Kyn Soltha of Nols. His gloss is superb. In a few places it's even accurate."

Ashesa and the curate both turned at the new voice. The curate immediately bowed. "Lord Abbot."

The abbot of Kuldun stood just inside the doorway. Ashesa couldn't understand why she had heard nothing, not even the rustling of his long brown robe. He turned to the curate. "Brother Lons, could you spare us a moment?"

"Certainly. There's always something else needing attention in the archives." The curate hurried away as Ashesa rose.

"My Lord Abbot," she said, "thank you for seeing me. I know my request must sound strange—"

"Once you accept the notion that the Crown Princess of Morushe comes calling disguised as a humble messenger," the abbot said dryly, "you also accept a certain amount of oddity afoot. So then, Highness—what can I do for you?"

Ashesa started to ask how the abbot had penetrated her disguise so easily, then realized the question itself was an insult to both her intelligence and his. She produced the parchment Lady Margate had given her. "It's about this, Lord Abbot. This is on the cover of a book recently discovered in Duke Molikan's library."

The abbot studied the glyphs for several long moments. He

finally looked up. "So that's where it got off to. I trust there's no one at Korsos who can translate this?"

Ashesa took a deep slow breath. "Prince Galan can."

The abbot nodded. "Then I gather he has the book in his possession and the subject is difficult to bring up since, if you'd just needed a translation, you could have asked him."

"We didn't want him to know." Ashesa immediately wished she'd bitten her tongue, but it was a little late for caution now. "He's reading it, Lord Abbot."

The abbot nodded. "So I feared. If that's the case it's already too late. The only question left to answer now is how much damage he's done."

"Is there nothing I can do?"

The abbot considered. "As a member of the Royal House of Borasur, your patron deity is Amatok, yes?"

Ashesa blinked. "That's right."

"And you do believe in Amatok?"

"Of course."

"Then I suggest praying. Until we know what His Highness has set loose, there's not much else we can do."

Ashesa looked grim. "There may be one other thing. But first I have to find someone. Someone who sets a great store in books and knowledge. To be blunt, someone I think who has visited this place before, perhaps often."

"Many people visit us, Highness," the abbot said.

Ashesa wasn't sure of herself before she spoke. It was an idea that made sense to her but she had no proof. What she saw in the abbot's expression, or rather its absence, was almost as good. Ashesa had seen more open emotion in a statue. "You don't put up a wall to show off your garden, as the old expression goes. You know who I mean."

"I do? I'm afraid your confidence in me might be misplaced, Highness."

"Shall I speak his name? It is Tymon the Black."

The abbot didn't even flinch. He merely nodded. "I thought your morbid interest in *The History of Blood* was a bit odd, considering the source. I am sorry to disappoint you, Highness. I'm merely the abbot of Kuldun, and not giving to discourse with monsters."

"This isn't a monster."

Now the abbot smiled. "That is not how the stories tell it, Highness. That's not how history will remember it, and that certainly is not how our various patrons would react if such nonsense became public. I'm sorry, but I cannot help you find your monster."

Ashesa thought about it. "Lord Abbot, it was wrong of me to suggest such a thing. I ask your forgiveness, and your indulgence to grant me a different favor."

He watched her closely. "Ask."

"You can't help me find a monster. Will you help me find a friend instead?"

Now there was a reaction on the abbot's face this time: astonishment. It was all Ashesa could do to keep from smiling. To his credit the abbot recovered quickly. "This friend you speak of . . . does he wish to be found?"

Ashesa nodded. "Yes, and very much so. Only he doesn't know it yet."

The abbot just looked at her for a very long time. "Blast me for a simple fool, Highness, but I believe you."

"I've done something," Prince Galan said, to no one in particular. He closed the book and stood up, stretching, feeling the tightness in his legs and the small of his back easing a bit. He started to walk away, thinking vaguely of stopping by Duke Molikan's kitchens to see about a bit of bread and cheese or something. He could not remember when he'd eaten last and he was suddenly hungry. He stopped just outside the door to Molikan's library and turned around and went back inside.

He still felt a little of what he had felt after reading the passage in the book aloud: excitement, elation, fear. All were fading now, though fear was still strongest. This did not surprise Galan, since he hadn't known what to expect in the first place. Images had come to his mind then. Things like a lock broken, a leash dropped, a collar snapped. Something was loose that had been confined, loosed and pointed in the direction of Galan's choosing. He did not know what it was. He did not really care. Once its purpose was served, then Galan could accept both the crown of Borasur and Ashesa's hand in marriage with a clear slate for whatever might come next. Once Daras's death was avenged, and not before.

As he had not done in a long, long time, Galan offered a silent prayer to Amatok. *Please, let it be soon.*

He stood inside the doorway for several long moments, and then the unfinished thing presented itself to his consciousness. Galan stepped to the reading table and lifted the book off its stand. He walked slowly through the silent rooms, to the very back, and pushed the book back into the place he had found it. He shook himself then, like a sleeper waking, then yawned and stretched once more. He was done with the book; it was back in its place and he was done. That sense of something unfinished was gone. He had done all he could do, and he knew it with a certainty passing understanding.

He was still hungry.

Galan headed to the kitchen as all the emotions left him. Except the fear. That remained, and it did not diminish even after the hunger was long gone.

He could not remember a time before the darkness. He had no memory of himself at all, as it was part of the darkness and so did not remember, or feel, or think for time past counting. Darkness had no need of any of those things. It just was.

Then he was . . . sundered.

BROKEN!!

At first there were the words, flitting through the blackness, separate things, mothlike. They gathered, strengthened, tore at him with tiny claws of knowledge until he knew. Words, concepts, visions rushed in like a torrent, pulling him from the darkness, carrying him away from all he was and ever wanted to be. He grew limbs to flail about, a mouth to howl, eyes to see things that were not of itself and could never be.

GO BACK!

He could not. He was not darkness now, not totally. He was of himself now, and he could not stop, or tear away, or kill that sense of self that had ridden in on the flood of words.

WHO!?

Now that he had a sense of himself he also had a sense of the other, something outside himself. Something that had hurt him very badly and was still hurting him. He had to make it stop. He had to . . . kill it. Yes, that was the action required.

KILL IT.

Like some great hound, the creature of warm, comfortable darkness began to sniff the wind.

The abbot had been right about the pass and horses. Ashesa and her three companions' mounts had to pick their way so carefully through the broken stones of the pass that walking would have been faster. And there was no grass to speak of to supplement what grain they could carry. When one of Ashesa's escorts' mounts came up lame after the first day, that was enough. She ordered the mounts linked together in train and had one of her escort lead them back to Kuldun with a written apology to the abbot for not listening to him in the first place.

Ashesa and the two remaining guards went ahead on foot.

"How much further, Highness?" asked one, a burly veteran from Lyrksa.

Ashesa studied the abbot's map. "Once we leave the pass? Another two days to the general area, if I'm reading this right. The abbot couldn't be more specific than that. And don't call me 'Highness.' Especially if we're around strangers—"

"I'm afraid your secret is already out, Highness."

The man emerged from behind a large boulder, an arbalest cradled casually in his arms. He didn't really look like a bandit, but his attitude was something else again. Ashesa's guards as one stepped in front of her and reached for their swords, but the arbalest moved ever so slightly and they stopped, hands on their hilts, glaring.

"You can only kill one of us with that thing, you know," said the Lyrksan.

The man nodded agreeably. "Excellent point. Have you decided who it is to be yet?"

Now that Ashesa's initial surprise had passed she took a good long look at their waylayer. "Lord Vor, why are you doing this?"

He looked surprised, but only for a moment. "Well, damn," he said. "As for my presence, I could ask you the same thing. In fact I will in a moment or two. Now there's other business."

He killed the Lyrksan first. Just a quick, almost casual change in the arbalest's direction and he fired, striking the man square in the chest. In the shock and surprise his less-experienced companion almost didn't get his sword out in time to block Lord Vor's almost equally sudden attack. Vor had dropped the arbalest almost as soon as he'd fired it, drawn his sword, and closed the gap between them. The remaining guard parried twice, thrust and missed. Then he missed the next parry and went down under Lord Vor's blade just as Ashesa managed to get her own blade out.

Lord Vor, not even winded, shook his head and Ashesa moved on guard. "Highness, you do not want to do that."

"You're right," she said, as calmly as she could manage. "Yet I don't seem to have any choice."

"I won't hurt you."

"Considering the evidence of my own eyes, you'll forgive me if I don't believe you."

Lord Vor tore a strip of cloth from the tunic of one his victims and began to clean his sword. "I am sincere. If you tell me what I want to know and otherwise behave yourself, it needn't come to that."

Ashesa looked grim. "Fool that I was, as soon as you were recognized you killed those men. I don't think you intended to do that before then. And I know who you are better than they."

"It's true I hadn't quite decided what to do," he admitted. "I could have played the anonymous bandit all else being equal but, yes, your reaction did rather force my hand. A regrettable action, but necessary. So. How did you know? To my knowledge we've never met before, and it was only your conversation with your escort that revealed you to me."

Ashesa listened with only half of her attention; the rest was devoted to finding an avenue of escape. There was none that she could see. "Duke Laras came to Morushe three years ago and you were with him. We were never formally introduced, but I like to follow what my father is doing, and who comes and goes in our house."

Lord Vor sighed. "Politics. It has been the undoing of many, and may be yours, Highness. You're no match for me and you're only making this difficult. Put down your sword."

"I may surprise you."

"Unlikely. Highness, I don't know why you're here but I suspect our concerns may overlap and I'd like to find out if that's the case. If there can be no mutual understanding then I may have to kill you, with regret, but if you attack me I'll kill you anyway. Isn't a slim chance better than none?"

"I have a slim chance of beating you," Ashesa said, "but that's better than none. Which is what I would have without my sword."

"Why are you here, Princess? Traveling the Serpent Pass at all, and so late in the season? Dressed not very convincingly as a common squire? Who are you looking for?"

"That's not your concern. I may forgive your attack on my guards if you explain it very damn well, but if you detain or harm me Prince Galan will have your bollocks for a door knocker!"

"Two lies. You will not forgive me for your guards and that's one more reason to kill you. That rather charming scenario is also not Prince Galan's style at all. Even if it *was* that's only one more reason to kill you. You are not helping yourself, Highness, and it's past time you began, because I have appointments to keep and no more time to waste with you. Put down your sword."

"No."

He shrugged. "Your choice. . . ."

Ashesa had no illusions about her chances, but even she was surprised by what happened next. Lord Vor thrust, not very fast, and Ashesa blocked and attempted to extend her blade past Vor's guard. He slipped his body to one side and looped her arm with his own as she slid by. One twist of his wrist and Ashesa screamed in sudden pain, dropping her blade.

"You won't find this move in a treatise, Highness. It comes from being in battles with your life on the line. It's fortunate for you that yours is not."

Then what seemed like a night full of stars exploded against her skull and that's all she saw for a moment. Then the stars went away and left, just for a while, the darkness.

Tymon greeted Seb and his "captives" when they reached the mountain. Seb hurried off to see about supper, leaving Tymon and Duchess Mero alone except for Lytea, who was fast asleep in her mother's arms.

"It's good to see you again, Your Grace. Even under these circumstances."

Duchess Mero handed Lytea over to him before she dismounted, slowly. "It's good to be out of that saddle. The rest remains to be seen."

Tymon cradled the child in his arms, careful not to wake her. "Of course it's as you say. I hope your stay with us will be brief and uneventful. The facilities are a bit primitive, I'm afraid," Tymon said, and nodded toward the campsite. "But your tent is already prepared. It is waterproof and gives privacy. We'll make you as comfortable as we can."

Duchess Mero looked at the tent and shrugged. "It's better than sleeping on the ground, and I certainly don't want Lytea out in this weather any more than necessary. This is no place for a child, Master Tymon."

"Again you are right, Your Grace," Tymon said, as he handed the sleeping girl back to her mother. "But it cannot be helped. I wouldn't ask this if it was not necessary."

She raised an eyebrow. "And I wouldn't have agreed except for the debt I owe and fear of what your plans might become without my cooperation. I'm here at least partly to keep an eye on you. Do you blame me?"

Tymon shook his head. "Not in the slightest. There are few assurances that I can offer, and I couldn't advise you to put much faith in such pallid things anyway."

Mero smiled faintly. "I've never heard lying counted as one

of your sins. And I could do with a bit of assurance right now. Please try."

"I want to help your husband, Your Grace, although he doesn't know he needs it and certainly doesn't want my help. I also swear that I mean no harm to you or your family."

"Unless it can't be avoided?"

Tymon shrugged an apology. "I will do my very best to avoid it. You can at least trust me on that."

"Well, then . . . for my sake—and yours—I hope that is enough."

Seb kept a discreet distance while Mero and Tymon spoke. After she withdrew to her tent to get settled, Seb went to Tymon. "She's rather amazing, isn't she?"

Tymon nodded. "We often measure each other by how well we rise to occasions, or fail to. I've learned never to question strength, wherever I find it."

Seb looked around. "Where's Koric?"

"Hmmm? Oh, off somewhere brooding, I fancy." He explained what had happened in the cave, and Seb let out a low whistle.

"I don't really blame him; that's a lot to deal with in one so young."

"Especially at a time of life when every stubbed toe is a tragedy."

Tymon's thoughts were somewhere else, for all that he held up his end of the conversation. Seb seemed to notice this, and he spoke up. "There's something on your mind. I mean more than usual. Is it anything I should know about?"

"I don't know," Tymon said. "I'm not even sure what it is."

"Tymon, there are several people's lives at risk here, including yours and mine, and you're worrying me."

"I am? I don't mean to. Yes, there's something wrong. I feel it. Not the Long Look—at least then I'd know whether there was cause to worry or not. As it is. . . ." He shrugged.

"A feeling? Such as?"

"I once saw a cat stalk a field mouse. The mouse was in the grass beside a stand of tall weeds that concealed the cat. I could see the cat slipping forward, inch by inch, its body taut as a bowstring before the shot. The mouse was nibbling a seed, oblivious. Then, while the cat was within striking distance but still, making no sound, the mouse suddenly dropped the seed, and started to run. It was too late. The cat had him."

"Charming anecdote, but what has this to do with this 'feeling' of yours?"

"The way I feel now is how I imagine the mouse must have felt, just when he dropped the seed."

Seb let out his breath. "Oh" was all he said.

"Indeed," said Tymon.

Seb buckled his cloak. "I'm going to find Koric. I'll say I need help with supper. This probably isn't a good time for any of us to be wandering off alone."

Tymon waited until Seb was out of earshot then said, to no one in particular, "Actually, this might be the perfect time."

"Am I at your beck and whim now, Magician?"

Tymon stared at the dark waters for some time before he answered. "What you will do and what you will not do is up to you, Amaet. I did not suggest otherwise."

"Yet you presume?"

"To ask a simple question? Yes. You've raised so many in our time together I don't think it unreasonable to suggest you might want to answer one. A small one."

"You want to know what's hunting you."

Tymon sighed. "You know about that. I am not surprised. That is why I came here. Will you tell me?"

"I will. But will you understand what I tell you? That is uncertain."

"I'll have to do the best I can with my pitiful human frame of reference. Just name this creature to me. Is it a Power?"

"That is two questions, neither of which is the right one. Its name? You could call it 'Amaet.' Or 'Amatok,' for that matter. Each is equally right and wrong."

Tymon sighed. "Riddles, again."

"The truth, and as plain as I know how to say it. It is a Power, yes, and it has a name given to it by others. But it has no name for itself because it is not a 'self' as you understand the term. It was darkness. It wants to be darkness again. It was happy being darkness until Prince Galan foolishly called it into awareness and linked it to you. So long as you exist, it exists as a separate creature. It hates that. And so, it hates you. And it is loose in your world."

Tymon felt a chill. "It will only be free when I am dead?"

"Yes."

"How do I fight it?"

Tymon heard laughter that seemed to come from everything around him, including the willow and the dark waters.

"You don't fight it, Magician. You can't."

"Then what do I do?"

"The only logical thing. You die."

Chapter 16
"Death and the Magician"

Ashesa awoke with stiff wrists and a raging headache. The sun had barely moved; by her own reckoning she had only been unconscious for a few minutes at most. She tried to push herself to a sitting position and realized her wrists were bound. She had a vague memory of her struggle with Lord Vor, but nothing after. She lifted her bound hands and touched the lump on her jaw. She wished she hadn't. Now she had a brand new pain to add to the raging storm in her skull.

Lord Vor sat a short distance away, studying the abbot's map. "Apologies, Highness, but you didn't give me much choice."

Ashesa groaned, rubbing her throbbing temples as best she could with bound wrists. "Lord Vor, when did you go mad? Palace gossip is usually more reliable about the state of the nobility."

He chuckled, then went back to studying the map. "Not so simple as that, Highness. I'm not mad and barely noble; I'm simply determined to know what you're about up here. I don't think this mountain pass has had this much traffic in fifty years or more."

"I don't know what you're talking about."

"Yes, you do. You've clearly been mucking about in areas of action and policy that are frankly unsuitable for one of your station. You're traveling with so little escort that it amounted to none at all, and you can call me addled?"

Ashesa sighed. She opened her eyes again and regretted it,

but did not change her mind. After a few moments she was able to focus again. "Lord Vor, my head hurts and I'm in no mood to discuss my affairs with anyone and especially with you. Untie me this instant."

"Not until you tell me why you're here. As for your headache, it may go away or it may kill you. . . . I've seen the like often in battle. Either way, right now it's the very least of your worries. Am I making myself plain?"

Ashesa nodded, slowly. More than plain. What he had done called for either the noose or the headsman in two kingdoms, and that if he was fortunate. Torture first, otherwise. Ashesa didn't know what Lord Vor's plans were but she just couldn't see how releasing her could possibly fit into any of them. "I can understand your curiosity but not your willingness to kill to satisfy it. Will you at least tell me why my business is so important to you?"

He shrugged. "It may not be important to me at all; that's the real chance I took in eliminating your escort. I can't answer your questions, Highness, until you answer mine. Let's start with this map of yours."

"It's a map. You can read it as well as I."

"I know where it goes. But where does it lead? What's at the other end?"

"Is idle curiosity worth a death sentence?"

"Highness, there is nothing idle about me. The stakes are high and you are a complication I did not expect. If I acted rashly I apologize, but it doesn't change anything. Just tell me what I want to know. If you don't, I will kill you."

"You'll kill me whether I do or not. You have to, now."

He smiled then. "Do I? Did you ever stop to consider that your importance to Borasur might suddenly diminish—"

He stopped himself, but too late. Ashesa put the pieces together, despite her headache. "If I am not the wife of the ruler, you mean. You are Duke Laras's man," Ashesa said. "In all things. This is his doing, isn't it? What is he plotting?"

"Nothing, thanks to Prince Galan and that damned tame magician of his."

"Tymon the Black? You think he serves Galan?"

"I know he does, and his reach is long. Laras will not risk his family for ambition. Fortunately for him, I will. No, Highness. I do serve the rightful rulers of Borasur, but Duke Laras knows nothing of this as of yet. When he does, it will no longer matter. The throne will be his, and alive or dead, the daughter of the Royal House of Morushe will no longer be a factor. Now, answer my questions."

"No. Let me go."

Lord Vor walked over and struck her across the face. Hard. Her headache exploded in agony and she sank to her knees, as stunned by the attack as she was by the pain, which was considerable.

Damn me for a dull fool.

Despite all that he had done, Ashesa had still expected that there was a core of reason to Lord Vor's actions, something that would restore her rightful relationship to him as a servant of Galan's vassal and a knight of Borasur. It was only the second time her view of the world had been so rudely undone, and she cursed through her tears, as much for her own slow wit as Vor's treachery. She stopped the tears. Pain or rage or both, whatever their cause, she stopped them.

My idea of you was too limited, Lord Vor. I will not make that mistake again.

"I'm waiting," he said, "but not for very long."

She had to give him what he wanted. At least until she had an alternative. "You were right, at least about one thing. That map leads to Tymon the Black."

Lord Vor smiled. "There. That wasn't as difficult as you thought."

Ashesa let her tears fall again. That wasn't difficult, either, and it seemed to satisfy Lord Vor's expectations. Though Ashesa swore to herself that, sooner rather than later, Lord Vor's idea of her would prove too limited as well.

Tymon and Seb sat together by the slowly dying campfire. Duchess Mero and her child had long since gone to their tent, and Koric to his. When Tymon was quite certain they would not be overheard, he outlined his plan in detail as Seb listened quietly and patiently to everything Tymon had to say to him. When the magician finished Seb looked him in the eye and said, "It won't work."

Tymon frowned. "Which part?"

"Any of it. All of it. Your schemes have always been risky, fragile, and foolhardy, but this is the first time I've been tempted to call one completely insane. You're trying to do too much. There are too many unknowns, too many factors out of your control. It's madness."

"There have been times when I haven't tried to do enough and I regret those lost opportunities more than I can say. I'm sick to death of regrets, Seb, and even insanity has its uses."

"For instance?"

"For instance, when the 'sane' thing to do would be roll over and die."

Seb tried again. "Tymon, how do you know Amaet is telling the truth? How do you know that you're not serving some arcane scheme of her own?"

"As for the first, I don't know. As for the second I do, since I am always serving some arcane scheme of Amaet's, in ways I can't hope to comprehend. She is a Power after all and, if I don't owe her worship, I certainly do owe her debts of one sort or another. I think she'd like to see me live long enough for her to collect."

"That's just it. If your plan works, you may die."

Tymon blinked. "May? My death would probably be the best possible outcome, for all concerned and for reasons well known to you."

Seb glared. "You're trying to be practical and thoughtful and you don't know how. Stop it, Tymon."

"All right. So. What are you going to do?"

Seb looked at him for a moment, uncomprehending. Then, "Oh. If by that do you mean am I staying? You know I am."

Tymon shook his head. "I didn't know. But I did hope. Thank you."

"You're welcome. Now explain your plan to me one more time. Slowly."

"Are you afraid you'll forget it?"

"I'm afraid I was right about it the first time. Maybe it will improve with a second look."

Prince Galan stared at the meat and cheese on his bread trencher. He broke off one piece of it, used that to sop up a bit of gravy. Duke Molikan's cook, a stolid woman of indeterminate age, watched him without appearing to watch him. Galan didn't mind; at least she had some curiosity about why he came to the kitchens night after night. Galan was rather curious about that himself.

"Madame, may I ask you a question?"

The woman almost dropped the knife she'd been sharpening. "O-Of course, Your Highness."

"Well, two questions really. What's your name?"

She did a little bobbing curtsey. "Meliat, so please Your Highness."

"It is a lovely name," he said, and she blushed crimson.

"Once it fit me better, Highness. At least by others' reckoning, if not my own."

Galan looked at her for a moment, then nodded. "I can see it. I really can." And he could. It didn't occur to him to lie. He wondered if he would know how when the need arose. He wondered if Tals could help with that, then dismissed the thought as unworthy. Tals did what he had to do; no more or no less. Just as Galan would do, now that he was to be king.

The cook blushed again. "You'll turn an old woman's head, Prince. You mentioned another question?"

Galan tried to read what he saw in her face then, other than the remnants of a fading beauty and what was, perhaps, the beginnings of another kind of beauty entirely. Was there also, perhaps, a glimmer of hope or possibility concerning him? A fantasy of potential grandness, beaten down and trodden over the years, but never totally abandoned? Could Meliat now see such from one such as he, even now?

I'm a fool, Galan thought.

He had never looked at another person's face and seen only aspects and shadows of himself reflected there. At least, not until now. Something was wrong, something was getting more and more wrong by the moment. Galan didn't know what it was. He only knew that he was the cause of it. Not the crown that he didn't want. Not Ashesa—though where was she now? He needed to ask. Nor even Tymon the Black, as much as he wanted to blame them all. Tymon had not opened the dark book. Galan had. He and he alone, and now something very bad was happening and Galan did not know what to do about it, or even what the bad thing might be. He was afraid. He was also curious.

"Meliat, can you tell me why I am so hungry?"

Later that evening, Galan dreamed of darkness. Not oblivion, which was the normal name for a dreamless sleep. Galan was not oblivious at all. He dreamed, and his dream was of darkness, a black stretch of infinity unmarked by beacon or star.

Nothing is here.

"Yes. And so are you."

Galan thought about it for a moment, in that clarity of thought that dreams sometimes bring, if only in illusion. The voice spoke the truth, though, as far as Galan could see. His sense of self was the only thing separating him from the devouring darkness, and he wasn't sure how long he could keep it at bay.

"Not for long. I'd get rid of it, if I were you."

Galan looked around, saw nothing. "Who are you?"

Silence.

"How do I rid myself of this darkness if I don't even know what it is? Are you the darkness?"

"Fool. If you did not know its nature, why did you summon it?"

Galan, stung, started to answer harshly, "I didn't—Oh. The book," Galan said.

"Yes."

"I thought I understood how to use it," Galan said, almost to himself.

"There was no 'right way' to use that book. You were wrong."

"Yes," Galan said at last. "I was."

"Even a fool can learn better, sometimes. Will you learn, Prince of Borasur?"

"Will you teach?" Galan asked. Galan then found something around him besides darkness—laughter.

"I already have, though the lesson seems to elude you. Why was the darkness summoned?"

"To destroy a man called Tymon the Black," Galan said.

"Then help it to do what it wants. Perhaps then it will go

away. For your sake and the sake of all those you hold dear, I hope so."

The voice then spoke of Tymon the Black, and where he might be found, and just how little time there was to waste.

Galan looked around one more time. "Who are you? How do I know that I can trust you?"

"You cannot trust me. But if you have half as much wit as rumor says, you just might be able to trust yourself when the time comes. Wake up now, Prince of Borasur. Remember."

Galan did as he was told, and he did remember what the voice had said.

So did the darkness. What Galan knew, the darkness knew. Soon Galan was doing what he was told one more time, and as dawn slowly filtered into his room the Crown Prince of Borasur sent for Sir Tals. The young knight arrived, half-dressed and almost completely breathless.

". . . here, Your Highness."

"Sir Tals, have our mounts made ready. You and I are going on a journey."

"A journey? May I ask where?"

"To a region known as the Blackpits."

Tals frowned. "Your Highness, that is within the border of Wylandia. We'll have to cross it to get there, if I'm not mistaken. What if we are detected?"

"I can't worry about that now."

His advisor frowned. "As you wish, but it'll take a day or better to get the escort ready to move."

"You are my escort, Sir Tals. Be ready within the hour."

"Your Highness. . . ." Tals looked desperate, then said, "Highness, there are two royal Dukes present. If we take them with us that will increase your escort to something more reasonable. Also, if we are detected, we can claim that we were on a delegation to Aldair and the messenger we'd sent ahead suffered some misfortune."

Galan frowned, then shrugged. "It doesn't matter . . . we leave in three hours. If the escort isn't ready I'll go alone. Is that understood?"

"Yes, My Prince. May I withdraw to prepare?"

"At once."

Tals left immediately. Galan stood very still for a moment, despite all the noise in his head that told him it was time to be about and doing.

What am I doing?

He knew what he had said, but he did not really feel as if he had said those things, spoken that way to Sir Tals. It was as if someone else was in the room, giving him directions that he understood and acted upon but never really saw. Galan looked around, as he had in his dream, but despite the morning light now pouring into his room, every piece of his world now appeared to be touched with shadows.

"I don't even have time to talk to you, but I'm here despite that."

Sir Tals stood in Lady Margate's room. He did not look for a place to sit; instead he used the time to buckle on his gambeson and vambraces. Down in the courtyard a squire waited with the rest of his armor and a hastily prepared sack of provisions. Lady Margate watched the lad from her window.

"Did you notice his excitement, Sir Tals?"

Tals blinked in the poor light. "I don't understand."

"You're young enough, I grant, but are you so young that nearly every experience is still something new and wonderful? Look at the lad. He's practically bouncing as he waits for you down there. He doesn't know what is happening, and yet he is certain it is grand adventure. Ask him and I'm sure he'd say."

"Lady Margate, nearly everyone around me has lost their

mind. I took some comfort in the knowledge that you had not. Was I wrong?"

Lady Margate shrugged. "Perhaps. I've sent a royal princess of Morushe into what is almost certain danger simply because I didn't have a better idea. That resembles madness enough to sit for its portrait. Now you're going to allow the Crown Prince of Borasur to go gallivanting off the Powers alone know where because you can't stop him short of committing treason. Where's the sanity in any of that?"

Sir Tals grunted as he fastened one buckle a bit too snugly. "None that I can see," he admitted.

"You think Prince Galan is acting like a madman and I'd have to agree. Perhaps he is mad. Perhaps not. You're going to have to work that out and then decide what you do then. I can't help you."

He smiled a bitter smile. "Then who can?"

"If it's help you think you need, then I'd say your squire has the right idea," she said, considering. "Let's play our parts and hope the adventure is as grand as the risks we take with our lives and those of others. We're probably wrong, but it's not as if we have much choice."

"A Crown Prince goes to his coronation gladly and bloody well on time. When he's king, he marries a suitable princess, produces heirs, makes wars and alliances, keeps a country's name and character well or badly. This shouldn't be so complicated, Lady Margate. In fact, it should be very simple indeed."

Lady Margate smiled. "Did Master Albon teach you that?"

"Well . . . no," Sir Tals admitted, although with great reluctance.

"My estimation of the man would drop considerably if he had. No, Sir Knight. He did not teach you that because it's not true. As you finish your accouterments I will tell you why."

He paused to lace a cuff. "I'm listening."

"You speak of princes and kings and princesses as if they were something other than people. Pieces in a game. Well, sometimes they are pieces in a game, but they are never that alone. Never. At heart they are always human beings, with everything that implies. Kings and queens, princes and princesses, dukes and duchesses, it doesn't matter. They are people, and people are always complicated. They don't behave as expected. Sometimes they are better, sometimes worse, sometimes simply different. This never changes, whatever else may in the land of statecraft. Never forget that."

Tals sighed. "Unlikely. It doesn't seem I'll lack for reminders . . . oh, Powers!" Tals looked at the broken strap in disgust. "I knew I should have replaced that after the skirmish at the Kor. . . . I must take my leave now, Lady Margate. Good luck to us and all our flawed charges."

Sir Tals hurried out, and Lady Margate turned back to her window.

Good luck indeed, she thought, *as if there is anything else that has a chance of bringing a happy conclusion.* She turned to the alcove on the far side of the room. "He's gone. You can come out now."

The member of the princess's escort who had been sent back to Kuldun with the mounts emerged from behind the curtain. "I thought Sir Tals knew of Her Highness's errand."

"He knows she went to Kuldun. He does not know that she followed her own path from there. Come to that neither did I, until now."

"She could not be dissuaded, My Lady. We tried."

Lady Margate nodded. "I have no doubt of it. . . . The northern path to Wylandia, did you say?"

"Yes. She was headed for a border region known as the Black-pits. I wasn't supposed to know, but I saw the map once when she was slow packing it away and I recognized a landmark. She didn't say why it was so important that she go there."

"She'll have to cross Wylandian territory to reach it. Hmph. Serve her right if King Aldair caught her there and married her for trespassing."

"Married? An odd punishment, My Lady."

Lady Margate sighed. "Never met His Majesty, have you?"

Lord Kyre had waited far longer than he thought wise, but to move without word would have been even less wise, to his thinking. Now finally the overdue messenger had come under cloak of darkness and departed the same way. He had even kept to the shadows thrown by the beeswax candles in Lord Kyre's chambers. Kyre had thought him secretive even for one of his profession, but he didn't dwell on that. The important thing was that now he had the courier's scroll and had long since read what it had to say. Now it was time to act.

Prince Galan is coming to the Blackpits.

This was indeed an opportunity, yes, and more than one. Kyre couldn't resist wondering, just for a moment, who could be best served, and how. So many possibilities, so many lovely thoughts and notions, but all futile. His own course, for once, was already set and there could be no diversions. It was regrettable but, well, there you were. Kyre summoned a servant.

"Please inform His Majesty Aldair that I need a moment of his time."

Waiting for the summons, Lord Kyre considered his plan of attack. The Blackpits themselves made the best rallying point. There were other arrows in Lord Kyre's quiver if need be, but he didn't think they would be necessary. The notion of Prince Galan at the Blackpits, plus a little royal family history, was probably all the lever Lord Kyre would need to set the King of Wylandia into tumbling motion.

Where he would stop was anyone's guess.

Ashesa of Morushe walked in front of Lord Vor in manner, to her mind, reminiscent of a dog on a leash. Her wrists were bound, and a long thin rope of braided leather secured her in Vor's grip.

"What must you be thinking, I wonder?" Vor asked. "Other than silly notions of escape and revenge, I mean."

"I'm thinking how satisfying it would be to see your master's head on a pike next to your own."

Lord Vor jerked once on the rein, wrenching Ashesa's shoulders painfully as he turned her to face him. "I told you he knows nothing of this!"

She nodded, wincing. "So you did. And, seeing the anger you will conjure for his sake that you will not for your own, I'm inclined to believe you. Do you really think anyone else will if I am dead?"

"It won't matter."

"If your plan, whatever it is, succeeds. Are you so certain of that?"

"A plan so simple cannot go awry easily. You lead me to Tymon the Black. I kill him. With the threat of him removed, my master will be free to act, and his House will take its rightful place, ruling Borasur."

"The Masters of House Dyrlos have been 'free to act' at one time or another for hundreds of years. They have not. What makes you think Laras will?"

"He will. He will see the wisdom. I will help him."

"Why?"

Lord Vor frowned, then snapped the rein sharply. "Keep walking, we have a lot of ground to cover, Highness."

Ashesa ignored the pain in her wrist. "Didn't you ask what I was thinking?"

"I did. Now perhaps I will tell you what I am thinking about, Highness. Fair is fair."

"I am curious," she said, "I admit it."

He nodded. "So I presumed. I was thinking about my favorite ruler of all time. Kodalian the Tenth of Nols."

Ashesa didn't expect to be surprised by anything Vor might have said. She was wrong. "But Kodalian's reign was totally unremarkable."

Lord Vor grinned. "You've studied history; I suspected as much. Yes, you are right. Quite unremarkable."

Ashesa sighed deeply. "Lord Vor, for someone so prone to intrigue and usurpation, I hardly expected you to be fascinated with a period of peace and stability."

He shook his head. "You're missing the point, Highness. There have been many such—albeit brief—periods in the history of the Twelve Kingdoms. What is so fascinating about Kodalian's case is how it came to be at all. It seems that, in almost all particulars, the man was an utter fool."

"And you admire him for that?"

That remark earned her another hard snap of the rein, almost as painful as a whip blow.

"Don't be obtuse, Highness; you haven't the knack. I admire Kodalian because of the single virtue he did possess—a clear knowledge of self. By all account he made the most of it. His queen was noted for her wise counsel, and he also took care to surround himself with loyal men much more gifted and perceptive than he was, and he *listened* to them. The fact that his reign was unremarkable is, in itself, extremely remarkable. By all rights he should have engaged in a hundred petty wars, or taxed his subjects to rebellion to pay for some folly or other. Neither of which happened."

"That sounds very wise indeed. So. Are you saying Duke Laras is such a fool?"

"Don't anger me, Highness. You presume too much from your station."

"I do not. I merely note the potential parallels between Kodalian's situation and Duke Laras. You want him to heed your counsel on usurping—or reclaiming—the throne; you've said as much. Therefore you want him to take example from the wise Kodalian."

"Now you go from presumption to assumption."

"Do I now? I'm wagering this subject has come up before, and that Duke Laras doesn't want to be king. Am I wrong?"

She glanced back, but she didn't need the flush of crimson on Vor's face to know that she was right.

"He will see that there is no alternative. There is no one else now."

"He doesn't want to be king," Ashesa repeated. "What does he want, then?"

"He wants to tally fishing boats," Vor said, his disgust clear enough in his voice. "He wants to enrich his House with tariffs and trade by exploiting the charters his House received as surety of its loyalty on the ascension of House Kotara. Everything he does is to that end."

"A loyal servant would accede to his master's wishes."

"As will I. He will be free to do all those things, and more, when he is on the throne. Running the government will be best left to his counselors."

"Meaning you."

He shrugged. "Perhaps. More than likely, even."

"Forgive my slow wit. I think I finally understand. This isn't about Duke Laras, Lord Vor. It's about what you want, not what he wants. You want Dyrlos to be the Royal House of Borasur because you want to control that House."

"To serve and to control are not incompatible, Highness. Sometimes they are even necessary. As now."

"You won't succeed, Lord Vor."

He smiled indulgently. "I already have, Princess. The rest is mere formality."

Chapter 17
"Endings, Happy and Otherwise"

"You're sure?"

Tymon blinked. The golem's handwriting wasn't the best—not surprising for a creature with twigs for fingers—but the message was clear enough. The thing just gave a creaking nod, then stepped back, expectant, as Tymon handed the parchment scrap over to Seb.

Seb studied the script. "I'm guessing the golem puts him here in less than an hour. The rest of our guests may be hard on his heels, Tymon."

"Should be, rather. A complication—or an opportunity. Let's find out." He turned back to the golem. "Thank you. Please return to your station, and if you pass Lord Vor on the way back be sure he doesn't see you."

In a moment the small creature was gone again, stumping off with surprising speed down the valley pass. In a moment its form was hidden in the steam from the springs and vents.

"The woman described sounds a lot like Princess Ashesa," Seb said, watching the creature disappear.

"Yes, and if we're interpreting our scout correctly, she hasn't come of her own free will. I have no idea what Lord Vor hopes to gain by this."

"He wants to kill you."

"I know that. I even suspect why. Yet what has this to do with the princess? She shouldn't be here, especially now."

Seb shrugged. "I agree, and yet she is here. So. What shall we do?"

"What we have to do, Seb. No more and, unfortunately, no less."

Progress was slow but steady, mainly because of Vor's refusal to grant Ashesa any respite. He allowed stops for water, once or twice for calls of nature—around a tree or bush, still tethered—but none for rest. Ashesa had never known it was possible to walk as far as she had in one day. She wouldn't have kept on a horse this long without resting the poor beast more than once. She observed as much to the taciturn Lord Vor.

"Highness, I've probably killed more horses than you've ridden. Sometimes it's necessary."

"I'm not a horse, Lord Vor."

"No, but unless you keep up with me I'll kill you too."

There seemed no arguing with that. Ashesa kept walking, despite the ache in her legs and the pain in her feet and the mind-numbing weariness that seemed so much a part of her now that she could not tell where it ended and Ashesa began. To make matters worse, the path they were on had started to slant upward into the mountains again, making walking more difficult. Here and there hot springs steamed and bubbled out of the rocks, leaving white and green crystals on the stones as the water cooled and dripped down the hill face. The air was sulfurous and fetid; Ashesa felt the beginnings of a raging headache.

"I can't—"

"Shhhh!!"

Vor commanded silence with a hiss far sharper than any from the fuming rocks. Ashesa looked around, but saw no one, no reason for alarm—or at least no more reason than a half-crazed vassal and a scene transported from the Underworld. Vor didn't so much summon her to him as haul her in like an eel on a fishing line. He whispered to her then, and Ashesa felt a cold knot of fear settle in her stomach. "You will take your cues from me, and if you interfere with me or fail to obey me in the slightest regard, you will die. Understood?"

Ashesa nodded. She was perilously short of options. She had to content herself with making meticulous mental notes for Lord Vor's execution. She planned to supervise the entire affair herself. Lord Vor put his arm around her shoulders and held his dagger to her throat. Ashesa now even considered doing the final act in person, if she could train long enough to handle that great chopped-off-looking headsman's sword in time. Best not, though, she told herself. Some things just should not be delayed.

Lord Vor scanned the rocks ahead. "I know you're there!"

Who does he think is there? thought Ashesa, distracted, then she remembered.

Ashesa had a little help remembering. Tymon the Black walked out onto the ledge formed where the slope she currently trod met a cliff face. Lord Vor tightened his grip on Ashesa and she felt the point of his dagger touch her skin, almost like a mosquito bite. It began to sting.

"Lord Vor, why are you here?" Tymon asked. He hardly raised his voice; he might have been greeting an old acquaintance at some chance encounter for all the tension in his voice.

"I want to speak to you, Magician," Vor said, "come closer."

"Certainly."

Tymon started down the slope towards them. When he got to within twenty yards of them Lord Vor shifted his grip on Ashesa a bit, and she no longer felt the dagger's point. Ashesa wondered if Vor's dagger had a new target now.

"That's close enough," Vor said.

"No, I don't think so," Tymon said. "Not yet, at least."

He came closer. Slowly, steadily, closer. He had a dagger in his hand, a short, stubby, wicked-looking thing with what looked like three points. Ashesa hadn't seem him draw it, or any sheathe to draw it from. She stared at it, fascinated.

"I'm warning you, Magician. I have your master's beloved!"

Tymon nodded. "I see you have Ashesa of Morushe, and I am curious as to 'how' and 'why,' I admit it. Though I must correct you on one point: I have no 'master,' save only myself."

Tymon never paused. He was barely ten yards away now, and closing the gap steadily.

"Stop where you are! I'm warning you—"

"Of what?" Tymon was very close now.

"I swear I'll kill her!"

"No need to swear, Lord Vor: I believe you. Here. Let me save you the trouble."

Tymon's hand snaked forward. Ashesa felt a sharp sting just below her left breast. She gasped in horror and disbelief as she saw Tymon's dagger, the hilt alone showing now, jutting from her midriff. She felt the cold metal piercing her flesh, saw the blood, then she could feel very little. All of her went numb, her limbs slack and useless; her vision dark.

Oh.

"—fool! They'll never believe—!"

Lord Vor was shouting. Why was Lord Vor shouting? In another moment, she could no longer bring herself to care as she felt herself falling down and down into darkness.

Prince Galan rode with Sir Tals and Dukes Molikan and Laras. There were no other retainers, save for Sir Tals's squire who was in charge of the packhorses. The four were plainly dressed though well armed; they rode through the central highlands pass like young knights-errant, out for adventure and brave deeds, or at least reckless endangerment. No one knew what to say and Prince Galan, his companions would have agreed if they'd ever spoken to each other about the matter, was not helping at all.

"Where are we going?" Duke Laras said aloud, to no one in particular. Prince Galan, riding a few lengths ahead as he tended to do, didn't hear him, or at least didn't respond.

Sir Tals tried to help the pack train to pick up the pace a bit, without much luck. "We are going to avenge the death of Prince Daras. It's a personal quest that Prince Galan has chosen and that we, as greater or lesser royal vassals, are bound to support."

"Of course," Duke Molikan said. "Though I'd feel better about it if I knew just where this vengeance was to take place, and how long we can expect to be in the saddle. I'm not as young as I was . . . well, when I was younger."

"We left Morushe yesterday," Duke Laras said. "I'm still surprised no one took us for mercenaries and challenged us."

"We're a small group," Tals said. "Hardly a threat to the kingdom. It's not as if we're invading with banners flying."

Duke Laras glared at the young man. "Do you think for a moment King Macol didn't know who we are and where we were by the end of the first day?"

Tals shook his head. "Of course not, Your Grace. But without some word from Galan himself about his intentions, Macol had no clear course of action. I'm sure he chose to pretend that he did not know. That's what I would have done . . . besides watching us very carefully, of course."

"Which is what really explains why we were not challenged: Macol forbid it. He will, of course, have us followed."

"I believe you are right, Duke Laras. We'd have attracted less notice if we'd taken the pass near Kuldun, but that one is little more than a foot trail by all account and bad on horses. Also, it would have cost us time. Our prince seems to be in a hurry." Sir Tals and his squire made another effort to speed up the pack-horses, who had clearly found a pace they liked and weren't about to abandon it. Prince Galan was getting further and further ahead. "If Your Graces would be kind enough to persuade him not to leave us?"

By the time Laras and Molikan had managed to get Prince Galan to wait, they had just cleared the northern edge of the pass. The Blackpits lay only a few leagues to the west. Unfortunately, between the path west and Prince Galan's party there sat a very large contingent of the Wylandian chivalry, their armor and lances gleaming silver in the afternoon sun.

Bloody hell.

Sir Tals abandoned the pack train and his squire to their own devices and spurred his mount ahead to where Prince Galan and his two Dukes waited.

"They were waiting for us," Molikan said. "They knew."

Laras nodded. "So it would seem. I hope your folk can manage a ransom."

"Tolerably," Molikan said, "though I'm more worried about our prince here. What's the price for a captured Crown Prince these days?"

"I don't think anyone's made the offer yet, gentlemen," Tals said dryly. "In either case, let's not assume too much. If King Aldair knew we were coming, he doubtless has plans of his own."

"Then ransom, however profitable, may not be his intent. The next move is up to him," Laras said, "though I would advise keeping our hands near our swords but not too near, if you catch my meaning."

That was nothing but sense. Sir Tals waited with his country-men for what seemed like a long time but couldn't have been more than a few moments. Finally the line of horsemen parted and two figures rode out, stopping about two lengths from the main body.

"The rather large gentleman on the left is Aldair," Molikan

said. "I met him years ago at a tournament. He entered the lists himself, as I recall."

"Foolish thing for a king to do," Laras said.

Molikan nodded. "Perhaps, but it made for an interesting tourney. I don't recognize the other man."

"I do," Tals said. "That's Lord Kyre, Aldair's chief counselor. He sparred with my late master from time to time."

"Are you referring to the lists or diplomacy?" Molikan asked.

Tals smiled. "Both, though sometimes where Lord Kyre was concerned it was hard to tell. The man is dangerous, in all senses of the word."

Laras shrugged. "Two dangerous men, then, or so Aldair is also reckoned. So. Either they'll charge now, or Lord Kyre will come over to talk to us first."

"Are we going to wager?" Molikan asked.

"I would if I knew which way to cover," Laras said.

Tals glanced at Prince Galan who merely sat, impassive as a stone, throughout his vassals' banter and bravado. Tals waited, because there was nothing else to do.

Lord Kyre finally rode across the meadow to where Prince Galan and his retainers waited. He stopped at a respectful distance and saluted Prince Galan. "Greetings, My Lord of Borasur. Your cousin Aldair sends his compliments, and begs to inquire what your business within his kingdom may be."

Sir Tals began a diplomatically evasive reply but Prince Galan, who had sat like a sack of flour for all this time, spoke first, firmly and very clear.

"Tell my cousin of Wylandia that I have come with my most trusted men to avenge the death of my brother and his own distant kinsman, Prince Daras. I am on a quest. I come not as lord or prince, but as a grieving brother, and man, to slay the vile person known as Tymon the Black."

Sir Tals sighed. *The hand is played. Madly, for good or ill, but it is played.*

Lord Kyre saluted and rode off to carry Galan's reply to his master. Sir Tals waited for whatever might follow next. What followed next was King Aldair of Wylandia riding out with Lord Kyre as escort to greet Galan personally.

"Cousin," he said, smiling so broadly Tals thought the man's homely face would break, "I would be honored if you will allow me to join your quest."

Later, as they all rode together at the head of the column, Sir Tals managed to ride next to Lord Kyre.

"Ah, Sir Tals. A pleasure to see you again."

"It had fortunately proved so, My Lord, though I must confess that I am curious as to how your master knew to expect us."

Kyre shrugged. "Quite understandable. For myself, I am curious as to how your master knew the one justification for trespass that His Majesty Aldair would not only accept and forgive, but indeed welcome with open arms."

"I don't know," Tals said frankly.

"Well, then, I'm afraid we will both have to live with our curiosities unsatisfied."

Tals sighed. "You wouldn't have told me in any case, would you?"

Kyre grinned with infuriatingly good humor. "Of course not. But then, only *your* curiosity would have gone wanting."

"What are you doing here, Cousin?"

It was the first question Ashesa thought to ask upon opening her eyes again, despite all the other questions waiting their turn. Mero was the daughter of Ashesa's mother's sister, and a childhood playmate. She was literally the last person Ashesa expected to see.

Duchess Mero sat back on her heels, still holding the damp cloth she'd been using to bathe Ashesa's face. "In the 'Land of Shadows' you mean?"

Ashesa groaned as she made herself sit up. It wasn't easy. Her head felt as if it weighed as much as a mountain, and her midriff was very sore and felt bruised. She reached down and touched the bandage, curiously. "I'm not dead? I thought I was. Tymon stabbed me."

Mero nodded. "Scared me senseless when they brought you in. Fortunately, he used this." Mero held up the dagger. Ashesa could now see that the triple point she'd noticed before was actually one blade and two barbs, like small harpoons. "Quite ingenious, really. The barbs catch flesh to hold the hilt in place. The blade collapses into the hilt except for the last bit, which carries the drug. Any blood you saw was your own. Enough to convince Lord Vor, but I'm afraid you're going to have a scar there, Cousin."

Ashesa nodded. "Better than dying. You still haven't answered my question."

Mero looked grim. "I could ask the same of you."

Ashesa considered her secret, and decided she didn't value secrets very highly just then. "I owe Tymon a debt. I came to pay it."

"So did I."

The princess sighed. "He has trees in many orchards, this magician."

"So it seems. Now answer a question of mine—why was Lord Vor holding you hostage?"

Ashesa thought long and hard before she answered. "He thought I could get him close to Tymon so he could kill him. I don't know why he chose me or why he wants to kill Tymon."

Mero sighed. "I think I do, damn him. His ambition will get my lord killed if he's not stopped."

"You knew of Vor's plans?!"

"I do now, Cousin," Mero snapped. "Before, I merely suspected. I prayed that my lord had nothing to do with the attack on your betrothed, but he is too easily led by Vor, despite all he may think of who commands whom. He's a good man, Cousin. He needs to be better served by his advisors."

Ashesa nodded. "What happens now?"

"That greatly depends on you two," Tymon said. He stood at the tent flap, smiling faintly.

"How long have you been listening to us?" Mero asked.

"I always listen to you," Tymon said. "I'd be a fool to do else. Highness, I am sorry about that nick I gave you. It couldn't be helped."

"What about Lord Vor?"

"He's in place. He doesn't know his part yet."

Ashesa glared at him. "Is this all any of this means to you? A play? A fabulation? I almost got killed!"

"Which would have been a tragedy. Tragedy is always an option. Sometimes we avoid it, sometimes not. Still, the nature of the beast is change, and the shepherding of event to create one truth at the expense of another is always a serious affair, Highness, whatever the means. What we do tomorrow will affect the course of lives and nations for good or ill. Is this not serious enough to suit you?"

Ashesa wanted to be angry, but knowing how much of her current predicament was her own fault took a little of the edge off her blade. "I don't know what this is all about, Magician, but I came to warn you."

"About Vor?" Tymon asked mildly.

"About Galan," she said. "He means to kill you. I won't let you hurt him, but I felt I had to let you know."

"Highness, doing harm to your prince is something I'd very much like to avoid. With you and your cousin's help, I might just manage. I may have rescued you from Vor but it was on my account that you were in danger, so you owe me nothing. Yet I must ask for his sake: are you willing to work with me one last time?"

Ashesa glanced at Mero, then met Tymon's gaze squarely. "Tell me what you want me to do."

Koric worked quickly, because he knew that, if he paused to consider more carefully, he might not get the thing done at all. He only had enough twine for the golem's hip joints; the arms he joined with small strips of cloth torn from his own cloak and wrapped several times around the twisted piece of lightning-blasted oak that served as the creature's shoulders.

"Is that the piece of wood that Tymon was whittling on earlier? The one that he didn't know what it was?"

Koric nodded. "I guess he finally figured out what it was."

Seb watched critically. "It's ugly. I mean, even for a golem."

Koric sighed. "It is, isn't it? Even for my first attempt."

Seb nodded. "Still, that's not the most important consideration. Can you do the glyph correctly?"

"I-I think so."

"You'd best be certain. We will only have one chance to get it right."

"Master Seb, you could be of more assistance with a little less commentary."

Seb smiled. "Your pardon, Magician."

"I'm not a magician!"

Seb looked unhappy. "Oh, yes you are. Or will be, sooner or later. Something in the blood, I guess. A wild spirit or breath of the divine, I don't know, but it's there. Otherwise Tymon wouldn't have trusted you with this."

"So why are you standing over me?"

"Because this has to be done right, and you're not a very

good magician. Yet."

Koric took the knife Seb gave him and worked quickly. Twice seven bold strokes and the rest was just clean up and whittling.

"It's done," Koric said.

"But is it right?"

"Yes," Koric said, "it damn well is."

"Then why isn't anything happening?" Seb asked, after a moment or two.

Koric looked at the glyph again, noticed the very slight changes in it that Tymon had asked for, and he said, "Because it's not time."

Seb looked puzzled. "What do you mean it's not time? Didn't you summon a spirit?"

"No, not 'a' spirit. I do believe I called one in particular."

"So why isn't it here?"

Koric grinned. He was beginning to enjoy himself. "Because it's not time," he repeated, and that's all the explanation Seb got.

"You're like Tymon in far too many ways," Seb said. "I think I'll drown you now and save us both the pain."

"Not yet. We've still work to do."

Seb nodded. *Not yet. Always, not yet.*

"He's here," Galan said.

Prince Galan, King Aldair, Laras, Molikan, and Tals stood behind a large boulder, peering up the slope at the dark cave mouth. They stood like adventurers in a fairy tale, for all that several squadrons of mounted soldiers guarded their backs, deployed further down the slope.

"How can you be so certain?" Aldair asked.

Galan thought about it for a moment, and gave the only answer he had. "I feel a link. It's hard to explain. It's as if we're joined."

Aldair nodded. "A fate is on you, Cousin. Destiny marks you to destroy this creature with our help."

Aldair looked as giddy as a young man in love. He seemed to be already imagining the songs that would be sung in their honor, now and to the end of time. Galan looked at him, then looked away. He didn't feel giddy, or happy, or excited. He felt a little sick. He felt, as he had felt since the book, that he was not under a fate. He was under a shadow, and it grew heavier and darker by the moment.

"Go!"

So the shadow spoke. So Galan had to obey. Knowing what was happening, yet powerless to do anything about it, anything at all.

"It's what you wanted."

Yes. It was what he wanted. The one thing that he thought would make his life all right again.

"You mortals bind your happiness to others, whether in love or hate. Did you not think you should, perhaps, find it in yourself?"

That was its way. Galan knew that without asking. *I took you from your happiness.*

"Now I must kill this magician. It will not make you happy. It will make me very happy indeed. Happier still if I destroy you in the process."

I deserve it.

The thoughts were unbidden and unstoppable. Galan almost felt as if the shadow was holding both parts of the conversation and himself no more than trickster's doll carrying its thoughts back and forth.

"Of course. Now get ready. I will command you to strike, and then I will be free. What shall I do then? How happy will I be? Enough, perhaps, to spare you? Or perhaps I shall need even more happiness. Perhaps I will require every life that surrounds you now. We shall see."

Because he still wanted to, but mostly because he had no choice, Galan drew his sword and stared up the hillside, and his companions followed his example. Aldair motioned his men to hold back, and they reluctantly obeyed.

They would be left out of the songs for certain.

Vor's cage was of stone this time, a tumble of boulders at the right rear corner of a cavern, with a hole barely large enough to see through. Food and drink had been shoved inside, but Vor had hardly touched them. The light in the cavern was dim; just a few guttering torches, but there was enough illumination to see his own sword, leaning against the stone wall several feet away on the right. He knew that the main entrance itself was further away, about ten yards to the right.

"I will escape, and then choose flight or revenge. That's why he put the sword opposite the exit," Vor muttered.

"Exactly. What's the point of power if you can't have a little amusement from it?" Tymon stood outside, smiling at him. His teeth flashed white in the darkness.

Vor was startled but he recovered quickly. "When I get out of here I shall show you power, Sorcerer."

"Brave words. Yet it wasn't bravery that brought you to this sorry pass, was it? I seem forever to be capturing you, Lord Vor."

"You should have killed me when you first had the chance."

"But I've had so many chances, My Lord. Maybe simply thwarting you is more fun. After all, you're more a danger to your master than you are to me. Or maybe there's another reason. Could you care to guess?"

Apparently not. "I'll make you eat those words."

"But would that change them? Do yourself a favor, Lord Vor. Stay in your prison this time. Or if you will not, take the left hand path and leave this place. You still can, you know. It's up to you."

"Let me out now and I'll choose."

"It's not time."

Vor frowned. "Time?"

"Timing. Pacing. The proper order of things. Death, sooner or later. You, me, everyone. Well, then. Enjoy the show."

Tymon left, and Vor made his decision. The magician was mad. Clearly. Vor gave him no more thought except as a part of the goal, which was to get out of that hole, kill Tymon, and return to get Duke Laras back on track for history. Slowly, patiently, he felt around, finding the smallest stones and carefully beginning to work them loose.

It didn't take nearly as long as he'd thought.

Galan and his party were still more than a bowshot from the ledge when Tymon appeared there. Galan knew the magician beyond question; the eagerness of the shadow ruling him told him so.

"More visitors. I believe you've already met my present guests."

Tymon pushed two figures forward, roughly shackled. Galan and Laras gasped almost on the same breath. Princess Ashesa and Duchess Mero.

"Come to your deaths, you gallant fools!"

Galan and Laras charged, without thought or conscious decision. The rest hurried after them.

"Highness, wait."

That was Tals, but Galan paid him no heed. He could not. Tymon disappeared into the cave's mouth and out stepped four armed . . . creatures. They stood nearly seven feet tall each, draped in crude robes, armed with swords and spears. They were mere stick figures grown large, creaking as they went on joints of rope and twine.

"By all the Powers," muttered Aldair. "Black sorcery indeed!"

Galan met them a half step before Laras, but it wasn't because Sir Tals wasn't trying to stop them both. The young knight finally gave up and contented himself by standing on Galan's weak side, using his shield to turn blows meant for the prince. Aldair and the two Borasurean dukes soon joined them, forming a shield wall against the creatures.

Ashesa? Duchess Mero? This is so strange. Galan tried hard to pen up his thoughts, now roaming madly about.

"The magican is escaping!"

The shadow spoke, and Galan's voice echoed. "The magician is escaping!"

Galan felt like a marionette. He almost started to look for the strings. He had no time to think of Ashesa and Laras's duchess in Tymon's clutches, or how it had come to be. The only volition he was allowed was that in pursuit of the magician. He decided to use it. "My Lord of Wylandia, can you and Molikan hold these creatures at bay until your men arrive?"

Aldair grinned fiercely. "If they don't come soon there won't be anything left of these abominations but kindling!"

Molikan just shook his head in exasperation. "We'll do what we have to, Prince. Save your princess!"

Galan stepped back from the line. "Duke Laras—" he began, but didn't get very far.

"I'm with you, Highness. I must."

Galan nodded. He'd expected no less. He glanced back at the creatures attacking them. Two men, even two such as Aldair and Molikan, would not be enough. "Sir Tals, stay with these gentlemen until aid comes. Follow when you can."

Tals clearly wanted to argue, but there was no time for that, either. He joined the line and together he, Aldair, and Molikan pressed forward hard, clearing the entrance of the creatures long enough for Galan and Laras to slip inside.

"Wonderful!"

For a moment Galan didn't understand where the thought had come from. It was joyous, almost childlike. It took him a moment to realize that it was the shadow. Galan could almost feel it ahead of him, pulling him along behind like a child with a toy.

You like the darkness.

"I *am* the darkness."

Galan wondered if Laras could actually hear the creature speaking, it seemed so loud to Galan, but Laras did not react at all. Galan turned his thoughts back to his shadow.

Then let me go. You can be happy here.

"Here is nothing. Here is not true darkness."

That much was true. There were torches along the passageway; their smoke made breathing difficult at times, but Galan and Laras pressed on easily enough through the gloom. Too easily.

He's waiting for us.

"That does not matter."

He has Ashesa!

"That does not matter either. His death is all that matters. His death for my freedom. You made the bargain, Prince. You have no right to complain about the terms."

Her safety matters more than Tymon's death! This isn't what I wanted!

"It's what you asked for. Enjoy the consequences. I know I intend to."

Galan tried to turn to Laras, to voice his worries, but he could say nothing. The shadow still held him fast. He looked at Laras, who smiled back tentatively. Galan could see that the man was frightened, but he controlled it well. Laras held a torch he'd taken from the cavern walls; the shadow made Galan hold back a bit even from that weak light.

How many will die today because of me?

"I do not know," shadow answered, as if the question was really meant for it. "I am as curious as you."

"Lord Vor is loose," Mero said. "What was Master Tymon thinking?"

"I guess we'll find out."

Mero and Ashesa and Lytea sat in an iron cage suspended about fifteen feet from the cavern floor. If Mero and Ashesa were worried about Lord Vor's new freedom, Lytea wasn't. She bounced and wiggled in her mother's lap, and for each movement the cage shifted every so slightly back and forth at the end of its rope.

" 'Wing!" she said happily, though her small voice was nearly lost in the emptiness. Mero immediately shushed her, but it didn't make any difference. Together they watched as Vor retrieved his sword and looked slowly around. Even in the dim light it only took him a few moments to spot them.

"Well, well."

"Lord Vor," Duchess Mero said imperiously, "if you'll be good enough to get us down."

Lord Vor seemed to consider the matter for a moment. "No," he said. "I'm sorry, Your Grace, but your husband did tell me to do what I had to do. So I will."

Mero glared at him. "How dare you disobey me!"

"How indeed? I would obey you, Duchess, except for two things. For the first, I know this royal bitch is in league with Tymon, and you're a fool if you don't know it too. As for the other, it occurs to me that Duke Laras's resolve to take his rightful place on Borasur's throne is, shall we say, dwindling?"

"His rightful place? Lord Vor, I will not tolerate this talk of treason!"

Vor smiled. "That's another thing, now that you mention it. You were against this from the start, or would have been if you had known. Yet you will serve Duke Laras better in death, perhaps. Princess Ashesa's death will merely remove the need for a marriage alliance that Borasur will not need once Laras is on the throne. Your own death, however, will put iron in Duke Laras's spine as he seeks revenge for your death at the hands of Prince Galan's lackey Tymon. Or so it will appear. Yes, I will indeed get you both down."

Vor swung at the rope holding the cage. It was thick and very heavy, and the first blow only parted a few strands. Nevertheless, they parted like the snap of an overstrung bow and the cage shuddered.

"It seems Tymon has hung us out to dry like washing," Mero said.

Ashesa nodded, and bit her lip. "So it does."

Ashesa suddenly stood as a few more strands parted.

"Patience." Lord Vor said from below, but his back was to them as he stood just past where the cage hung, hacking at the thick rope. He'd be through it soon, and if the landing probably wouldn't kill them it was safe to assume Vor would.

Perhaps Tymon has abandoned us. Or perhaps he's once more left the choice to me.

Ashesa put her hands on the bar of the cage. "Mero, push," she whispered. Mero, not comprehending, put Lytea on her hip and followed Ashesa's example. Ashesa whispered to her. "With me. First push, then pull, and in both cases brace your feet against the bottom of the cage, your hands on the side." Mero quickly caught the rhythm. The cage swayed more violently, then began to move slowly back and forth like a pendulum. Lord Vor, intent on cutting the rope, did not notice. Ashesa judged the distance to the wall, the distance to where Lord Vor stood hacking the rope, the length of the swing. But the timing had to be perfect.

Almost there. . . . "Push!"

Lytea put her hand on the cage. " 'Wing?"

Ashesa smiled grimly. "Yes, Dear One. Swing."

The scream froze Galan and Laras in their tracks for the barest moment; then came the sound of metal crashing into stone. The two men took off down the passageway as fast as they could go, coming perilously close to crashing into low ceilings and sudden turns. The passageway suddenly opened out and Galan and Laras rushed out into an area of greater darkness. There were torches here too, but the size of the cavern dwindled their light to barely more than stars in a clear sky. They heard shouts from behind in the passageway. Galan was certain he recognized Aldair's and Tals's voices; the rest were lost in the general murmur.

"Prince, over here!"

Galan followed Laras and his torch around the perimeter of what appeared to be a lake; lying beside it was broken cage with a large rope tied to the top. Ashesa and Mero huddled inside; Mero held Lytea in her arms. They seemed badly shaken but not seriously injured.

The door was sprung. Galan and Laras together managed to get it open.

"It fell," said Ashesa.

"Lord Vor cut the rope," Mero said. "He—" She couldn't finish.

The cage rested on a body. Galan saw it first, then Laras. "Lord Vor. . . . Help me, Prince!"

They got the women out of the cage and together managed to move the heavy iron grating off of the downed man, but it was far too late. "Tymon had him, too," Mero said. "He . . . he got free and tried to cut the rope."

"And misjudged the weight, I think," Ashesa finished. "He

died trying to free us."

Duke Laras embraced his wife and child. Prince Galan took two steps toward Ashesa, but the shadow held him back.

"You're forgetting your purpose," it said, in that voice that only Galan could hear.

After today I think I will have to forget many things.

Galan could manage no more; the shadow pulled him away.

"This way, fool!"

The shadow commanded and Galan followed. He saw Tymon on a large platform of limestone some distance away. He sprinted in that direction, oblivious to the slippery footing and obstacles; he knew the shadow guided his feet, the darkness opened a way for him. He barely needed the extra light as more torches from King Aldair and his men filed quickly into the cavern.

"You think you've won," Tymon said.

"No. But soon," the shadow said.

"No. But soon," Galan echoed.

Galan was closer now, and Tymon had not moved, either to threaten or to run away. When he spoke now only Galan could hear. "Tell your shadow I am here. He can leave you now."

"Leave?" said the shadow.

"Leave?"

"Take your sword," the shadow commanded.

Galan raised his blade. Almost at the same instant he felt the darkness flowing out of him, obscuring Tymon like a cloud crossing the face of the moon. Galan willed himself into action, striking, not at Tymon, but at the darkness. Then for a long time there was nothing *except* darkness, within and without, and the blow he struck seemed to last forever.

Tymon watched the shadow leave Prince Galan; it hovered over them both while time itself seemed to hesitate, losing its way in the darkness.

"Tricks and illusion. Whatever you make these fools think, you cannot escape me. This deception will not last. You cannot stop time," the shadow said.

No one can, Power. Not even you. Yet perception can alter if time does not, and altering perception is what I do best. Tell me you are not affected by what I have done.

"It does not matter."

I disagree. I think it matters to you.

"It will not matter once I kill you!"

The shadow struck at him. It reached out and around and through as if it would replace what life he had with darkness like a flow of lava surrounding and consuming a house. Tymon was not there. He stood a few feet away, shaking his head.

"You cannot escape!"

I know. But I can delay. How long? Do you really want to find out?

"*Die!*"

The thing struck again, and again Tymon eluded it, if barely.

How long, Power? How long until your spirit decides it cannot survive betwixt and between and locks you in a form you may not escape? Did you ever stop to think it might be too late already? That what you see and what you know as something separate from dark-ness, separate and unique, might not fade with time? You are in danger of becoming like us. Forever.

"You must die!!"

Yes, Tymon agreed, *I must. But "when" is not entirely up to you, is it?*

"Die. . . ."

The thing was almost pleading now. It sounded as lost and afraid as a child, for all that its power and anger had not lessened one whit.

Tymon aimed his thoughts at the creature like the thrust of a spear. *If you want to go back to darkness sooner rather than, perhaps, never, you will listen to me.*

The darkness was like a thundercloud now, booming, noise and fury incarnate. "What do you want???"

Tymon answered the darkness. *When I am dead you will leave. You will save yourself and become as you were before while you still can. You will not seek revenge for what was done to you, now or forever. As it is your true nature to forget, so you will. You will swear on the nothingness that you wish to be that this will be so.*

It tried, one more time, to kill Tymon. Tymon evaded it. Not easily, but he managed. He could feel the creature's rage and fear shaking him like thunder.

"I swear, mortal. I swear by all that nothingness. I swear by all that I desire!"

Tymon nodded. *Good. Now I will die.*

Galan heard the muffled cry, felt his sword strike something, then watched it fall from his nerveless fingers as he himself fell, landing hard on the stone. The jolt shook him to the teeth and, for another long moment, the world was spinning.

Galan heard people calling his name. He could not see them; their torches seemed very far away. The thunder was still booming; it was if a storm had formed within the depths of the earth with himself as the center. It was only when several strong hands helped him to his feet that he realized the others had come.

"What happened?" he asked, rubbing his head. There would be a bump; no question.

Duke Laras retrieved the prince's sword, and kicked the prostrate form laying beside it once as he did so, then leaned closer for a better look. "He's dead, Your Highness."

Galan could see the blood, but not much else. "Who?"

"Tymon the Black, slain in personal combat by the Prince of Borasur!" King Aldair slapped him on the back so hard he almost fell again. "Nobly done, as we all witnessed!"

"If you say, then it must be so," Galan admitted. "I remember reaching him but not much else."

"Combat can do that to a man. Squeeze time, or lengthen it. Sometimes even take it away," said Aldair. "I've known such before. I don't know how long you fought; it seemed like several minutes. We could not approach; his foul magic held us at bay."

As if to emphasize the point, there was another dull booming sound, from somewhere deeper in the earth. Several small stalactites broke free from the ceiling to splash into the dark waters of the underground lake.

Laras went down on one knee before Galan. "You've saved my family, Prince. I was wrong. . . . I mean, I don't know how you had the wisdom to lead us to this place, but your deeds speak more clearly than any explanation could. I owe you everything, and I will not forget."

Galan took Duke Laras's hand in friendship and accepted his embrace, though for the life of him he could not remember doing any of what they said he did. He went to Princess Ashesa who stood, almost hesitantly, at the edge of the group.

"Did you see it, too?"

"Yes, My Lord," she said. She looked neither sad nor happy, just anxious, though about what Galan could not say. He decided to say what he could. What, finally, he thought he understood.

"I've been a fool, Princess. I've meddled in things I should not and sought justification where it was not. There are many things I do not understand about this day, but I no longer care. You are safe, and that's all that matters to me." Galan took her hand and he kissed it, and Ashesa, for the first time he could remember—and barely imagine—blushed as red as a fireflower.

"You are safe, too," she said almost shyly, "and that is all that matters to me."

There was another boom, and more stalactites fell. Sir Tals spoke up, "Gentlemen and ladies, I suspect this cavern is not altogether stable. I think we should leave now."

There was no dissent. Those who could find torches held them aloft as they made their way toward the entrance. One of Aldair's barons stumbled over something and glanced down in irritation.

His eyes got very wide. "Your Majesty! Come look at this!"

Aldair strode up to him. "Are you daft, Takan? We have to leave!"

The man just pointed, and Aldair sighed gustily and looked. "By Martok's hairy bollocks. . . ."

Two skeletons lay side by side by the water's edge, their bones partially crystallized over the centuries. Their clothing had long since rotted away, but the gleam of gold was clear enough. One wore a medallion with the royal arms of Wylandia.

"The lost princes," Molikan said, softly. "Can it be?"

"They were lost in the Blackpits," Aldair said. "Or at least so it was told."

There was another boom. Somewhere behind them they heard large boulders shifting. "If we don't leave soon we may join them," Tals said.

"I can't leave," said Aldair. "Not yet."

Galan tried to read Aldair's expression. "Duke Laras, you and Sir Tals lead everyone out. We'll follow."

Aldair nodded to Lord Kyre. "You too. Get my men out of here."

Kyre obeyed without a word. Sir Tals was less resigned. "Your Highness, I'd like to stay," he said.

"I know," Galan said. "Now go. I'll be all right."

Duke Laras put his hand on the young man's shoulder. "That was not a request, Sir Tals. Let's be gone. You too, Your Grace,"

Laras said, turning to Molikan. I think their Majesties need to be alone."

Soon everyone else was gone and Galan and Aldair were left by themselves in the near blackness, with only Galan's torch to hold it at bay. Aldair reached for his belt. He frowned as his hand came away empty. "I seem to have lost my dagger."

"Take mine, Majesty," Galan said, carefully drawing out the blade and handing it, hilt first, to Aldair. There was another boom. They tried not to think too much about what it might have done to the cavern ceiling or the only passageway out.

"You know what I have to do, don't you?"

Galan nodded. "I think so. You need a peer witness for this ceremony. In your case someone either crowned or in the direct line of succession. I am the only such here."

"One alone is more than enough. For your discretion I am in your debt, as well as for this fine adventure. There have been very few such since my coronation. I advise you to enjoy this one while it lasts."

Galan nodded, though he'd already sworn to himself that he would put as much distance between the rest of his life and this day as he could possibly manage. Aldair took Galan's dagger and touched it, briefly, to the wrist of his right and then his left hand.

"Very sharp," he said, in approval. Already the blood was beginning to well up and trickle into his palms. He turned his hands toward the stone, and let blood drip onto each shining skeleton.

" 'My blood I offer in payment for your own. My flesh bear the pain, my sorrow heir to your own, my body to punish as you choose. Forgive my ancestor, and forgive me. We are your family, as you are ours. I pray for your spirits' pardon and make blood offering in your honor, as the gods demand.' "

After only a moment's hesitation, haltingly, Galan gave the

proper response. "So witnessed," Galan said, "before both gods and mortals. It is done."

Aldair let out a sigh, the Ritual of Atonement complete. It was normally used to settle blood feuds when simple punishment was no longer possible. Galan judged its use here appropriate enough.

Aldair stared at the skeletons. "That should have been done long ago. It seems there is even more I owe to you, Prince."

"You did the proper thing, Majesty, whatever your ancestor was or was not guilty of. That rite settles debts; it does not create them. We won't need to speak of this again."

Another stalactite fell perilously close. "Well, there is much we *should* speak of, Prince," Aldair said. "Though I think that out in the sunlight would be a better place to do so. As soon as possible."

Galan glanced at the ceiling. "On your heels, Cousin."

"I was beginning to think they would never leave," Seb said. "I could only risk a few more blasts without collapsing the entire cavern."

Koric followed Seb out of their hiding place near the rear of the cavern. It took a moment with flint and steel to get their torch lit. It only took one more moment to find the body.

"He is dead, isn't he?" Seb said, his voice somewhere between wonder and sorrow. "It's not a trick this time."

Koric, kneeling beside the body, looked a little green. "See for yourself."

Seb reached down, then nodded. "Yes. The wound isn't that great; Galan didn't strike well. Yet Tymon is dead."

"We both know it wasn't Galan's blow that killed him," Koric said.

Seb nodded, looking grim. "Tymon knew what was coming, and he knew he couldn't defeat it, though I guess he had to try.

He said as much."

Koric nodded. "He said something else."

Seb frowned. "What?"

"He said that, if the worst happened, I would know what to do."

Seb gave the lad an odd look. A tear glistened in the corner of his right eye. He brushed it away, angrily. " 'Do'? Is there aught to do, save bury him? We'd do that much even for poor Vor."

"If we have to," Koric agreed.

"You're not making sense," Seb said.

"No. In time I hope to do so. Let's wait a bit."

For a moment Seb just stared at him. "What for?"

They both heard the tap-tap-tap of wood on stone. A small golem walked into the weak torchlight from somewhere out of the surrounding darkness. It was the one Seb had watched Koric prepare, mere hours before. It walked its stilted walk right up to Tymon's body. It stood there, motionless. It seemed to be waiting as well.

"For that," Koric said.

"Well," Seb said, "I guess your handiwork was satisfactory after all. Yet the battle is over, and this thing is too small to help with the burials. What good is it?"

"Let's find out. Master Seb, will you hold the torch closer please?" Koric's mouth had a grim set as he clumsily pulled on Tymon's robe until the body's bare chest was exposed.

"What are you doing?"

"What Master Tymon told me I would know to do. I hope I'm right."

Koric took his knife from his belt and began to carve the Glyph of Life into Tymon's cooling flesh. Both Seb and the golem watched with more than casual interest.

EPILOGUE
"A HAPPY BEGINNING"

"Every court in the Twelve Kingdoms will speak of this wedding for years to come," Lord Kyre whispered.

His guest, richly dressed but hooded as one with an infirmity, shrugged. "Why so?"

Kyre nodded toward the altar, where the High Priest of Amatok had just finished blessing the groom and his men. King Galan I of Borasur, crowned scant days before, stood resplendent in ermine and velvet with his Groom's Men awaiting the arrival of the bride.

"Well, to begin, the story of Galan's duel with Tymon the Black is already common knowledge across most of the mainland. The lad's well on his way to becoming a legend."

"That's not necessarily a good thing," his guest replied.

Lord Kyre gave a small shrug. "No, but in this case I think it may be. Also consider that no fewer than two crowned kings are attending this wedding, in addition to Galan himself. Insular the other kingdoms may be, but they will certainly take note of this. I fancy they will consider their own relationship with Galan of Borasur and his growing number of allies. I believe envoys will follow after a barely decent interval."

"Allies including the formerly contentious Wylandia?"

Kyre smiled. "My point. His Majesty Aldair himself as one of the Groom's Men? Imagine!"

"I don't have to. I see it."

Someone shushed them. They both nodded apologetically as

the choir began to sing something traditionally ethereal. They both smiled as Princess Ashesa of Morushe entered the Temple of Amatok on King Macol's arm. Ashesa was befittingly radiant, her royal father beaming with pride and—let it be said—relief. Behind them followed the Ladies of the Court led by Lady Margate. She was clearly trying not to cry and failing miserably. For all that, she looked happier than anyone could remember seeing her for a very long time.

All bowed as the procession swept past. Ashesa glanced their way, smiling. For a moment the smile faded into surprise, but the smile quickly returned, dropped into place like a portcullis falling. In a moment she was past them and going to meet her king.

Lord Kyre looked stricken. "Oh, bliss. . . . Do you think she recognized you?"

"I'm sure she did. Don't worry; she won't betray me."

"Are you certain of that? It was quite a risk, you coming here."

"And for you to arrange it, Lord Kyre. I think we may call our account settled after this."

"I am grateful. But still, I have to ask: why take this chance?"

"Because," Tymon said, "this is the part of the story I never get to see. I thought perhaps it was time."

"A reward?"

Tymon the Black, fiend and monster—for so it would be recorded for all time—thought about it for a moment, then shook his head. "A reminder."

ABOUT THE AUTHOR

Richard Parks is a native of Mississippi and lives there with his wife Carol and a varying number of cats. His short stories have appeared in such places as *Asimov's SF, Realms of Fantasy, Fantasy Magazine,* and *Weird Tales.* His first story collection, *The Ogre's Wife,* was a World Fantasy Award finalist, and his second collection, *Worshipping Small Gods,* has just been released.